GONE GREEN

ALSO BY BETH BARANY

GONE GREEN

A JANEY MCCALLISTER MYSTERY, BOOK 3

BETH BARANY

FIREWOLF
BOOKS

FIREWOLF BOOKS
771 Kingston Ave., #108
Piedmont, California, 94611
www.firewolfbooks.com

SIGN UP HERE FOR NEW RELEASE NEWS:

http://bethb.net/ggfr

PUBLISHER'S NOTE: This is a work of fiction. Names, characters,
places, and incidents are a product of the author's imagination. Locales
and public names are sometimes used for atmospheric purposes. Any
resemblance to actual people, living or dead, or to businesses,
companies, events, institutions, or locales is completely coincidental.

COVER DESIGN by Nada Orlic
BOOK DESIGN by Beth Barany

ISBN: 978-1-944841-36-2 (ebook)
ISBN: 978-1-944841-37-9 (print)

To all the young dreamers out there, never give up. Even in our darkest moments, the dawn is coming.

ONE

"WHAT ARE YOU DOING HERE?" THE QUESTION just popped out of Janey's mouth.

Orlando Valdez leaned against the wall of her boss's office, obstructing the live feed of the space station's massive docking bay. He watched her with a piercing gaze, cool and mysterious, giving nothing away.

Anger flared, ballooning hot and itchy all over, even though she'd known he might show up on L'Étoile unannounced.

Venus Hells.

Lead Investigator Janey McCallister faced her boss, Security Chief Daniel Milano, who was seated behind his desk, his rotund middle stretching his red Turkish coat. "What's he doing here? Is this what you called me in for? I thought we had an urgent briefing."

Thirty-five minutes ago, Milano had called an earlier-than-usual security briefing without an explanation, other than to hurry her ass to his office, stat, cutting short her morning plans. She'd been scheduled to talk to a medical researcher about her mom's condition. If Janey could get her mom on a new experimental drug before the current medical trial ended in ten weeks... Those calls regarding her mom could wait but not for long.

Orlando Valdez, Sol Unified Planets special investigator, straightened from the wall and opened his mouth to speak, but the chief waved him off.

"Yes, that's why I called you. And we do have a briefing," the chief said to her. "But firstly, you should know that Special Investigator Orlando is here on a top-secret Sol case and has a job to do."

"I can appreciate that, but so do I," Janey said, prickles buzzing under her skin like a million hopped-up electrodes, urging her to storm out of the small office. She kept herself in place. "We'll be at capacity soon, and we still have final prep for the gala."

Milano knew all this. And so did Orlando. He heard all her news in their regular evening vid calls.

"I'm sorry, Janey," Orlando said to her, a serious look on his face. Looked like he meant it. Micro tension tightened the corners of his lips.

"There's another matter," Chief Milano said, weary.

"What's your case?" Janey asked Orlando, ignoring her boss.

Orlando shook his head, his dark wavy locks falling over one eye.

Stars, he looked great in that fashionable, shimmery blue suit, with a pale pink pocket square, his creamy white silk shirt open at the throat. Yet he held himself with uncharacteristic rigidity in his shoulders, unlike the last time she'd seen him, been with him—a whole week together over three long months ago.

Now he was all business, secretive and tense. His missions for the Sol that took him all over the star system were more than top-secret and politically sensitive. He wouldn't read her in unless he absolutely had to.

Would he this time?

"McCallister," Chief Milano said and cleared his throat, breaking her focus on Orlando. "Per inter-Sol regulations, Agent Orlando is to report to you for all security matters. It's up to your discretion on whether or not you need to clear any of his actions with me. Got that, Investigator?" Her boss gave her a hard stare over his faux antique eyeglasses no one used anymore.

As if he needed to remind her of the rules that governed the private corporate city-state of Bijoux de L'Étoile, this hotel-casino in space.

A jurisdictional dance, every time.

A former investigator himself for various companies and state governments, Milano was a stickler for the rules and spent more time behind his desk filing reports for the hotel owner than another else—other than gambling. Yet he treated her and everyone else fairly.

"Yes, Chief." Even though she felt Orlando peering at her, willing her to look at him, she kept her gaze on her boss.

Orlando would officially be her direct report, and she'd be *his* boss. So, she had to keep things professional between them if she was to follow regs. Could she? She had to. This job was her mother's only financial lifeline. All those expensive medical treatments for her mother's hard-to-treat disease.

But Orlando didn't often follow regs during his undercover work.

"I'm sure you two will work well together, as you have in the past. Yes?" Milano lifted an eyebrow at her. Orlando had helped her on two murder cases on L'Étoile.

"We will, sir." Janey snapped to attention, chin up, shoulders back. Her Space Wing training second nature.

"Chief Milano, it would be my utmost pleasure to work under the investigator," Orlando said in a silky warm tone.

Cheeky bugger. What happened in the bedroom between them was private.

Milano nodded at Orlando in acknowledgment and fussed with his dancing figurines that lined the edge of his desk, tiny models he created in his off-hours.

"Sir, a word," Janey said. Had he received the ping about the unidentified vibration she'd felt on her way to his office?

"Just a moment. One more thing." Milano lifted a finger to cut Janey off, then said in his comm, "Kim, send them in." Kimani Iona was the station security operations manager, handling the department's communications for Janey and her team. She was a tech and systems whiz and had become one of Janey's closest friends at L'Étoile.

A moment later two women entered Milano's office. Chief Milano stood.

"To start this special briefing, Investigator McCallister and Agent Orlando, I'd like you to meet Veronica Ladipo, a journalist with *The Tell Papers*, and her business partner, Monica Farmingham. They are here to cover next week's gala."

Veronica Ladipo reached out a hand to Janey. She was as tall as Janey was, with an open, friendly smile, striking green eyes, and dark brown hair, a halo around her head. "Investigator McCallister, it's a pleasure to meet you. I appreciate you taking the time."

Like Janey had a choice.

She shook the journalist's hand, exchanging a firm

grip. The business partner, Monica Farmingham, nodded in greeting to her and the two men. She was dressed in a grey suit jacket, a cream blouse buttoned at the throat, and a matching grey pencil skirt. In expensive strappy black spike heels out of place with the conservative suit, Monica wore no jewelry and carried a thin real-leather briefcase. Shorter than Janey by at least six inches, coming to Janey's shoulder, the petite woman had sharp cheekbones, almond eyes outlined in kohl, reminiscent of an Egyptian princess, and had a quiet, powerful look about her. As if she could dominate any boardroom and get her way.

"I'll stay out of your way as much as possible, though I would like an hour or so of your time soon to interview you and your team," Veronica said, bringing Janey's attention back to her.

"I don't have time for media interviews, especially now," Janey said. "And it's abnormal to have a working journalist on board. L'Étoile's owner, Frederick D. Schoeneman, is a well-known recluse and never grants interviews to the press."

Veronica smiled, nodded, confidence oozing, and glanced at Monica. They shared a secret smile.

"A pleasure to meet you, Ms. Ladipo. Ms. Farmingham." Orlando smiled with sparkling charisma and shook the journalist's hand, nodded at the business partner, his body tension gone, replaced with languid fluid ease. He turned his full attention on the journalist. "I'm one of your most ardent fans. I read your column regularly."

Janey frowned. He hadn't greeted her with a smile like that, and they were dating.

"Call me Veronica, please." The journalist offered Orlando a bright smile of pure joy and unnecessarily straightened the jacket of her bespoke black suit, primping under his gaze. Monica watched, seemingly unaffected by Orlando's charm.

An angry, territorial beast roared in Janey's heart. She rammed it down, then spoke, keeping her tone neutral.

"I'm surprised to see someone from *The Tell Papers* covering—" Janey swirled her hand to encompass the luxurious surroundings beyond the small security office.

"Social engagements and parties at high-end resorts?" Veronica said. "I know. Not my usual beat of exposés on despots, corporate greed, and industrial cover-ups." She gave a tinkling laugh. "Monica thought it would be a good change of pace. I agreed, and so did my editor." She shrugged. "Plus, I was curious to check out the Starry Jewel in the Sky, cover the gala prep and then the gala itself, and congratulate Mr. Schoeneman for his ten years of success. Bijoux de L'Étoile is quite something. Ten years of constructing in high-Earth orbit... Now this..." The awe in her voice sounded genuine.

"It is an impressive feat of engineering," Janey said. "Schoeneman knows you're here, I presume."

"They've signed all the right paperwork," Chief Milano gestured at his screen, gave the requisite commands, and the customs checklist ballooned to fill the wall screen beside him. "Her team was approved by Zurich. Schoeneman informed me personally that she and her camera crew were coming for the gala."

Schoeneman was due to arrive any day now—another security task on her long list.

"You have a crew with you?" Janey asked Veronica. Great, more people to keep tabs on.

"Yes, they're waiting in your conference room to meet you." Veronica offered a smile, open and inviting.

"I don't know when I will have the time." Janey glanced at Milano.

"Yes, we need to organize ourselves, our work arrangements," Orlando said and scrutinized Janey, his gaze intense as if he was trying to communicate a serious message to her.

"I understand," the journalist said. "We're here for the entire week. I look forward to speaking with you when you have the time."

"We don't have the time," Janey said.

"We will make sure you get your interviews, Ms. Ladipo," Milano said, as smooth as any diplomat.

Veronica addressed Milano, determined and peppy, seemingly unfazed by Janey's refusals. "I'd love a tour of the lower levels for our B reel and then the out of way—"

Whatever else Veronica said and was about to say was drowned out by a deafening high-pitched alarm blaring from Janey and Milano's wrist comms. The journalist slapped her hands over her ears, wide-eyed shock on her face. The business partner backed up against the wall, her face pale.

The high-pitched alarm shrieked off and on, like a wounded animal screaming in fear, jamming clear thought for a split second. Adrenaline flooded her system.

Orlando rushed to Janey's side, a question in his eyes. Janey had the same questions he probably did.

What tripped the alarm?

Where?

How?

The red flashing code on her comm was unfamiliar at first. Then her ocular implant decoded it. The alarm was from a normally quiet and out-of-the-way section of the station.

Hells.

Janey waved over her comm, inputting the command to open a channel to the entire security department, and shouted above the horrible din. "We have to go. Now! All hands on this one." She bolted for the office door that opened on approach.

She rushed into the corridor and raced toward the staff elevator, side-stepping the cleaning bots.

"What is it?" Orlando sprinted into the elevator beside her. "Where are we going?"

Fear tightened her ribcage. The elevator door closed, and she shut off the alarm. "The casino vault. It's a 10-18. Officer down. Needs immediate assistance."

TWO

"The triple redundancy casino vault, guarded twenty-four-seven?" Orlando asked in the elevator.

"Yes. How do you know?" Janey eyed her holo screen for more information, but there was none. She commed the guards on duty in the vault, Ed and Kosi, but they didn't answer either.

He shrugged, tense and tight. "I studied the station's schematics. You're being robbed?"

"Unlikely. No, impossible. State of the art, triple redundancy." Janey glared at her holo. The camera feed on the lower level showed no movement at the vault's entrance. The feed of the vault door inside the monitoring room showed no action either.

"Yet—" Orlando broke off.

"We'll see soon enough." Janey stared at her screen, again. Nothing new. Useless thing. She snapped at it so it would refresh. No new information.

Venus Hells.

She blinked to access all the security cameras on her

ocular implant, but the feed showed no one in or out of the vault room in the last hour since the shift change. One hour ago Security agents Eduard Kou and Mandlenkosi Dube had entered the vault room, and a minute later, the two guards coming off shift had exited into the corridor.

Before her mind could go spiraling into what-ifs, the elevator door whooshed open. Janey rushed down the narrow empty corridor, Orlando beside her, grim.

"What were you going to say to Milano back there when you first came into his office?" Orlando asked.

Janey glanced over her shoulder, a half step ahead of Orlando. "Later."

Halfway down the corridor, she stopped at an inconspicuous grey door. No signs of tampering.

Was that a good sign?

Possibly.

She palmed the door so it could take her palm print and record her pulse. At the same time, she squared her face with the center of the door and stared at a pinprick dot—the retinal scanner.

Wait to worry, Mom always said. Her stomach shimmied with nerves.

The door slid open to reveal a room empty of people, as she expected. She whooshed out a breath.

"This is normal?" Orland spun in the small room designed to hold a maximum of six seated people, chairs against the walls. "A waiting room in case guests stumble in?"

Janey nodded. On one wall, a small window was covered with a grey curtain as if to receive customers. A few chairs and a side table with reading material populated the space. In front of them was another nondescript grey door.

She used her wrist comm to unlock that door and it slid open. She took a step in and gasped, stunned.

Triple Venus Hells. No!

Her two agents were down, and the vault door was cracked open.

Security agent Eduard Kou was on the floor at an odd angle as if he'd collapsed off his chair, his face ashen, one arm bent under him. Security agent Mandlenkosi Dube was slumped over the table, unmoving in front of a bank of wall monitors as if napping. One hand was bent to wave in the alarm command.

Ignoring protocol to sweep the room first, Janey rushed to Ed and checked for a pulse. But she knew before she touched him. No heartbeat showed up on her ocular implant screen. Her touch at his neck revealed the same. There was no pulse, his skin papery dry and cold to the touch. Out of habit and the need to do something, she rolled him flat on his back and started CPR, to no effect.

No, not Ed. The quiet, sweet man didn't deserve this. No one did.

He had aging parents in New Macau and a cousin and other family in Amsterdam.

Ed's face was pale grey, almost white, his expression slack as if he hadn't been aware of what hit him. She commanded her ocular implant to scan at the micro-level. No visible marks on his face, neck, or hands, his black shirt and slacks not torn or smudged. She'd ruled out natural causes as soon as she'd seen him; his skin didn't look right.

"This one is still breathing." Orlando bent over an unconscious Mandlenkosi, checking his pulse. "Pulse seems faint though."

"Call him Kosi. We call him Kosi."

Orlando called the agent's name gently, but Kosi didn't stir.

Please be okay. Janey sent out a prayer to the stars and to Kosi's ancestors who, he'd told her, watched over his family and the whole Zulu Nation.

She didn't want to have to notify his ten siblings in Cape Town.

Janey continued chest compressions on Ed. With a mental command, she opened a comm channel to Medical and spoke in an urgent low tone, "Emergency in the vault. Eduard Kou's not breathing. No heartbeat. Doing CPR. Mandlenkosi Dube is... down, still breathing."

"On our way. Arriving in two minutes," Medical replied.

"Hurry." Janey stayed steady with the manual CPR, wishing she'd gone directly for the auto-compression equipment right away. The box was on the wall, outside of reach, and she didn't want to stop. Yet she was too late. Hopelessness crowded her for a moment, black and heavy.

Ed's face seemed to grow greyer and whiter like ash by the second, abnormally quickly. The pallor of death usually arrived after thirty-six hours or so under normal conditions. What had caused this?

Then Orlando came over to Ed. "I'll work on him."

Grateful, she gave him room. She rushed to the emergency box on the wall, palmed it open, grabbed the box, and opened it on the floor in the center of the room, equidistant from her two downed agents. There had to be something she could do.

She opened the emergency medical sensors and set them next to Ed. He was flatlined and brainwave activity was null. According to the protocol on the screen, there wasn't anything they could do for him.

"Venus Hells."

"Can Medical revive him?" Orlando stopped CPR and sat on his heels. "What else can I do?"

"I hate to leave him. I don't know." Janey glanced at an unmoving Kosi. "But there's hope for Kosi." Had to be.

The medical sensors showed that Kosi was breathing but needed oxygen. She handed Orlando a one-inch circular patch. "Put this on his neck near his arteries. That should push more O_2 into his system."

Orlando used a fingertip to place the dot on his neck. On the medical monitor, Kosi's O_2 levels went from red to orange.

"Better," Janey huffed out in relief.

"What else?" Orlando stood and eyed the open slivery vault door.

"Don't move him."

"Wasn't planning on it."

Janey studied the emergency box readout.

"The medical sensors say to wait for medical evaluation," she said. "Wish we could do more."

"Janey, the vault door."

She checked the vid that still showed the vault door closed. Sabotage. The door was cracked open, wide enough for a person to slip in and out. She stood and peeked in, careful not to touch the thick door. A stone in her gut.

She peeked in. "No," she breathed. "Emptied completely."

"How?"

"I don't know." She set her wrist comm and ocular implant to read for residual heat signatures, other than

BETH BARANY

hers, Orlando's, Ed's, and Kosi's. "I'm not going in yet. Better to take readings from here."

"Is the casino in the mierda?"

"Yes. By Sol law, we need hard currency if ever there was a demand to cash out by everyone on the casino floor."

"What kind of hard currency?"

"Precious gems guests used to secure their bets, plus lingots strips of asteroid metals."

"My scan picks up two biosignatures. Unknown idents." Orlando peered at from his wrist holo, his screen shimmery in the room's low light. "You?"

"Yes. What the regolith!" She should have checked right away and seen the biosignatures. "Couldn't be more than an hour old. But they're faint." She shook her head. "Not in the guest roster. Not on the staff list. Where did they come from?"

Orlando looked grim. "Not in any of our databases either. Probably fake biotags."

She frowned at the empty vault, the floor-to-ceiling shelving.

"We're not going in?"

"Not yet. Let's search this room first."

"How could this happen?" Orlando said under his breath as if he was working the puzzle.

"That's what I want to know. Two assailants—one to subdue Ed and Kosi, another to open the safe?" Janey signed the wake command in front of one of the wall panels to open the screens and gather what she could.

No reaction from the screens. She punched in her security override to unlock them, but nothing happened. Not good. Not good at all.

"Who could have done this?" Orlando asked.

"Someone smart. Someone who knew our systems."

14

"Maintenance staff?" Orlando asked.

"Possibly. Only those on staff could get into this room or the vault. The deterrent system would have kicked up an alarm if any of the biometrics didn't match. Someone had to have turned off the biometric scan, rigged it, fooled it somehow, or bypassed it."

"With those protocols, had to be staff."

"Or someone allowed in by staff." She glanced at Ed and Kosi. "I just don't see them capable—so loyal, long-time staff."

"Robbing the vault on the eve of the gala." Orlando shook his head. "That's cold."

"If that's what happened." Janey returned to the thick vault door at the far end of the monitoring room. Time to examine it.

There were no signs of tampering on the enormous vault door. Still, she took detailed footage of the wide facade, checking the face scanner and tube hand reader that took a pinprick of blood from a finger and scanned fingerprints and blood vessels. Blood, heartbeat, and DNA analysis. They weren't messing around.

"No signs of tampering on the security protocols," Janey said. "They were smartly bypassed."

"Someone with high-tech knowhow."

Janey nodded. "Right. Could there be another way through the door?"

"What do you mean?"

"Overrides. Like a back door that hackers leave."

"Not that I know of," Orlando said, grim. "So two people break in, attack the guards, hack an impenetrable vault door, rob the vault, and leave with hardly a trace."

"And Ed paid with his life," Janey said. "Where's Medical?"

It was time to examine the vault. The empty vault.

THREE

THE   THIEF—OR   THIEVES—HAD   TAKEN
everything.

Venus Hells.

All gone. All the winnings from the day before in the
form of gems and casino chips, plus the asteroid precious
metals that secured all the currency used for all casino
transactions—gone.

The black disks that contained contracts and backup
transactions—gone.

The grey recyclo-metallic floor-to-ceiling shelving—
empty. Janey circled the twenty-by-twenty-foot vault and
kicked up dust bunnies that must have hidden amongst
the vault's contents.

No, not this.

With a tight pit in her stomach, she waved the bad
news over to Kim and Milano.

"How did they get in?" Orlando asked as he stared at
his holo.

"I don't know," Janey said and adjusted the settings
on her wrist comm to pick up bioelectric and heat signals

her ocular implant didn't scan for. With her ocular implant, she scanned light waves beyond the normal human capacity. She also swept for objects on the micrometer scale, setting her implant to log everything.

Readings rolled in on her comm's holo screen and her internal ocular screen. Then her internal screen went fuzzy and grey. She sucked in a breath. So much visual noise like audio static in a darkened room in a snowstorm. Dizzy. Stomach didn't like that. Reminded her of her first days and weeks with the ocular implant when she was a teen. Too much input for her brain to sort through.

"What's wrong?" Orlando asked and touched her arm. She grasped his hand, warm and steady, a lifeline, bringing her back to reality.

"Something's overloading my visual field. Some kind of interference." Janey blinked to fine-tune the image. It stayed fuzzy. She pushed a thought command to Rhea, her personal assistant AI synched into her room controls. Rhea could work on the analysis and keep her findings private, off the work networks. "I can still see."

"I thought you got that checked," Orlando said, concerned.

"I had."

"You need to again," he added, his voice soft.

"I will. Not now. I have Rhea working on it. Besides, it's gone," Janey said and huffed out a breath, focusing her attention on the holo screen, the details clear. "Biosignals are faint, but at least two warm bodies have been in this room recently—within the last hour, I think."

"Can you tell whose?"

"No, the data isn't that precise. No discernible idents," Janey said. "And it's odd they're so faint." She glanced at Orlando. "Don't say 'ghost'."

"I won't," Orlando said. "Maybe teleportation? Though that tech doesn't exist outside of the lab."

"Great, some teched-up thieves. Let's stick to evidence collecting.

"I detect no fingerprints or skin cells," Orlando said. "Here or in the control room."

"Me neither. They probably had full body clean suits on." Janey sighed. "Soren can double-check our readings. His scanners are more refined than ours. Maybe he'll get something." Soren Stinson, their crime lab tech, had been bugging her to upgrade her sensors for better sweeps, so they could get to the answers that much sooner. Where was he?

"He can check your implant too, yes?" Orlando asked. "I thought you'd worked out all the glitches."

"Me too." Janey rubbed her temples, more from frustration than fatigue. "There's nothing else to see here."

Orlando spun in a slow circle at the empty vault and whistled. "Schoeneman's going to be raging."

"No doubt."

"Does he have a backup, enough hard currency, gems, lingots, on hand to cover the casino?"

"I don't know. He should, back in Zurich. But if gamblers rush to cash out or investors think L'Étoile can't cover its debts..." Janey exited the vault and stepped into the control room, light-headed and sick to her stomach.

Chief Medical Officer Tseng and her team had arrived and were speaking softly to each other in medical terms. One assistant worked on Kosi. The other covered Ed with a black body bag. Beside Ed's shrouded form, Tseng glanced up at Janey and shook her head.

He was gone.

Janey tightened her lips against the anger and sadness storming inside her.

Tseng came beside her assistant, conferred with him, and ran her medical handheld over Kosi.

"Mr. Dube is critical," Tseng said, her voice more clipped than usual, tension in her clenched jaw and rigid spine. "We need to get him back to medical to stabilize him."

"What happened to him?" Janey asked.

"Something is interfering with normal organ function. If we don't stop whatever it is, he will die." Tseng motioned for her assistants to lift Kosi onto a stretcher.

Kosi's face was pale and his breathing shallow. He was hooked up to an IV patch, and a monitor was beeping softly at his side. The assistants lifted the stretcher between them, and it hovered above the floor. On a voice command, the stretcher glided out of the monitoring room toward the corridor. The doctor turned to follow.

With a hand on the petite woman's shoulder, Janey stopped her. "Doctor, what killed Ed?"

Edouard Kou was—had been—her friend.

The doctor flinched ever so briefly, then regained her composure. "Everything just stopped. Heart. Lungs. Nervous system." Tseng frowned and stared at the stretcher floating away.

"Suspicious death, then." Janey clenched her hands into fists.

"Not my call. I've called Doctor Wellesley Running Feather. She'll have to give you an answer to COD." Cause of death.

Doctor Wellesley Running Feather was the station's coroner and medical examiner and rarely came on scene herself.

Janey nodded and let Tseng go. Hopefully, Kosi had a chance. There was nothing more Janey could do for Ed, except catch the thieves, recover the stolen items, and find out how Ed was murdered and Kosi harmed.

Orlando approached the wall monitors. "Janey, can you unlock this for me?" He waved at them. The screens were blacked off. "I can start with a timeline analysis and check the cameras."

"I tried earlier," Janey said. "They weren't responding. But I can try something else…" She came alongside him, standing at the table that ran along two walls. The wall screens covered the entire width and breadth of the walls in the ten-by-ten-foot room.

Her current security codes had done nothing. Maybe an older code would. She tried one and it worked. The wall monitors flickered to life. She synched her wrist comm with it, but the local memory had been wiped. No video footage of the last hour. Not good. She checked the backup bucket and hit a firewall that wasn't supposed to be there, requesting a password. Not good at all.

"The system has been tampered with," Janey said.

"That's what I noticed too," Orlando said.

Janey waved over her wrist comm. "Kim—"

"I can't get any footage from the vault and surrounding corridor," Kim said, voice tight, her breathing rapid. "As if the last hour has been wiped. I wasn't notified. If the system's been tampered with, I can't tell."

"Doc's on her way. Ed…is gone," Janey said.

"Oh no." Kim gulped. "What about Kosi?"

"He's critical. Heading to Medical with Dr. Tseng."

"What can I do?" Kim asked. "What happened?"

"There's a firewall that shouldn't be here," Janey said. She waved over a wall screen again to be sure and glanced at Orlando who frowned and shook his head. He couldn't bypass it either, and he excelled at backdoor hacking.

"It should be secured from the outside." Kim sounded angry. She'd set up most of the security systems on L'Étoile when it'd opened ten years ago.

"I know. Can you determine what happened from one of the backups?" Janey asked. Every screen and work portal on the space station had at least three backups that she knew of. "Can you find out how those monitors could have been sabotaged from there? I'll do what I can on my end."

"On it." Kim closed the comm.

"Okay, Mister full of surprises—showing up today in my boss's office—any thoughts? Any rabbits to pull out of your hat to shed some light on what the ersatz happened here?" she asked Orlando. "We need to see what happened. The monitors track all transactions from the casino and the hotel. Plus, the room AI tracks whoever is in here. And I can't reach any of it."

"No such luck. My bag of tricks is emptied—nothing I try works." He ground his teeth. "I could call in my division's tech team."

"No, let's wait and see what Kim can uncover. She knows the system better than anyone."

Just then, Doctor Wellesley Running Feather, or Doc as most people called her, swept into the room. Her statuesque presence filled the small office, her thick black hair in an elaborate braid wrapped around her forehead like a crown, a white lab coat covering a colorful floor-sweeping garment. Without speaking, she surveyed the scene, then knelt beside Ed's inert, covered body. She scanned him with her holo screen, her black case of instruments at her side.

Janey let her work. When Doc did show up on scene, she didn't like to be disturbed.

After a few minutes, Soren Stinson arrived and stilled as he surveyed the scene, buttoned up in his white lab coat, his blond spiky hair his only nod to current fashion. "Janey, where do you want me?" He noticed Orlando. "Hey, Valdez, I didn't know you were here. Sparkly." Soren faced Janey, expectant.

She led the tall tech into the vault. He whistled. "I always wondered what was in here. Guess now I'll find out the hard way." He set to work, placing his specialized tools on shelves and on the floor. Janey watched for a moment, but it would be a while until he gathered his data. She left to confer with the Doc.

Doc was standing, frowning over Ed's body.

"What is it?" Janey asked softly.

Doc shook her head. "Something is very odd about this one."

"Odd in what way?"

"Don't know. I'll know more when I get him on my table."

"Time of death?" Janey asked.

"I'd say just before oh-seven-hundred."

"Why do you say that?"

"Body temp down by point-zero-three. Livor mortis hasn't set in yet, neither has rigor mortis. Way too soon. Also, I scanned his chip. You didn't scan that?"

"No. People's ID chips usually don't mark the time of death, they just hold identifying information and credits." Janey stared at Ed's right wrist, where his chip was lodged. She rubbed her wrist, the faint ridges pebbly under her fingertips.

"His had a bioelectric trigger in his, connected to his medicine," Doc said.

"Right." Janey nodded. "Ed had time-released allergy medicine. Something about being allergic to dust mites on the station." Janey had overheard some of his buddies teasing him about his allergy, Kosi included. The two were—had been—inseparable, always taking their shifts together and doing better work together than split up. Ed loved tinkering and was often—had been—the casino repairman as his cover during stings. She was going to miss his steady presence.

"The bio-chip registered his heart stopped at 6:58 a.m. Could be time of death," Doc said.

"We got the alarm at 7:03. Maybe Kosi tripped it," Janey said. "How, specifically, did he die, Doc? What caused his death? Some kind of poison? And why is his face so grey? His skin is so dry and crinkly. I've never seen that." Ed had been a vivacious, healthy man in his fifties, but now he appeared to be over a hundred and twenty, without rejuvenation treatments. "It's as if he aged after death. How is that possible, Doc?"

"I don't know the answers to your questions, Janey. Not yet. Never seen anything like it." Doc stared at the body as if Ed would open his eyes and tell her. "Have you run a basic bioelectric and olfactory scan on him?"

"No. I was waiting for you." Janey waved open the comm to the right functions and gulped against the sharp lump in her throat.

"I know he was a trusted colleague," Doc said gruffly.

"He was." Janey blew out a breath. "I can only gather the standard minimum range with this device." She waved the functions to run and then shook her head.

"That's strange." She eyed the data on her holo that shot vertically from her wrist comm. "bioelectrics actually reveal he's over one hundred years old." She frowned at the wavering screen. "The olfactometer is registering some unusual readings too." She double-checked the readings on her optical screen, but the readings were identical.

"My bioelectrics confirm that age analysis." Doc's specialized device could analyze over one thousand scent accents and determine the health or disease of a body.

"As if he died of old age," Janey spoke in a whisper. No one died of old age anymore. "What could cause that?"

"His organs were in senescence. Again, I'll know more when I get him on my table." Doc pursed her lips. "Soren here?"

Janey pointed to the open door of the vault. Doc called out to Soren for him to return with her and help transport the body to the lab.

"I need five minutes, Doc," Soren called out from the vault.

Janey moved into the small waiting room to get out of Doc and Soren's way. And she needed to comm Kim another update.

Orlando was sitting on a chair, waving at his holo screen. She'd lost track of him while talking with Doc. Janey stared at the way his dark wavy hair fell over his strong jaw, at the way his hair brushed the long column of his neck.

Stars, she'd missed him.

How were they going to work together? She let out a sigh.

Moment by moment, that was how.

He looked up at her but wasn't really seeing her. "Just checking in with the home office."

"What is it?" Janey asked.

He finally focused on her. "I'm sorry I didn't tell you I was arriving. This case—it's more need-to-know than usual." He searched her face. "Sometimes this job—" He didn't finish the sentence.

"Compounded with mine...I know. But we can do this."

His gaze deepened, tugging on her like the magnetic pull of the nearest star. Her body responded with a flare of desire at her center. It had been three months since they'd been together during their vacation Earthside. Nightly vid calls just weren't the same.

"Hey, the case," she said softly, more for herself than him.

"I know. Right." He waved over his holo screen and stared at it, brow furrowed as if it were the most important data point in the world.

"What did you see that I didn't?" Janey asked.

"I was starting the search for similar cases when a case-related message came through." No subterfuge showed in his expression or his pulse. His bio-signals were all normal on her ocular screen, a comforting beacon. They were together in the same location, the same time zone.

"Thanks. Find anything?"

"Not yet."

Janey spun and paced the length of the small waiting room, the curtain fluttering in her wake. "We have to catch these people. Two maybe four people involved. Maybe more. And fast."

"If guests catch wind of the theft, they'll panic. Not to mention the investors," Orlando said.

"Yes, and that's the last thing in the Sol this place needs or Schoeneman wants. The gala in one week. I was hoping you saw something I didn't because we have few clues and a big problem."

He shook his head, no. "Sorry, nothing yet. But my offer still stands to call our tech team."

There. His pulse increased. Her ocular implant didn't lie, but it didn't tell her why something had shifted in Orlando. He was covering up something—about his tech team? Or his case. Probably his case. She wanted to ask about the deception but knew better. He'd tell her when and if he could. It was his right, but the secrecy still irked her.

When all they did was carry on via vid calls, it was easy to push aside the unseen, but when he was with her —the fire of frustration flamed again.

She'd clear the air with him later. Now she had to get this case rolling and catch the murderers before they tried to get off the station.

Janey commed Kim. Kim picked up, her voice tight. "It's not good."

"Tell me."

"All the crypto-currency is gone, contracts too. All have been wiped off the network," Kim said grimly. "I notified Schoeneman." Kim lowered her voice. "Do you think the heist has anything to do with that unidentified vibration we felt?"

"Don't know. Have you determined its source yet?"

"No, I was in the middle of gathering reports. Then the alarm…"

"I know. Thanks. Set the station on lockdown," Janey said. She should have thought of that as soon as she'd arrived on scene.

"Already done."

She glanced at her holo. Oh, it was right there. This case had her rattled. "Right, of course. Thank you." Janey gathered a breath for the next words she had to say. "Kim, sorry to tell you, Doc pronounced. Ed is dead."

Kim had known them both longer than Janey, had worked with them, played cards with them, and sang silly karaoke with Ed after dinner at the commissary.

"Oh dear." Kim sucked in a breath. "I didn't want to believe… His family will be devastated."

"You knew them?"

"I met them a few times on leave over the years." Kim pushed out a sigh. "Did you want me to tell them?"

A familiar face would be good. "Let's do it together when I get back."

"Okay."

"Kim, please send Natalia and Clark to guard the scene."

Their daily security checks on incoming guests in advance of the gala would have to wait.

"Will do," Kim said, her voice firm and all business again. "Do you have any leads?"

"Not yet. I've sent you all I have, so far." Janey rubbed her temple. "We're looking for two, possibly four, unknowns. I need to know if everyone is accounted for, staff and guests."

"I'll get on it. Top priority." Her voice raised in pitch, angry. "How could someone break into the vault unde-tected, bypassing all our security protocols, and shut down the vids? And why the vicious attack on Ed and Kosi?"

"I don't know." Janey blew out a breath and paced the small room.

Orlando was staring hard at her like he wanted to say something.

Kim didn't speak but Orlando did. "Cloaking tech."

"Possibly. We'll consider all angles," Janey said, her voice hard.

"I'll get on it," Kim said again, her voice tight, sad. She commed off.

Schoeneman would be beyond apoplectic.

Someone had just taken billions of credits, valuable mining contracts, all the backup currency on hand L'Étoile had for all the gambling and slot machines, precious asteroid metals, and killed one person in the process, with another at death's door. They had robbed the operating credits. The casino dealers had maybe twelve to twenty-four hours' worth of credits in their independent chip system. Once that was gone, the casino would have to shut down—if there wasn't a general panic before that. Either way, this was a PR nightmare on the eve of the tenth-anniversary gala.

She and her team had to find the killers, the gems, and the contracts before they fled the station. And before anyone else got hurt.

FOUR

"You going to be all right? Need me for anything?" Orlando stood and waved his wrist about in the small waiting room, grey walls, grey recyclo floor, all grey. "I got a lead. On my case. And I need to—" He gestured toward the door. "But I could... if you needed me."

She nodded, numb for a second. Leads, she needed leads.

"Go. Work in the conference room until Kim assigns you a desk. Or you could work at Ed's desk in the bullpen," Janey said and immediately regretted it. Her throat tightened. "Too soon. Sorry."

"Nothing to be sorry to me about." He reached out to her but didn't rub her shoulder like she thought he would. Instead, he stared off into the middle distance. For a moment, he seemed lost, not the self-assured, cocky investigator he normally projected. Then he took a breath and nodded to himself as if he'd made up his mind about something. "I only got to know him a little.

He seemed like a good guy, hardworking, good at bocce ball."

"He was all those things," Janey huffed out. "He was stubborn and nice, diligent, kind, solid."

They'd need a memorial karaoke party. Ed would have loved that.

"You sure you don't need me for anything?" Orlando eyed her lips and then met her gaze, a kindness there. "If not, I have plenty to do." He lifted his wrist again.

"Send me the data you collected from the scene. I would like your help with the timeline and anything else you—" Janey started, but Soren interrupted as he burst through the door from the monitor room.

"Janey, I've got some strange readings." He waved his hands in the direction of the vault behind him.

"What?"

"Trimethylamine." He wrinkled his nose.

"You smell something?"

"I smell something fishy. That's from the trimethylamine, an organic compound. Did you smell it?"

"No. What's it from?"

"Don't know yet," Soren said.

"What's it used in?"

"As a plant growth regulator, herbicides, making dye, among other things."

In the waiting room threshold behind Soren, the stretcher floated and gently bumped into him.

"Stinson, move," Doc barked. Doc was done with her preliminary on Ed's body.

"Thanks, Soren," Janey said, not wanting to stare at the black shroud that covered Ed but couldn't stop herself. "Comm me the minute you have something. I have no leads on these bastards." Her throat tightened again.

"You got it, Janey." Soren gazed down at the body on the floating stretcher too, fists clenched, a look of bewilderment on his paled face. "Poor Ed. We will find out who did this to you."

"Let's go, Stinson," Doc said more softly and waved Soren forward. Doc and Soren left the grey, drab, pointless waiting room to head back to their labs.

Orlando stood and stared at her.

"What?" Janey tugged at her standard black jacket. Was it not fitting correctly?

"I am sorry for not letting you know I was coming. I'd been fighting with the bureaucracy, both mine and Schoeneman's office, to get me back on L'Étoile for a few months. I didn't want to say anything." Orlando closed the two feet between them, hunger in his gaze as he drank her in. He lifted a palm to her cheek but didn't touch. "I didn't want to get your hopes up. Plus, 'need to know'." He dropped his hand. "Now this."

She gazed into his hazel eyes, and then spun away from his heat. She had to do something to distract herself from wanting to lean into him for his warmth and his strength. She crossed through the monitoring office and re-entered the vault to resume the necessary and urgent work of finding out what the Venus Hells happened.

"We need to confirm the trace Soren mentioned," she said over her shoulder.

"Wait," Orlando said from behind her in the monitor room.

"I can't," Janey said. "Work first, play later, once the case is closed." Who knew when that was? But it had to be soon or everyone on the station would be out of a job.

"Not that. There's something here. Must have been under Ed's body."

Janey returned to the control office, scanning all spectrums again. "What? I don't see anything."

Orlando snapped on gloves and crouched under the table connected to the wall. Janey did the same and bent to see what he was looking at. Grey granules the size of grains of sand were barely visible against the grey recyclo carpet. Beside the granules was a small canister that easily fit into her palm.

"Must have been hidden under Ed's body when he fell, then thrown aside when Doc moved his body." Janey scanned the grains. "This dust is from some kind of metal compound."

She'd been searching the light spectrum and not for any particulates.

"I'll document." Orlando prepped his wrist holo.

"Great, thanks." In her haste, she hadn't had a chance to grab her gear with her kit. But she always had a few extra evidence bags in her jacket pockets. She pulled out a few now and handed them to Orlando. "Bag the canister and granules, and we'll get them to Soren as soon as the replacement guards arrive. Be careful with the canister. No telling what it contains." She swallowed against the bile rising up in her throat. Ed dead, Kosi down, the vault empty.

"It's probably spent." Orlando bagged the items, wrinkling his nose. "But spent from what?"

"Good question. Thanks for doing that." She didn't notice any odd smell.

Janey entered the vault again, scanned, and recorded the areas Soren mentioned, checking the shelves and the floor again. On the tile floor, there were fine granules she'd overlooked—dust and some trace of metal grains in patches. Similar to the trace Orlando spotted. Surely, Soren had bagged the trace. Why he left these behind she didn't know.

These granules were grey, beige, and black, and so very fine, like specs of dust in motes of sunlight, they'd blended into the grey recyclo-flooring of the vault. No wonder the specs had shown up as dust in a basic scan.

She stared at her holo, comparing it to her ocular implant screen.

The metal analysis they showed her was confusing. The granules were comprised of different metals found all over L'Étoile, commonly used to manufacture structural elements, such as the walls and doors, chairs, and tables—their entire surroundings.

Could the metal particles be left over from when this part of the station was built years ago?

She headed back into the monitoring office and paused. Orlando was peering behind the removable wall monitors, panels attached to the walls.

"Found anything else?" Janey asked.

Orlando put a finger to his lips for her to stop talking and waved her over, gesturing at something on the back of the paper-thin monitor—a small dot, nearly invisible against the back of the screen. Janey scanned it. Yes, it was still transmitting. She examined the data streaming from the microdot, pursed her lips, and rushed to check the rest of the wall monitors, detaching them from the wall. They each had this dot on the back—all unregistered data transfer devices.

"Are they listening to us?" Orlando mouthed.

"No, thank the stars," Janey said.

"Sure?"

"Yes, but worse. They're pulling data out of the vault monitoring system."

"Maldición," Orlando swore in Spanish.

"And it's worse. They stole not only the contents of

the vault but also all the data pouring through the control room—the hourly security codes, the security rotation, the transfer times off-station. Venus Hells. Someone has been watching us for some time. Who knows how long the dots have been here, bugging this room?" She sank in a chair, her legs rubbery. Panic fluttered in her chest like a caged bird trying to escape. "Kim didn't see this."

Spies, in their midst.

"Your security cams in the corridor…" Orlando bit his lip, worried too.

"Show nothing. Kim said." Janey rubbed her temples, a throbbing headache forming. She sighed and pushed out of the chair. This had to have been a carefully orchestrated and well-planned heist. "Kim can trace the feed of the microdots at her workstation better than I can here." Hopefully.

The thieves had circumvented their security. Had all security L'Étoile had been compromised? She tamped down on the urge to yell and throw something. This wasn't the time.

"I'll take them off." Orlando reached over to pull one off.

"No. The data could still be transferring. We don't want to alert them that we are on to them."

"Whoever they are," Orlando said grimly.

"And wherever they are," Janey bit out. "We need to catch them."

FIVE

THE MONITORING ROOM WALLS SEEMED TO press in on her. The whole situation was terrible. Ed dead, and Kosi in intensive care. L'Étoile's vault robbed, the operating credits siphoned off, and their vault security breached. No one had ever dared rob them before, not even attempted. And Janey had read all the case files from the last ten years on many a quiet duty shift.

Her headache getting worse by the second, Janey shoved the pain into a black hole and commed Kim, for the second time in fifteen minutes.

"Could the data still be siphoning off L'Étoile?" Janey asked. Her heart squeezed. Where would it be going? The where could help determine the who and the why.

"No, not that I can tell," Kim said, her voice tense, thankfully interrupting her worst-case scenario conjecture. "I'll dive into it."

Janey waited, rolled her shoulders, and stared at the grey fuzzy screen walls.

Without working credits on L'Étoile, the casino would have to shut down. Then there'd most likely be mass panic, angry demanding customers, and a PR nightmare. When customers were angry and panicked they did stupid things that could jeopardize the safety of the station. Locking down the bar and the escape pods wasn't her first choice. Her first choice was catching the murderers and retrieving the credits before the end of the day.

Luckily, there were up to twenty-four hours of working credits in the holding caches of the casino itself. Plus, a nightly transfer of credits to and from the head-quarters' bank in Zurich.

Two minutes passed before Kim came back on the comms.

"Janey—" Kim's voice was low, a raspy whisper. "The credits—the data's all gone. What the—" She swore in Kiribati and then in New York street slang.

The vault's precious gems and collateral and contracts and now this?

"Are you sure?" Janey asked, then mentally kicked herself. Of course, Kim was sure. She was one of the smartest techs Janey knew. "Can you see where it went?"

"No, because—that's odd."

"What?"

"All outgoing transmissions from L'Étoile are accounted for."

"That *is* odd. Or a point in our favor." Janey blew out a breath of tiny relief. "That means the digital and hard currency and other items stolen are still on station. But where? Who has those skills?"

"That's your department," Kim said glumly. "And it's not even 8 a.m. But the fact that the stolen credits are still on board, that's got to mean something, right? A small thumbs-up on an otherwise horrible day."

"Right." Janey scrubbed her face. If the perpetrators

were waiting for some point later in the day to flee, then maybe they had transport arranged. "Kim, have the Hanger Chief scan for any small craft out beyond."

"On it." Kim's comm went silent. Janey could imagine her signing the information in front of one of her wall screens set to translate into text and send.

"I'll also send you vids on what we found. Please send them to the team." With a flick of her wrist, Janey transferred the stills and a short vid of the dots on the backs of the office monitors. "Where are the guards anyway?"

"Natalia and Clark should have arrived and checked in with you by now."

"For star's sake." Janey went to the waiting room entrance, and there they were. Natalia and Clark worked often together, and well—though they were opposites in temperament and styles. Natalia Goldberg was graceful and tall, dressed in a tailored shimmery brick red silk suit as if ready for the casino floor, while Clark Alexander Bernard was short and stocky and dressed in a grey jumpsuit. Both had been off-duty for the morning shift. "Guard the door. Thanks," Janey commanded, and they nodded their assent, alert and serious.

Back in the monitor room, she continued with Kim. "Got the data? See the small near-transparent dots, one-point-two millimeters across?"

She forced herself to exhale, panic rising like a wave across the back of her head. She was behind the eight ball on this case, from the moment the alarm sounded. One of her team had been killed in a brutal way and the hotel-casino robbed.

"Yes. Got it all. I'll sift through it and determine if I can discover what they were looking for," Kim said. "Have you seen this kind of attack before? Has Orlando?"

"Similar, but nothing this sophisticated. Nothing like this." Janey glanced at Orlando, who shook his head, a thoughtful expression on his face. "He says, no, but he's been digging into the Sol criminal databases."

Kim mumbled curses and commed off with a promise to get back to her with further analysis pronto.

"You've caught something similar?" Orlando quirked an eyebrow at her and waved over his comm, probably inputting the search.

"In my days with the Space Wing Command MP division, I caught an airman trying to sell military secrets to the Russian Empire. He'd stuffed the top-secret ion drive specs into a transparent cube about one-inch square." She illustrated with a small space between her fingers. "He was about to dump it into a cup of coffee at a spaceport café when I arrested him."

"Good on you," Orlando said.

"Thanks. And to my team." Janey checked the time. Only thirty minutes had passed, but it felt like a lot longer. "Orlando, how's that check coming along?"

He glared at the holo screen hovering above his wrist comm and paced the wallscreen monitor room, careful to avoid the spot where Ed had fallen. "Nothing so far."

Watching his movement made her head pound more. Something about the grey of the dead screens behind his vibrant, energetic body. She closed her eyes and moved them from side to side to reset her screen and her focus.

"Janey?" Orlando touched her arm. "¿Cariña? ¿Está bien?"

"I'm okay. Just a headache."

"Still? Can I help?" His voice was gentle, his warmth radiating, beckoning her like a moth to the flame. She shook her head. "Maybe the med kit has something for it." His warmth left her side. A moment later, the warmth was back. "Here."

She opened her eyes to a grey, fuzzy room. Orlando had a pain tab in his palm. She took the tab and swallowed it. She sent the command and blinked again to reset her ocular implant. Her vision went back to normal, her headache receding. "Thank you."

"Your implant? I thought you just had your monthly medical."

"I did. I told you." A sharp bite crept into her voice. It was the pain talking.

"I know what would make you feel better," he said, ignoring her jab, his voice a warm rumble, his gaze caressing her.

She shook her head, not bothering to look away, drinking in his desire. Then she spun away, closed the vault room, and reset the locking mechanisms. "Later." She strode across the crime scene, staying clear of where Ed had fallen, and crossed to the waiting room.

"Natalia, Clark, seal the doors. No one in except for our team."

"Yes, ma'am," Natalia said and popped open her crime scene kit. Clark had his too. She could rely on them.

"Let's go," she said to Orlando and exited the scene, Orlando at her side. She led the way down the narrow grey corridor to the service elevator, pipes overhead painted grey to match the walls and floor.

"What part of the station is this?" Orlando asked as they stepped into the elevator. "It doesn't show up on any maps I've studied."

"I know." Something wasn't sitting right with her, an unease stalking her like the remnants of a bad dream. She fiddled with her pearl choker at her throat. Mom had given it to her as a high school graduation gift, packed it with photos and holos of her childhood. She hadn't been able to make the medical calls for her mom as she'd hoped to be doing this morning. That dragged on her, but that wasn't it.

"You're worried about your mom?"

"How'd you know?"

"You're touching your choker." Orlando mirrored her move. "¿Qué tal?"

"Later."

"Okay, about the maps then." He nodded.

"I told you last time you were here." Janey shrugged, breathing out to release the stress of her mom's situation. "Schoeneman is cagey that way, making sure the maps are a little off until you're cleared as an employee. Even then, the in-house staff maps aren't one hundred percent accurate. I've mapped the station extensively and charted every inch of this place." She hoped she had.

The secretive—even paranoid—actions of the station owner. What could she do, except what she'd done? Knowledge was power.

"So, where are we then?" Orlando studied his holo.

"Five levels below the lobby and a half-floor down from the maintenance level on the left aft dorsal side."

"And half a level up from the machine shop." He nodded. He'd helped out on the last big and dangerous case that had taken them to the lower levels, including the machine shop.

The station map discussion jogged something free that had been niggling at her since she'd arrived at the vault and resisted stating so baldly.

She said at the same time as Orlando did: "It's an inside job."

He whistled.

She held up her hand in a stop sign. "What if it only seems to be an inside job?"

"Okay, I get where you're going with this." He leaned against the elevator wall and faced her. "Everyone has to know there's a vault."

"Yes, only not where it is." Janey stared at the panel of lights, tugging on her pearl choker again. "Why do you think it's in a grey tiny out-of-the-way service corridor on this half level?" Her nerves fluttered up and down her spine, the certainty of it being an inside job flooding her system. "We need evidence."

"What evidence do we have so far?" Orlando asked.

"So you're going to help me?"

"Yes. My case can wait. Go on. I know you like to talk it out."

Janey nodded and proceeded. "The mysterious dots, the unknown way Ed was killed, the dust particles, the canister..."

"Right. And who could know the vault's location?" Orlando crossed his arms.

"Security personnel—our team, the casino pit bosses, Schoeneman. Maybe his executive team."

Orlando chewed his lip, uncrossed his arms, and waved the information into wrist holo comm.

"Adding that to your search parameters?"

He murmured his assent.

The elevator arrived at the main level. Janey hustled to the conference room, across the corridor from Chief Milano's office, Orlando at her side, quiet, practically vibrating with something to share. She sensed his shifts in moods as if they were the subtle changes in wind direction off the San Francisco Bay sea walls.

"What?" she asked as she unlocked the door with the eye scanner.

"I'll tell you later." He shook his head. "We're not going to your office?"

"We can both work in here, plenty of space."

The door whooshed open. The wide room was empty of staff. Most security staff was securing the station's three exits: the SkyEl elevator to the Earth's surface, the hanger for the guests' arrivals via space jet, and the exits to the escape pods.

The coffee maker was percolating. Morning buns, cream puffs, and other pastries had been stocked in the bin. Janey commed Kim to let her know she'd arrived. Orlando sat at the far end of the conference table, nearest the far wallscreen set to pipe in the real-time morning sun, its warm glow burnishing his face and neck. Head bent in concentration, he seemed to be folded in on himself, his whole focus on processing, connecting the dots, and gathering puzzle pieces.

She approached the wide wallscreen and cleared it of a swirling starscape of the Andromeda galaxy. With a horizontal cutting gesture, she started a timeline of the crime and waved in the details.

Five minutes later, the door whisked open, and in strode Chief Milano.

"Report," he said, jaw tight. "The vault emptied? Operations currency disappeared? Ed deceased? Kosi critical? And what's this about an unidentifiable vibration you felt?"

Janey paused from her waving and addressed Milano. "Yes, to all of it."

Chief had never shown up for an in-person verbal report right after her visit to a crime scene. Then again, no one had ever robbed the station before and killed one of their own.

"No news on the vibration, yet. I felt it on my way to

our meeting this morning and commed Kim. She was tracking it down when—the alarm."

"Quello è strano," he muttered. That was strange, in Italian. He had a faraway look in his eye as if he were someplace else.

"Chief?"

"Proceed, Investigator," he said, snapping out of it.

She nodded and walked him through what they knew. The alarm at 7:03, their arrival at the scene at 7:05 and no trace of the intruders, Ed and Kosi down, and their attempts at first aid. At 7:08, she'd examined the vault to find it emptied of all contents. She showed him the vids and stills of the evidence they'd collected that Stinson was analyzing in his lab—the minute granules and the canister that had been under Ed's body. And about the microdots.

Milano shook his head, frowning.

"Doc pronounced Ed on scene and said his TOD may have been 6:58 when his med tracker registered no heartbeat. Tseng said Kosi is still in critical. No word yet on the cause of death or the cause of Kosi's illness," Janey said.

"What about vid?" Milano asked.

"Someone cut the vid in the hour before the alarm. We see Meilani and Antonia leaving and Ed and Kosi arriving. Then nothing."

"How convenient. Have you talked to Meilani and Antonia?" The chief sounded tired and disgusted.

Janey nodded. "I'll wake them up." She requested for Kim to have them report. Kim acknowledged.

"What about this? Inside job." Milano tapped the board where Janey had written that. "What's your evidence?"

"So far?" Janey exchanged a glance with Orlando.

"They knew where the vault was. They overrode the vault with some backdoor hack not even Kim knew. The microdots. The siphoning of funds from operations..." Her stomach clenched. They would find these bastards. The credits had to be in some kind of impenetrable black box somewhere on L'Étoile. The vault contents in a room somewhere.

Before arriving at the station, all staff were thoroughly vetted, but it was possible that people had falsified records and had deep covers. Janey had seen it herself.

Kim strode in, nodded a sober hello at Janey, and spoke, reading off her holo. "I have the snapshot of where everyone was from between 6 and 7 a.m." With a flick of her wrist, she sent the information to the board. Her ruby red tunic dress was one of the few bright spots of the morning—one of her own creations, most likely.

Janey rearranged it to sit below her timeline of the vault crimes and studied the map of the station—an accurate one—with red and blue dots all over it. A side box tallied the totals. She rolled the timeline.

Janey watched timeline progress sped up, and the dots jiggled on the screen. For the first forty minutes, the red dots of Ed and Kosi didn't move much, and no other dots came in or out of the vault.

Red dots for staff—all 2,000 of them. Blue dots were for the guests—900 of them, at the moment. There was one white dot in a Platinum guest suite at the topmost level, and a few more white dots in the staff areas. White dots were for VIPS that didn't fall into the first two categories.

"Who is that?" Janey tapped the white dot by itself in a guest suite.

"That's Schoeneman," Kim said. "He was in his

suite."

"I didn't realize he was on board." Janey tightened her jaw.

"He's often here without notifying anyone except me and the chief," Kim said. "I was going to let you know after the morning staff meeting. Then…" She shook her head.

All hell had broken loose.

Janey was glad not to cross paths with the reclusive station owner. She'd only seen him at the very end of a few of the previous cases, and he was always throwing his weight around, showing what a big shot he was, interfering in her cases without explanation. His right and privilege, she supposed. It was his station, his hotel-casino, after all. But still, she didn't like his interference. He was an industrialist, a capitalist, and a CEO, not an investigator.

At the 6:40 a.m. timestamp, two white dots showed up in the vault, but not in the corridor or monitor room. Their mystery assailants and thieves appeared as if out of thin air.

"What was that? Did they just enter through the walls? How the hell did they get in there?" Milano burst out.

"I don't know, Chief, but we'll find out."

"We're running them down now," Kim said.

"So am I," Orlando chimed in.

Milano frowned.

"I think they're dummy idents," Janey said.

"They're mocking us," Milano grumbled.

"You could be right, sir."

"So what? They waltz into the safe, take the goods, attack our guys, and waltz back out?" Milano asked, glaring at the wallscreen timeline.

Janey sighed. "Looks like it, but they only show up for a few minutes, fifteen at most, in the monitor room and vault."

"Planning." Milano shook his head. "Lots of coordinated, careful planning. The vault must have been robbed a different way. Have you figured out how?"

"Not yet. Soren has particulates, a canister. Doc's with Ed's body." Janey shook her head. "So far everyone is where they should be, except for our unknown assailants."

"I can't find any other heists with this MO in our database," Orlando said.

Everyone looked at him. The sun rays cast a golden halo over his head and shoulders, brightening his dark brown hair and skin, shimmering onto the wallscreen behind him, whitening it out.

Janey sucked in a breath at the flair of attraction in her belly. She blinked to adjust the filter to dampen the light and her fire.

Orlando had two table holo screens open, one on either side. As a third screen, his wrist hologram hovered in a central position in the form of a flickering face—his AI bot interface. The AI holo face was of a beautiful woman who looked like a cross between an Ethiopian and a Celt—a lot like the journalist on the station, in fact. Bright blue-green eyes on an angular brown face, a corona of brown hair surrounding the vibrating holo.

Jealousy bloomed in Janey like an overnight orchid coming to life. She squelched it—old fears flaming to life, nothing more—and addressed Kim. "Where is the journalist and her crew?"

"I sent them to the casino for their B reel. Anahi is babysitting them," Kim said.

"Who?"

"Anahi Prentice, one of the new agents. She's a recent grad from Space Wing Academy. You vetted her last month."

"Right. Good, we want a security agent with them at all times. I'd send the journalist and her cameras home, if I could."

Chief Milano cleared his throat. "Not your call, McCallister."

"I know, Chief. The coincidence of the coming celebrations, the heist, and the journalist's arrival…" She shook her head. "I don't like it."

"Me neither. But they're only persons of interest at this point. Any other suspects?"

"No, Chief. Not yet."

"I want you to update me every hour." Milano hunched a little, then expelled a breath and straightened, a fatigue in his gaze she hadn't seen before on him. "I'm passing my updates to Schoeneman. It goes without saying that he's more than concerned."

"I'm surprised he's not here, breathing down our necks in person," Janey said.

"He's probably in frantic business meetings, assuring his partners and investors that everything is okay," Milano said with a sniff of condescension or was that hostility? While he continued to file reports as always, ever since Schoeneman's interference in the last murder case, Milano hadn't been his boss's biggest supporter.

"How do they know something isn't okay?" Janey asked.

The chief waved a hand as if to bat away his words. "He knows. Somehow. Didn't say. He told me he was conducting business as usual. I'll be in my office, McCallister. Get me a list of viable suspects, presto." Milano stomped out of the room.

"Milano looks like he's aged a decade in the last hour," Kim said softly.

"He does. The weight of the job…" Janey tapped her chin, staring at the door. "What does he know that he's not saying?"

"Did you know that his wife was part of the team that designed and built the hotel and casino?" Kim spoke up.

"Including the vault?"

"Yes."

"Milano's been here since then," Janey mused. "So have you, Kim."

"I have, and I remember when his wife was designing this place."

Before you were working here? Janey wanted to ask, but now wasn't the time. Kim never talked about her past before working on L'Étoile, and Janey hadn't wanted to pry. "Can you get me the original blueprints?"

"Of course," Kim said.

"What are you thinking?" Valdez asked.

"Maybe the vault was robbed from the other side," Janey said.

"We didn't pull the shelving away from the wall." Valdez nodded, on her wavelength.

"Soren can check behind the vault shelving." Janey sent him a message, went back to the timeline she'd been building, and added more details.

For a few minutes, they worked in silence.

"I've finished scanning the news feeds, and there's absolutely no news of the theft," Kim said.

"That's good. We don't need a panic," Janey said. "Then how did Schoeneman find out?"

In his work corner, Orlando snorted but didn't look up from his work.

"What's that about, Orlando?" Kim asked, her tone

light, but Janey heard the steel beneath.

Orlando shrugged. "What I think doesn't matter. It's what I can prove."

"You're investigating Schoeneman?" Kim tilted her head and examined him with a coolness Janey hadn't seen in her before as if she were addressing a stranger she didn't like much.

"I can neither confirm nor deny…" he replied, lifting one shoulder in a mockery of the standard statement spoken by spies for over the last one hundred and fifty years.

"Okay." Kim adjusted a red hibiscus snug in her dark hair high on her head and said to Janey, "Need me for anything else?"

"Yes." She tapped the wall screen. "The other white dots? The journalist and her crew?"

"Yes." Kim nodded. "Their press passes are coded."

"Every single one of her crew has been vetted and cleared? It didn't come through our office." Janey frowned.

"Of course." Kim waved over a corner of the wallscreen, called up her workstation, and waved some more. "Says right here that Sandrine in the Zurich office cleared them." In a lower voice, as if to herself, she said, "I didn't vet Sandrine."

"When did they arrive and how?" Janey asked.

Kim waved her hand over the screen as if flipping through a book. "Last night. On Schoeneman's jet. With him, in fact."

Janey glanced at Orlando over her shoulder. "Were you on that flight?"

Maybe she'd catch him unawares, and he'd reveal something about his case.

He looked up from his three docile glowing screens.

"No, I took SkyEl up and got here last night." SkyEl was the space elevator staff took to the station. A five-day journey, it was a great time to catch up on your reading or sleep.

"And you didn't bother to come and see me." She sighed.

"It was late. I bunked with the staff dorm."

"Really?" Orlando seemed more like a high-flyer. He loved being a high-class spy. He wouldn't waste five days in the elevator or sleep in a dormitory. What was his case? Though they had enjoyed a humble hotel in her hometown on their vacation.

"Hold on—" Orlando tapped his earpiece as if he was listening to something, so Janey went back to her time-line and to Kim.

"Who else was in that SkyEl car with Orlando? I want to get a sense of the recent arrivals."

Kim waved and snapped her fingers at the wallscreen. "Seven new housekeeping staff, two new engineers, and five new kitchen prep chefs."

They were expecting one hundred more guests for the party in seven days, filling the hotel to its capacity of three thousand souls—staff and guests.

Janey paced in front of the board. "Right. I saw those vetting reports."

"I can double-check them," Kim offered.

"No, that's fine. I'm just grasping at straws here. Our suspects could be anyone on board this morning who had the gumption to wear a junk ident. There's no footage of our crime scene. No DNA evidence. Nothing that links back to anyone." She stared at the board. She needed evidence, something solid to follow. "A ghost didn't kill Ed. A real live human being did. And by Saturn's Rings, I'm going to find out who."

SIX

"Not human beings, Janey. Bots," Orlando said grimly and swore.

"Bots?" Janey frowned. "Those are hard to trace."

"You got that right. There was this one case in my art heist days—"

"Stealing or investigating?" Janey asked. He'd done both. It took a master thief to catch the thieves.

Orlando gave her a bland look, revealing nothing.

"Bots, really?" Kim said, not believing. "Bots unaccompanied are illegal except under the strictest controls. Section Thirty-One."

Orlando crossed his arms. "Despite Section Thirty-One, bots are hard to regulate and trace. Politicians don't seem to realize that."

Janey's heart sped up. "But that could fit. The metal compound granules, the speed of the heist, and the probable murder. Unless Soren finds a damn tunnel behind the walls." She waved a hand over her wrist comm. "Soren, anything?"

"No." He coughed. "Unless you count all the dust as something."

"Another dead-end," Janey said. "Bag and tag."

"On it, boss." Soren commed off.

"The bots couldn't have acted alone," Orlando said. "Someone has to oversee them for something as complicated as moving all that loot out of the safe. That is a lot of loot—"

"Stop saying loot," Janey interjected and served herself a cup of coffee. "Ed died. Seems too cavalier. If bots are the culprits—" She leaned on the counter, hot coffee warming her palms.

Orlando nodded and continued, touching his fingertips in succession, enumerating his reasons. "One, they have to be programmed. Two, the programmer has to be nearby to monitor and direct the bot in the complicated task of lifting and transporting all the odd-shaped items in the vault. Three, I have never heard of a bot leaving trace behind."

"A possible theory," Janey said. "I've never heard of bots leaving trace behind either." She sipped her coffee and spoke to Kim. "Just in case, we need to track the bots on the station. How many are there, and who do they belong to?"

"I'll get the list for you," Kim said. "Not even sure why guests would bring their bots on board since they're not allowed in the casino. And our cleaning bots are the highest-rated."

"Wonders never cease," Janey said. "We could be looking for at least two suspects with bots that may have left traces, with the ability to travel undetected, and who managed to disable two guards, killing one."

"I'll add that parameter to my search," Orlando said. "That definitely sounds like the work of more than one person. And didn't the faint bio-signals in the vault indicate two people?"

"Yes." Janey set her coffee down on the counter and strode past the conference table over to her section of the wallscreen. She then did her own wave dance on her area of wallscreen.

"Okay. Updating our suspects parameters." Kim waved over her screen, calling up the stats for the bots on board like a conductor signaling the trumpets to a crescendo.

"Thanks, Kim. Anything?"

"No. No guests with registered bots, Janey," Kim said, frowning at the wallscreen. "Or staff for that matter. Though..."

"What?"

"Anybody with the right tech skills could reprogram the bots."

"Venus hells." Janey huffed out, spun away from the wall, and picked up her coffee, sipping without tasting. "Orlando, want any?"

"Yes, thanks." He smiled and gazed at her a little too long as if he had more to say.

"What?" she asked.

"Later."

"Fine." She topped hers off, poured a cup for him, and walked it over to him at the far end of the broad table. She sipped hers standing, not really tasting, but needing the warmth between her hands, feeling her pulse, her lifeforce, the energy that drove her forward. She stared out the window at the broadcast of the shaded sun. The window screen blocked out most of the sun's bright rays and all of the sun's harmful UV light. Brighter as it was nearly 9 a.m., the day was ticking down.

Leads, she needed leads.

Though no one had said it outright, there was pressure to close the case as soon as possible and before 6 p.m., when another batch of guests was due to arrive by space jet. If that flight was delayed, guests could talk, spread rumors, and tarnish Schoeneman's reputation.

Another thing normally happened at 6 p.m.: the daily digital transfer to and from the Zurich bank. Was that transfer compromised?

"Kim, we need to let the finance department know the nightly transfer could be compromised," Janey said.

"I've let them know. I've got a colleague earthside helping me sort that out." She looked worried, her lips pursed.

"Thank you." She put her cup in the sink, then headed for the door. "I'll be in the lab to check in with Soren about all the trace we collected. Follow the evidence to some suspects." She hoped. And to connect the dots. Dots on the station map. She stopped at the door, an idea forming. "Kim, could there be people on board that don't show up in the dots map?"

"It's possible," Kim frowned. "Yes..." She tapped her chin, catching Janey's thought thread.

"Undetected biosignatures?" Janey asked.

"Entirely possible," Orlando chimed in.

"You'd know," Janey said. In their last case together, Orlando had fooled their biosignature sensors with his sophisticated spy tricks. Everybody on board and most people on-planet had a registered identity chip with heart rate, fingerprints, and their medical history, usually as part of their identity bracelets or as a chip under their skin.

"I suppose it's possible, but I don't know how you could detect them," Kim said.

"I do," Orlando said. "If they've masked their biosigs, we can detect them only when we're in close proximity."

"How close? Five to ten feet?"

He nodded ruefully.

"And detect what exactly?" Kim chimed in.

"Bio-photons," Janey said to her, then to Orlando, "Manual sweeps of the entire station, then."

"Yes, that could work," he said, his tone doubtful. Janey gave him a hard look.

"Okay, yes, that close, those settings, that does work." He sighed and sat back in the chair. "But don't tell anyone else." He looked over at Kim, who nodded assent. And then at Janey.

"Seriously? I don't divulge your professional secrets to anyone," Janey said. He barely divulged any to her, as it was.

"I know. It's just that I can't be too careful. I need to be able to do my job undetected from my marks—I mean, targets. I mean, suspects."

"Are you planning on doing some sneaking around on my station behind my back again?"

"I hope not." Orlando looked pained.

"We'll need more of our people for the sweep," Kim said.

"You set up the grid search. Have people work in pairs, keeping an eyeline with each other."

Kim set about calling in off-shift security staff and all of their recently hired for the gala. They'd get to know L'Étoile quite well.

Kim cleared her throat, drawing Janey's attention. Kim looked like she'd just downed something way too sour.

"What's wrong?" Janey asked.

"Schoeneman just asked me when we can lift the

lockdown, reminding me about the scheduled arrivals at six."

"Really? Tell him—"

"We're working as fast as we can," Kim finished and waved over her wrist comm.

"Thanks." Janey expelled a big breath. Could they just reboot the day? No. She could—they could—handle this. Had to handle it. "So, if everyone's moves have been accounted for, and still there was a successful heist on the vault and attack on Ed and Kosi—"

"—Someone is hiding somewhere," Orlando finished. "Someones, plural."

"Right," Janey said. "Kim, have Larissa and Jintao sweep the station. Have them double-check all move-ments, even if that puts them on overtime."

"On it," Kim said. "And Milano and Schoeneman already approved all overtime for this case."

"Good. We're going to use a lot of it. Have them start from the top and work down."

"You need more than one team on this," Orlando said.

"Agreed." Janey studied the list of security agents and guards on her holo screen. "Let's ask the hangar chief to be on the lookout with his entire crew and add extra guards in the machine shop." She peered up at Kim, who nodded and input the commands, then at Orlando. "Ready?"

"For what?"

"You and I will start from the bottom of the station and meet in the middle. The thieves have to be hiding somewhere on L'Étoile," Janey said. Only twenty-five levels, one hundred twenty guest suites, a casino, multiple service areas, and several dozen staff quarters to search.

"Okay." Orlando closed his holo screens. "Lab before sweep?"

"Yes." Then Janey said to Kim, "Oh, and let the restaurant know what's happened and have their security be on extra alert." Janey rubbed her chest bone, aching from the stress.

The Phoenix restaurant had lots of in-and-out traffic. A potential place for suspects to hide, if they were wily enough to get past the restaurant's own security team. Janey had seen it happen before.

"I've already let them know." Kim signed over her holo. "Housekeeping too. They have one of their own people standing guard at the SkyEl lobby." Her comm beeped. "Oh, and the hangar chief is sending extra hands to back up for Liberosa because we're already maxed out. Unless you want me to get Meilani and Antonia on it. They're in the bullpen." Meilani and Antonia had been on duty in the vault room before Kosi and Ed had arrived for the 6 a.m. shift.

"Yes, but I need to question them first. Right," Janey said, "will you call them in?"

He nodded at her and went back to his holos.

Meilani and Antonia arrived. Meilani was five-foot-three and had been a gymnast in high school. Antonia was five-foot-nine and a former college basketball player. They'd both arrived at L'Étoile over two years ago and were good friends. They exchanged a somber glance.

"How can we help, boss?" Meilani asked.

"We can scrub footage, guard the vault, search the lower levels—" Antonia said.

"Upper levels?"

"Did you see anything out of the ordinary? See anyone?" Janey interrupted.

"No, boss," Meilani said.

"I feel horrible," Antonia said. "Ed—was my friend. And Kosi—he better recover. I owe him credits on the last asteroid race."

Meilani yawned. "If you need us..."

Antonia nodded. "Anything."

"Yes, I do. Kim will assign you for the sweeps we're doing."

"Yes, boss," Meilani said with a solemn nod, and the two agents huddled around Kim for their assignments.

Five minutes later, with Orlando, Janey entered Soren's lab and wove her way through his tall shelves of equipment. Soren was all the way in the back, huddled over his sonic microscope, his ambient lighting low, the only light focused on his work. The faint smell of antiseptic hung in the air. A jangly guitar tune played low, evocative of wind whistling in the trees.

Soren peered up at them and blinked, looking a little dazed. His blond spiky hair was aimed in every direction, more mussed than usual.

"Hey, Janey. Orlando." He frowned. "So sorry about Ed. How's Kosi?"

"Critical." Janey didn't like the tightness in her lungs, making it hard to take deep breaths. She forced air out. "I know it's probably too early for you to have anything for me, but we found some things after you left." She should have brought the items sooner. The feeling of being behind plagued her on this case. She needed to get ahead, get a lead, get something useful. Handling the evidence with a glove, she placed the canister and the granules on the table. "Maybe you can give us the skinny while we wait. We're thin on actionable evidence. And—"

"Clock's tick-a-tick-tick. Understood." Soren bent to examine the evidence bag with the granules, sniffing, wrinkling his nose. "I found minute traces like these in the vault room, too. That smell too."

"I don't smell anything through the bag. How can you?" Janey said.

"It's faint. Reminds me of fishing off the docks with my uncles." Soren pursed his lips in thought, slipped on a glove, and picked up the slim, grey canister, half as long as his large palm. "Where was this?"

"Under Ed's body, we think. We didn't spot it at first. We found it against the wall, under the tabledesk. When the medics moved Ed—" She shrugged, gulped.

Soren nodded. He got the picture. He brought the petite canister over to a protected box and carefully suctioned it into the vacuum chamber. He stuck his hands through the protected gloves, unscrewed the canister, and tapped out its contents into a dish. A fine greyish powder.

"What is that?" Orlando asked.

"The residue of trimethylamine, which is a gas after it evaporates," Soren said. "It's the trimethylamine gas that gives off the fishy smell."

"Is that the gas that knocked them both out and killed Ed?" Janey asked.

"Not sure. Possibly," Soren said. "I'll need to run it through the mass spec' for answers."

"Maybe Doc detected this on Ed." Janey glanced at the autopsy room. The light above the door was red. Doc was still working on Ed's body and wasn't ready to reveal her findings yet.

"Soren, that beer—" Orlando started.

"Will have to wait until after we catch these buggers." Soren frowned and shifted in his stance, his hands in the vacuum box.

"Of course. That was what I was going to say," Orlando said soberly.

"No one will get a beer if we can't catch the suspects and recover the money," Janey said.

"Folks, I need to get to work," Soren said.

"One more thing, Soren." Then Janey spoke to Orlando. "Didn't you want to tell me and Soren about the other heist-bot murder you found?"

"It doesn't have anything to do with the fish smell." Orlando rubbed the back of his neck, worry writ on his tightened features. "Yes, about five years ago, Sol agents arrested two engineers who were behind a heist on the Granton One Space Station. They used a series of bots to disable the security system, crack the station's vault, and make off with all the station's liquidity."

"Your buddies caught them quickly, I take it," Soren said.

Orlando smiled thinly. "My colleagues tracked the engineers to their escape pod hiding in the junk orbit. Their engine had crapped out on them. The engineers didn't know their bots had been tracked by the solar dust stirred up in the vault."

"The kind that shows up under a UV blacklight?" Soren asked.

"The very same," Orlando said. "An amateur job."

"Oh." Soren's shoulders slumped, disappointment on his face. "We don't use solar dust as a tracking device on L'Étoile." He bent to the microscope on the vacuum box. That closed the matter for him and was their cue to leave.

Out in the corridor, Janey spoke as she studied her holo for the sensor map where people were on the station and sighed. "That was a bust. Until Soren has some answers for us—"

"Just because we can't see the connection, that doesn't mean there isn't one." He gave her an astute look.

"I know, but we have nothing specific to go on."

"Yet," Orlando cut in. "In the meantime, we have a search to conduct for ghosts."

"Yep. This way." Janey led the way down the corridor into the service elevator and waved in the command for the lowest level of the station. "There shouldn't be anyone down here, but let's do a quick sweep anyway."

"It pays to be thorough." Orlando nodded and waved over his comm, setting his holo to screen for biophotons.

They exited into another grey corridor.

"I recognize this area. The weapons station is that way, right?" Orlando pointed down the darkened hall. "And the machine shop is that way, up a half-level. Yes?"

"Good memory," Janey said.

They proceeded down the narrow corridor toward the weapons station. Janey stood outside the grey door with no special markings—just a door at the dead-end of a tight hallway under drab ceiling lighting. And no bio readings. No one here. Thank the stars.

She pivoted and headed back toward the service elevator, passed it, and kept going down the corridor, her scanner quiet, the air musty as if no one had disturbed the area in a while.

"What are these for?" Orlando waved at the grey walls with inset panels, tagged with numbers.

"Water filtration, air circulation conduits," she said. Her ocular implant decoded the numbers. Any repair engineer would have the decoder in their comms.

"Any people supposed to be on this level?"

"No, not on this level. Why? You have something?"

Her heart fluttered. She stared at her scanner but saw no change.

"No. I was just wondering. The air smells stale."

"True." Janey picked up the pace to a drab stairway and hustled up to the next level. The corridor was warm, and there was a low hum vibrating through her boots. Here the air smelled faintly of lavender and light sweet soap. "Laundry is this way."

"Five people?"

She glanced at her map. Five red dots there, just as expected. "Mine too. Weird. Faint metallic readings, like the minute particles in the vault. Faint unidentified biophoton readings too."

"On the people?"

"Not sure. We need to get closer." She opened the door to the laundry and was hit with a blast of warm humid air. The lavender was stronger here but not over-powering.

The forewoman, Susan Duncan, glanced up from her seated work screen. "Janey! Come in. What can I do you for?" Susan's tone was full of delight. She bounced off her stool, her blue bouffant hairdo bouncing in her wake. "Is it true what I heard about Ed? Poor man! He always wanted his work clothes folded on top of his casuals. And Kosi, is he all right?"

"Susan, it is true about Ed." Janey grasped Susan's outstretched hands in hers. "Kosi is critical. Tseng and her team are on it. No news yet."

Susan hugged her and then pulled back, frowning. "And you're all right? Need anything special from us?"

"I'm fine. We're just doing a hotel-wide sweep." Janey let Susan fuss over her for a second, then stepped out of her embrace, her cheeks hot, and her heart beating too fast. It was all too much suddenly. She had enough aunties back home with Mom who did the same thing.

Susan offered an understanding smile. Janey knew Susan liked nothing better than to dote on the staff. Then she noticed Orlando. Janey monitored the minute readings but couldn't pinpoint the source.

"Well, well." Susan gave him an up-and-down appreciative perusal.

"Ms. Susan, nice to meet you." Orlando quirked his lips and made as if to tip an invisible hat in a courtly gesture. He enjoyed all female attention. "Sol Unified Special Investigator Orlando Valdez, at your service."

Susan patted her cheeks at the blossoming rouge there. "You are too kind, Investigator Orlando." She bustled back to her station and plopped back in her chair, eyeing her screen, fanning herself. "Everything is normal here." She whispered dramatically, "On the hunt? Shall I reprogram the machines to—I don't know—fold up the bad guys?"

"We are looking for some people." Janey stifled a smile. "We're tracking... The readings led us here."

Susan glanced about. "No one in or out this shift, except us."

"You touch all the clothes, right?" Orlando asked.

Susan nodded.

"How does the laundry arrive?" Janey asked.

"Through the chutes. The linens here. The personals through there." Susan pointed out the multiple chutes that were embedded in one wall and came from all around the hotel.

"The trace could have been on linens, tracked here, then laundered," Orlando said, glancing at Janey.

Janey asked Susan, "Can we scan you and the others

to see if you've come in contact with what we're tracking?"

"Of course." Susan held out her hands, and Janey scanned them and then the other staff. The trace remained faint. "Maybe we touched something..."

"Perhaps. What do you handle?" Orlando asked.

"Bedding and towels mostly. Personal items, sometimes, mostly of staff. Guests tend to bring or buy all they need from the clothes-maker," Susan said, and the other staff nodded in agreement.

"No traces on you," Janey said and ran her scanner lower to the floor. "Just specks, scattered in no discernible pattern."

"When we transferred laundry from the chutes to the baskets to the machines," Susan guessed.

"In parts per billion." Janey shook her head. "No way to tell—"

"Where they came from or when," Orlando finished her sentence.

"Somebody touched something and that got tracked here?" Susan asked. "Why that could be from anywhere in the hotel. Kitchens, the spa, staff quarters, guest suites..."

"I know, Susan. Just let us know if you notice anything out of the norm. I'm sending you the compound we're tracking. Are you able to notice such metallic particulates?"

"The washing machines can, but it sends everything to the recycler."

"But you know where the linens come from, yes?" Orlando asked.

"So you know where the bad guys are. Oh!" Susan's eyes went big, but not from fear, as Janey expected, but from excitement. She grinned. "Then I let you know if we find anything."

"We'll make a sleuth out of you yet." Orlando winked at Susan.

"It is my pleasure, kind sir." Susan nodded at Orlando, all business, her crush set aside for the time being. "Need anything washed in a particular way, young man, you let me know. Assuming you're here for any length of time."

"Yes, ma'am, thank you. I will," Orlando said.

"Good." Susan stared at Orlando a little too long, blushed again, and tore her gaze away to stare at her screen. She patted her blue hair.

"Thank you, Susan," Janey said. "We'll get out of your way."

"You better catch them, Janey. We're counting on you." She was fanning herself again.

Janey nodded, headed for the door, then paused. "Susan, who told you about Ed and Kosi?"

Susan considered, her head tilted, gaze wandering as she put her facts together.

"I was getting coffee in the break room on sublevel B and saw Al Horsely. She said something. She was pretty broken up about Ed. They were croquet buddies, or was it bocce ball? I can never remember one lawn game from another. Was she not supposed to?"

Alison Horsely, medical assistant, had been on the scene this morning.

"She should know better than to talk about a crime scene. What else did she say?" Janey asked.

Susan shrugged. "Nothing else, but I left soon after with my coffee."

"Did she say anything about the crime or about Kosi ?"

"Just that Kosi was in Medical, in critical but stable. And that she'd never seen anything like his condition like his organs were aged beyond his actual age. Weird, isn't it?"

"It is." On her wrist holo, Janey waved out a message to Tseng.

"Did I get her in trouble?" Susan asked worriedly.

"Tseng will take whatever action she deems appropriate, but she's not supposed to talk about patients," Janey said.

"But she was so worried about him and sad about Ed." Susan sighed.

"You sure she didn't say anything else?" Janey asked gently. "Anything about the location or…"

"No." Susan put a hand to her heart and pursed her lips.

"What is it?" Janey asked.

"You know when I'm not saying something?" Her eyes widened in surprise.

"It's my job."

Susan eyed Orlando. "Can you do that too?"

"He's an investigator, like me, Susan. Answer the question, okay?" Janey kept her tone soft for the older woman, as she didn't want her to feel like she was being interrogated.

"Al said something about a tiny gray room in an out-of-the-way area of the station. She was complaining about having to navigate the stretcher around tight corners," Susan said. "She's a good young woman. I don't mean to get her in trouble."

"Thank you, Susan," she said and softened her tone even more. "Anything else?"

Susan gulped. "She said it was the vault room. Was that wrong? She said we'd been robbed. All of it. Gone.

Is that true?" Susan whispered the last bit and glanced at the other four laundry workers at different corners of the room, monitoring their machines for the different washing-drying-folding stations.

"You mention anything about the case?" Janey eyed the older woman sternly.

"Heavens, no. I knew that much."

"Good. Thank you. Keep it that way, okay, Susan? We need to keep things business as usual, so we can catch these guys. If there's any kind of hysteria among the staff, the guests will catch on, and we can't have that, can we?"

Susan shook her head.

"You'll help us keep things calm?"

Susan nodded and stood, leaning into Janey and Orlando as if in a soccer huddle. "You can count on me, Investigator." She tapped her nose and winked. "I know how everyone likes their unmentionables folded, and I never tell how or what kind they are. I can manage this."

Everyone wanted to be a part of the investigation, to help uncover the truth.

"Thank you, Susan. I knew I could count on you. Comm me if you hear or see anything out of the ordinary."

Susan nodded, gave a little salute, and sat back at her station, attention on the screen.

Outside of the laundry room in the corridor with Orlando, Janey sighed and commed Kim.

"Janey, you found something?" Kim asked.

"No, not yet." Janey sighed. "Word is getting around. Susan knows, and I don't know how many others know. Any suggestions on how to contain the panic among the staff?"

"Probably not. I'll send a reminder to them not to talk

about the investigation, but it's a race against the rumors until you catch these guys," Kim said. "Anything?"

"No, but we have four more levels to go until we get back to you. I haven't heard anything from Larissa and Cho. Have you?"

"No news."

"I'll check in with them. McCallister out." Janey headed down the corridor to the next stairwell and commed Larissa. "Report."

"Nothing yet, Chief. Having to do a lot of 'no comment' to staff and some guests."

"What are they asking?"

"Guests are wondering what we're doing. I said it's routine surprise checks in advance of the party."

"And to staff?"

"That they should check with Kim. I knew you'd be busy."

"Good job," Janey said. "We're heading up to the sublevel B break room. Some gossip was there from Horsely."

"Jintao and I have three more levels to go," Larissa said.

"Good. Report anything anomalous."

"Will do."

Janey commed off. They were no closer to any suspects. On to more sublevels.

SEVEN

Janey and Orlando swept sublevels B and C, all grey walls and recyclo flooring. They got no abnormal readings from hydroponics and aquaponics. Both areas emitted bio-photons from the plant life, bugs, and fish, but nothing spiked out of normal ranges. The few workers there hadn't seen anyone out of the ordinary.

The staff exercise room was occupied by a few off-shift staff. They nodded at her and Orlando. Janey glanced at her wrist holo screen for the millionth time. Nothing.

Venus Hells.

All was within normal parameters. All living creatures accounted for. It'd be nice to see a spiked reading. That would indicate living beings who were in the vicinity but clocked or masked somehow.

Such tech was currently beyond their scanners and probably hot off the beaker in some obscure lab.

But no—no off-grid villains to confront.

Larissa and Jintao had nothing to report either.

Where could their suspects be hiding? What was she overlooking?

The sublevel B break room was empty by the time they got there.

"Frowning at that thing isn't going to make data magically appear," Orlando said.

"I know." Janey checked her settings again. "Maybe it needs to be calibrated better."

"Maybe. But I know you. I'm sure it's set at the maximum bio-photon setting the technology will allow. You tweak your comm in your off-hours."

She glanced at him. "So?"

He opened his mouth to say something else, but Janey's comm vibrated against her wrist.

She tapped the wristband to signal she was available.

Soren's face appeared on her wrist holo. Perhaps he'd found something they could use.

"You got something?"

"Yes. You need to see this." Soren's voice was tight.

"On our way." Janey commed off and hustled to the elevator, Orlando hot on her six. She commanded it for the next level up.

Inside Soren's lab, Janey glanced at the coroner's closed doors. "Doc come out of there yet?"

"No." Soren stared at his table. "She's been in there for over two hours."

"What could be taking so long?" Orlando eyed the shut double doors of the coroner's lab.

The red "do not disturb" light over the doors glared at her. Janey sighed. "Nothing good." She addressed Soren, taking in his countertop full of Petri dishes. "What's all this? I brought you grey granules, not all these colors."

No longer black, the granules were now different

hues. Each dish contained a solid color of either blue, green, or brown.

Soren pointed to the brown-tinted ones. "These were found on the shelves in the vault, yet appear to have originated from the machine shop."

"So bots used in the heist could have been made in the machine shop," Janey said. "If this residue is from bots."

"Right, might not be. But the material is the same used in making bots." He bit his lip.

"Spit it out, Soren."

"It gets weirder," Soren said. "These"—he pointed to the blue ones—"are from soil in the upper-level arboretum. And these"—he waved to the green ones— "are from the weapons range."

Janey firmed her lips. "How did they turn colors?"

"I was testing for different components."

"You sure all of these were found on the shelves in the vault?" Orlando asked Janey and Soren.

"Certain," Soren said.

Janey waved out a message, closed her holo, and glanced at Soren. "Larissa and Jintao checked the upper guest levels and reported nothing unusual. But I'll have them check the arboretum again. They may have overlooked something that could identify the culprits or find where they're hiding. What else?"

"The granules are crystalline in structure."

"Like salt?" Orlando asked.

"Yes, but more refined, smaller grains," Soren said. "Manufactured, not natural."

"Can you tell by who?" Janey asked, her heartbeat accelerating. A clue to follow, finally. "Can you confirm that these granules were manufactured in our machine shop?"

"All our fabricators are tailored to the space station. Everything manufactured by our machines contains the graviton signature from our generator."

"Even granules?" Orlando bent over the Petri dishes and sniffed, scrunching up his nose.

"Everything." Soren nodded and gently shoved away from his specimens.

"Which machine made them specifically?" Janey asked.

"I can't tell. The striation differences between the fabricators are so minute, even I can't measure it. We don't have the technology for that, yet." Soren waved over his work screen. "Here's the chemical makeup, but there's something weird."

Janey shifted from foot to foot, looking over his shoulder at the chemical formula. "What?" It all looked weird to her. Give her a physics equation any day.

"While these appear at first to be made here, they also look like they were made elsewhere." Soren scratched his stubble.

"What lets you know that?" Janey asked.

"I see the graviton signature, but the station's manufacturing mark for the base material is missing."

"Bring me up to speed," Orlando said. "I thought all objects were made on the station."

"Yes, but all raw materials are brought up by SkyEl or space jet," Soren said. "In granular form. Easier to ship that way."

"What are you saying?" Janey blinked rapidly to zoom in to see if she could see the lab markers or lack thereof in the granules. All was a blur. She'd gone too far, so she blinked to zoom out. The specks showed up as spiked squarish objects but told her nothing she could use. She blinked again to reset her vision to normal.

"I'm speculating that these granules could have been made in a private lab," Soren said. "Our top-of-the-line fabricators wouldn't be so...messy. But only the brown compound is from here."

"I don't follow," Janey said.

"The blue and green particles appear to come from the arboretum and weapons range, respectively. *And* they seem to be made elsewhere. Someone went to a lot of trouble to make them appear as if they originated here." Soren stared at the dishes as if they would speak up and reveal their origins.

Janey rubbed her temple and studied Soren's chemical formula on his screen. "My chemistry is rusty, but this looks nothing like an inorganic compound. Is it some kind of organic compound?"

"Possibly. There's carbon but no hydrogen. At least, not in its present form. There's an echo of hydrogen though as if it was once organic," Soren said and worried his lip. "I've never seen anything like it."

"Keep checking the database. Obscure science journals, medical databases, patent offices," Janey said.

Soren nodded. "Of course. On it already."

"The green granules from the weapons range... We checked there and found nothing abnormal," Orlando said.

"We'll check again. Maybe the culprits holed up there or went there for some reason," Janey said.

Soren picked up the canister that had been under Ed's body. "This canister was repurposed from the kitchen. I found trace of almond oil and higher traces of algae."

"What does that mean?" Janey asked.

"Does the algae match hydroponics?" Orlando asked.

"Some of the algae matches ours in hydroponics," Soren said. "And some doesn't."

"So, also from off-station," Janey said. "Did you check the arboretum's algae?"

"Of course." Soren frowned at his evidence. "But some algae are from—" He checked his notes. "A common form of macroalgae. It could have been cultivated in a lab off-world." Soren scanned the algae with the microscope, then studied the screen. A spiderweb of lines radiated outward. "Gravitons are near non-existent."

"What does that tell us?" Janey asked, trying to piece it together. Why were traces of algae at the scene?

"The algae were fabricated in a near zero-g lab." Orlando lifted an eyebrow. "How many of those are there? Could that be a way to track the culprits? Maybe former workers?"

"There's a handful of such labs around the moon," Soren said, "and I know of at least two space—"

Janey cut in. "Other space stations. Can you narrow down the location?"

Soren studied his readings. "No, but I can ask the other labs for matches."

"Who runs these labs?" Orlando asked.

"Right, follow the money," Janey said. "Get me a list of those labs, Soren, and I'll look into who owns them. Maybe find who is behind this." She eyed the Petri dishes. "Anything else?"

Soren shook his head. "No skin cell traces."

"What about definitive traces of bots?"

"No trace of them unless"—Soren stared at the dishes—"these granules are the trace."

"How likely is that?" Orlando asked.

Soren brushed a shock of blond hair out of his eyes with the back of his hand. "Bots usually emit and receive a specific carrier wave when turned on, but because the vault is shielded and the security room too..." He shrugged. "Maybe there was no transmission because of the shielding."

"Pre-programmed..." Janey said just as Orlando did.

Orlando lifted one corner of his mouth. Then he got serious. "A bot could have been programmed to travel without a transmission signal."

"Possibly, but bots can't travel far without their owners. Not out of their line of sight, per Section Thirty-One." Janey blinked to get Kim's results of bot movements without their owners. She frowned.

"What?" Orlando stepped toward her.

"No anomalies of bots out of control, Kim says."

"That would be too easy, but at least we have some locations to narrow down our search, thanks to Soren's work." Orlando nodded at Soren.

"Good work, Soren," Janey added.

"Thanks." Soren tapped on his screen. "I'll get you the names of those zero-g labs, find out what I can on their research focuses. My buddies should pull through for me."

"I hope they will—and quick," Janey said.

"If they're as outstanding as you..." Orlando said to Soren.

Soren beamed at the compliment and then bent over his instruments, back to work.

She glanced at the coroner's doors. "One more thing, Soren. Dare I disturb Doc? We need all the leads we can get. Clock's ticking."

It was now 10 a.m., and they had only these granules to go on to find the yahoos behind the murder-heist.

"You know Doc," Soren said.

"Thorough and likes her quiet and undisturbed workspace." Janey wouldn't distract her then. She headed for the lab exit, Orlando with her, passing through the narrow aisles of supplies and lab machinery, and she glanced at the Doc's closed door one more time. No, she'd wait for the Doc to call her.

She messaged for Larissa and Jintao to check the arboretum and weapons range again, to report any anomalies, no matter how small, when they were done with their primary sweep.

Back in the conference room, Janey poured a cup of coffee and reviewed the timeline of the crime.

"Need to talk it out?" Orlando stood shoulder to shoulder with her, not touching.

"Yes." She crossed her arms. "Ed and Kosi reported to the security vault control room at six. All is quiet. The cameras go dark in the corridor at 6:40. One of them triggers the distress beacon at 7:03. We arrive on scene at 7:05. Time of death for Ed was 6:58—according to Doc." She stared at the board without seeing it. "Who knows how long the suspects had been on the station before they hit?"

"Days? Weeks?" Orlando said softly.

Janey stared at the murder board—no suspects. Yet.

Orlando's holo pinged.

"What do you have?" Janey asked.

His jaw tight, he lifted a finger for her to wait and turned away from Janey to shield the visual. He listened, nodded, stilled.

After a few minutes, he exhaled and faced her. "Good and bad news. Which do you want first?

"I could use some good news right about now." Janey eyed the pastries shelf. Thin pickings.

Orlando read off his holo screen. "Another heist with bots just spat out of the database. This one was small but significant for the asteroid base. Happened two years ago. A bot and at least one suspect involved. Twenty thousand credits were stolen. Get this. Not even the whole amount kept there was stolen."

"That's the good news?" Janey refilled their coffee cups. "And why didn't this one show up earlier?"

"That's part of the bad news. The file was encrypted twice and made to look fake."

"Your own agency did that? Why?"

"Not sure. But now I can requisition the whole file and see if there are any similarities."

"What's the other part of the bad news?" She sipped the coffee. It was too hot. She set the cup down on the conference table.

"No one was ever charged with the crime. The case is still open. The suspect is still at large."

"Great. No direct leads there." She sat beside her coffee and stared into the brown liquid. But maybe that'd been a trial run.

"I'll dig into the case file. Maybe there's something in there we can use. Thanks for the coffee." Orlando took his seat at the other end of the table.

They were professionals. He was getting right to work, no small talk needed.

He caught her staring at him. "We got this," he said softly.

"Got what?" She got up and paced. "We have no suspects, the granules we found on scene are from all over the station, everyone is accounted for, and it's highly unlikely a bot did it. So who or what did?"

Orlando nodded encouragingly.

"Whoever did this is smart, had inside knowledge of the station, and has advanced tech from several domains." Janey strode back and forth, her boots shur-shurring against the rug. "Protocol demands we ask the hard questions and search for the unknown unknowns. What else is there? What are we missing? What did we not scan for?"

Her holo pinged—her reminder to check in with Milano.

She commed her boss and relayed the details about the trace. Talking it all out again gave her another perspective.

"Chief." She had an idea. "I need to talk to Schoeneman."

"Why?" Chief asked. "You know he doesn't like to be disturbed during work hours."

"I need to ask him about his enemies, dive into any hate mail he's received, beyond the usual public rants."

Milano made a considering noise. "Think this is personal?" His comm was silent for a moment. "Good idea. I'll let him know you're on your way."

"Thanks, boss."

"And, McCallister?"

"Yes, Chief?"

"Be on your best behavior."

"Aren't I always?" she said with a straight face.

He snorted and commed off.

EIGHT

FIVE MINUTES LATER, JANEY ARRIVED AT Schoeneman's suite with Orlando. They were greeted by a woman who introduced herself as the housekeeper, didn't ask their names, and led them to an elegant sitting room.

"Mr. Schoeneman will be here presently," the housekeeper said. Dressed in a grey Chinese mandarin collar dress, the tall, portly woman had her straight black hair in a bun at the nape of her neck. She nodded once to them as if that was that and left them alone.

The sitting room was decorated with a gold-threaded brocade couch designed for two and a pair of chairs, red silk walls, and plush carpet that muffled all footfalls. Janey sat on the plush couch and resisted the urge to lean back. Instead, she crossed her legs, straightened, and allowed herself to smooth her palm against the couch fabric. Nubby and unbelievably soft like the finest wool mixed with silk.

"Nice digs." Orlando sat beside her and eyed her, inviting her closer. He patted the space on the couch between them. She shook her head, though she craved his warmth.

The housekeeper bustled in with a tea and coffee service, set it on the coffee table, and left again without a word, though she did purse her lips at Janey for a split second. Janey caught the micro-expression just before the woman turned her back on them. That look of displeasure prompted Janey to check the woman's ident against the hotel guest and staff registries.

Her ocular implant flashed the woman's ID record. The housekeeper was Pamela Zasada, indeed listed as a housekeeper in Schoeneman's employ. Zasada's hotel entry held many arrivals and departures over the years. She probably kept to her room the whole time she was on board and not working. That would explain why Janey had never seen her eating in the staff commissary or enjoying the shows in the casino on a staff pass, as many of her colleagues did.

Twenty minutes later, Schoeneman breezed into the sitting room, bringing a rich cologne with him, evocative of jasmine and sandalwood. Styled in the latest tasteful fashion, his salt and pepper wavy hair suited his Roman nose and sharp cheekbones. His steel-grey silk suit was tailored to show off his broad shoulders, and he gazed at Janey like she was the only person in his world.

Oh, for star's sake.

What was the big boss doing making eyes at her?

As if nothing was wrong, she stood and held out her hand to shake Schoeneman's outstretched one.

"Mr. Schoeneman, thank you for meeting us," Janey said, her voice strong, authoritative. If he thought she could be swayed by his charisma... "The situation is—"

"Horrible," Schoeneman said. His voice rumbled like thunder in the desert, loud and startling, demanding complete attention. "What do you have so far, Investigator?"

When Janey didn't answer right away, he glanced at Orlando, squinted at him in a micro-second, and turned his attention back to Janey as if Orlando had been judged and dismissed as not worthy of his attention. Was that better or worse than how Schoeneman had ignored Orlando the last time they'd crossed paths when Janey was present? Then, as now, Orlando seemed unfazed, calm and cool, in his professional guise.

Janey spoke. "I thought Chief Milano updated you. I'm here to ask you—"

"Yes, he updated me," Schoeneman interrupted. "But I want to hear an update from you, my trusted lead investigator. I hear you've been training others. Trying to get out of your job?" He gave her a coy half-smile, still attempting his charm offensive.

"Of course, not, sir. I just want the station to have all the support it can get from security."

"Well done. I was teasing you. Relax." Schoeneman chuckled, released her hand, and gestured to sit, his grey gaze intense as if he was still trying to lure her into his fan club. She blinked, resisting, imagining there was a barrier of a screen between them. Seemed to work. She could look at him without falling in. He pulled back on his intensity and offered tea, perfectly politely.

"No thanks, sir." Janey glared at the red carpet, the color of brick. All the while impatience grew in her gut, and the flutter of nerves was back. They had to catch the killer and re-open the station to traffic, so the credits could be replenished. And here they were taking tea with the boss.

"I insist." Schoeneman's voice was deep and melodious. He poured himself tea. In a plush chair of red silk brocade, he crossed his legs and leaned back, forearms resting on the armrests. "Ms. Zasada gets upset if no one partakes."

Janey nodded, and Schoeneman poured them tea, graceful and efficient as if prep school trained. Janey helped herself to a flaky spiral-shaped pastry in a dainty paper cup but didn't eat. Neither did Orlando.

"Well," Schoeneman boomed.

She straightened her shoulders, set her tea on the low table, and looked him in the eye. He was just a man, not a god. She filled him in rapidly on what they had so far and ended with, "I need to know who you think may have done this. Does anyone hold a grudge against you?"

He chuckled, avuncular and a bit condescending. "Everyone. Just check my hate mail."

"Really? Who is at the top of the list?"

"I wouldn't know." He shrugged, looking relaxed. "My office can send you whatever you need."

She nodded. "Are you sure you have no one in mind?"

"No one. So many people have come after me over the years. I warn you not to take what you see in the mail personally on my part. People are always after the biggest shark in the sea." He showed his teeth in a feral grin as if to scare her since charm hadn't worked.

"Shark, sir?" She blinked again to read him through the spectrum, but he was sincere in his choice of words. No shame or hiding here. He seemed to take delight in his moniker of shark.

He rubbed his diamond-studded cufflinks. "I'm a very wealthy man. People want what I own. People always want what they don't have. Don't they?" He gave her a penetrating stare.

"Is that why they are after you? I've always thought sharks were predators." She held his gaze and ignored her increased heart rate—just her critter brain responding to what felt like a raptor's hunger, and she was the mouse. The red walls of the sitting room seemed to pulse in time to her rapid heart rate. She focused on her breath to calm her heart. Schoeneman probably thought he could intimidate her like he did to everyone else who wanted something from.

"Smart too," Schoeneman said quietly.

"Indeed. Sir, if I may say so, you don't seem concerned about the theft."

"I can cover the casino by tomorrow after you find the killers. You're all doing your job and will find my gems, lingots, and contracts. I have faith in you."

"I'd expect you to be raging right about now."

He narrowed his eyes at her. "And what would that serve? I hire the best. I expect the best. I get the best." He stood. "If you don't—"

Janey stood. "Then what?"

"You're all out of a job."

"I thought you had faith in me? In us?"

"I do. But law of the jungle…" He showed his eye teeth.

"Is it all a game to you?" she asked quietly.

"If I have to cancel the party and shut down L'Étoile, so be it." Schoeneman stood.

"That would be horrible," Janey said.

Schoeneman shook his head. "That won't happen. Like I said, I have my utmost faith in you, Investigator. I wanted to look you in the eye and tell you that."

"Thank you, sir," Janey replied coolly and blinked a few times, registering his behavior, tracking his breathing patterns and heart rate. What an odd character.

He smiled at her. He knew exactly what she was

doing—adjusting her ocular implant. He knew all about her. His biosignals hadn't shifted, neither to increase nor decrease. Steady. This man was probably lethal in negotiations. Hence his massive holdings and rating as one of the richest men on Earth and throughout the Sol Unified Planets.

Schoeneman blinked a few times rapidly too.

Oh. He must have an ocular implant. If he did, she couldn't see it.

"Ms. Zasada will see you out," he threw over his shoulder and strode away toward a back room.

He was gone. Janey let out a breath. She and Orlando followed Ms. Zasada to the door. The woman held open the door without a word or gesture, radiating displeasure with the slight downturn of her lips and cold gaze in her eyes.

Out in the corridor, Orlando opened his mouth to speak. Janey held up a hand to stop him and shook her head. She pointed to her and mouthed one word, "Bugs."

NINE

A FEW MINUTES LATER IN THE ELEVATOR, Orlando asked, "What's bothering you? The fact that Schoeneman bugs his own suite or that he's a hustler of the first order."

"Yes, to both. And there's something Schoeneman isn't saying."

The silver box whizzed downward to the security floor, making the barest of noises. A stone of dread churned in her gut. The recyclo flooring's diamond pattern held no answers.

"Hey." Orlando leaned on the wall. His dark brown eyes were full of concern. The heaviness in her chest eased a little. The walls nestled her. "When isn't he up to something?" He shrugged like Schoeneman's behavior was of no consequence. But that had to be an act. "What do you want to do next?"

"Dive into his hate mail. Maybe there's a lead there." She sighed. She'd have to run keyword searches, read every scrap for clues. Even if she divided the work amongst the team, it'd still be tedious and slow. "Unfortunately, I don't like the sit-and-search method."

"You much prefer the run-around-and-search method."

"I do." Janey stared at her holo, checking for Schoeneman's data. It wasn't there yet. She commed Kim. "Do you have Mr. Schoeneman's data yet?"

"It's coming in now."

"Thanks." Janey's comm pinged, interrupting her. "Another call's coming in. I have to take it."

"Of course, go." Kim signaled off.

Janey answered the new call. It was Larissa. "Investigator McCallister, you need to see this. I'm in the arboretum." Her voice was strained.

"We're on our way." Janey commed off and re-routed the elevator with a voice command. Her stomach felt the stop, then the tug as they went upward again. The arboretum clue could be the break for the missing thieves she was tracking. Sure, she could vid in and talk to Madge the gardener, but then she may miss something —the unexpected, the unaccounted for, the random.

Orlando waved his hand over his holo, inputting commands, and chewed his bottom lip.

"What are you doing?" Janey fidgeted with the band of her wrist comm.

"Studying the cold case files for anything more that pops."

"Found anything new?"

"Nope. Not yet."

The elevator arrived on the arboretum level. Greenery welcomed them, gracing the corridor walls with swirls of silver-green moss and air plants. Janey hustled down the wide corridor to the arboretum, Orlando matching her stride for stride.

Larissa met them in the arboretum lobby, frowning at her holo. "I'm getting strange bio-photon readings. They weren't here earlier. See?" Larissa held up her wrist for Janey to see the screen and pointed out the two graphs. One graph showed the bio-photon readings of four adults.

"That explains our presence and Madge's," Janey said.

Madge Fujimori was the Arboretum Master Gardener, probably somewhere beyond the lobby. On the ceiling high above, cumulus clouds floated by. The lighting was set at a bright afternoon Mediterranean glow, highlighted by the whitewashed lounge furniture and sky-blue walls.

"But look at the other graph, there's an increase of six percent. Weird," Larissa said.

"This is current?" Janey examined the data.

"As of ten seconds ago," Larissa said. "Live feed. I detected it at the entrance but didn't go in. I called you as soon as I saw this."

With her wrist holo, Janey took her own readings. "There's enough bio-photons for this to be a child or an animal. But neither are on board, as far as I know."

Pets weren't allowed on the station. Children rarely came aboard. The arboretum had insects, probably birds, but nothing that should emit so many bio-photons. What could be causing these abnormal life readings? Bots didn't emit them.

Janey fisted her hands, opened them, and shook out the nervous energy. Ready for anything. "Let's go."

Janey entered the arboretum proper, Orlando behind her, his footfalls as silent as hers as they were greeted by rich, loamy earth and the fruity aroma of blooming flowers and trees.

In her bright orange apron, the Master Gardener, Madge Fujimori, strode toward them, her gap-toothed grin wide in greeting, hedge clippers in one hand, basket handle looped over her arm.

"Janey, nice to see you! Haven't seen you here in a while."

"Madge, hi. Is there anyone else here?"

"Besides me and the insects? Not that I know of." Madge checked out Orlando and nodded at him impassively as if assessing but not making any conclusions yet.

Janey reviewed her holo. Besides their five dots, she read an uptick of bio-photons, by an additional five percent. "Something alive is showing up in the far corner, by the orange grove."

"What are you looking for?" Madge gazed at her evenly as if she was ready for anything. Only about ten years older, Madge had a way of taking on the role of the wise woman. Maybe it had something to do with her being in touch with the life and death cycle of plants.

"Not sure," Janey said. "Have you noticed anything unusual?"

"Now that you mention it…" Madge looked thoughtful.

"What?" Janey asked.

"Oranges have gone missing from the tree. No one picks the fruit but me."

"Has that happened before?"

Madge gave it some thought, eyeing the faux sky. "No, not like this."

"Like what?"

"Sometimes a guest will walk out with an orange or two. But this has been like two or three oranges over as many days." Madge took on a determined look, a twinkle in her eye. She shoved her clippers in the basket. "Let's go check it out."

"I'll stay here," Orlando said. "Cover the entrance.

We don't want anyone else coming into the arboretum just now."

"Good idea. It's the only public exit," Janey said. "Larissa, with me, please."

Larissa nodded and fell in behind her.

Madge trudged through the trees, her pink boots treading over mulched leaves.

Janey stepped around Madge. "I'll take lead, just in case."

"It's probably nothing," Madge said.

"No need to take chances."

In the rear of their little group, Larissa scanned as they tromped past the mini Japanese garden. White bridges arched over a pond of koi. Next came the ferns and baby redwoods.

Schoeneman wanted to represent as many ecological regions of Earth as possible, so his guests would feel more at home. He also wanted to show off that he employed one of the world's most renowned experts in habitat reformation, who created the first multi-biome garden on a space station. That was Madge Fujimori.

Heralded by the enlivening, pungent smell of oranges, Janey arrived at the orange grove and moved under the warm lamps. This was one of Janey's favorite parts of the arboretum. She often visited for the full-spectrum light, the aroma of orange and orange blossoms, and the calm buzz of bees. The balmy corner reminded her of her childhood, of Mom's boxes of oranges and homemade orange juice, and of eating oranges with her neighbor friends while they watched Saturday morning cartoons.

With her wrist comm, Janey scanned the area and found the source of the readings under a mound of dirt barely six inches high. "You have a mouse home on board. Or perhaps another rodent." She stepped off the path and knelt on the moist earth. "Strange how the readings appeared, then disappeared on the scans."

"I see that too, sir," Larissa said. "I'll run a diagnostic."

"Good idea," Janey said.

"Not mice, gophers more likely. Being underground probably masked the readings." Madge knelt too. "How did these little buggers get on the station?"

"A good question," Janey said, relieved.

"Their surprise appearance is a problem. I'll talk to the space jet baggage handlers at the Earth spaceports," Madge said. "But they're not bad for business. I've been lobbying Schoeneman for more bio-diversity."

"False alarm then," Janey said.

"Sorry, ma'am," Larissa said. "I thought it was something."

"Better we check out every lead. But that still doesn't answer why we found soil traces that appeared to come from here at the crime scene." She stood and brushed dirt off her knees. "Madge, have you seen anybody in here that looked suspicious?"

"No, but you know I mostly keep out of the guests' way."

"I do. We'll check the vid feed." Janey spoke to Larissa. "Please take care of that."

"Yes, ma'am," Larissa said and headed for the exit.

"You're taping people on the station?" Madge asked. "Is that really necessary?"

"Station security, Madge. But you knew that."

"Doesn't mean I like being reminded." Madge glared at Janey and mumbled the rest. "I thought privacy meant something. Apparently not." She stomped away and disappeared amongst the bushes and flowering trees.

"Come on, you know it's only in the corridors and

entrances," Janey called after her. An old argument with Madge. The gardener had her own bio-tracker. She knew security required everyone aboard be tagged, but she grumbled about it to Janey.

Janey hated that her job sometimes pushed her friends and colleagues away. Yet she wasn't here to please people but to catch the criminals.

Just in case the burrowing animals weren't the source of the elevated bio-photon readings, Janey kept one eye on her holo and one on the ground as she made her way back to the entrance. The levels spiked as she approached the Japanese garden. She stopped at one of the arching bridges where the signal was strong.

She commed Orlando, who'd been standing guard at the entrance. "I have something."

"I'll be right there," Orlando replied.

The compact arboretum was about fifty feet in diameter, the pond taking up at least a third of that space, three white stone bridges arching over it. Scanning the ground at high-magnitude, she stayed clear of the marsh grasses and wet earth at the edge of the pond.

Orlando arrived and joined the search. They worked in silence for a little while.

"Something's here." Orlando crouched beside a miniature Japanese maple tree, its red leaves rustling in a light breeze.

"No biophoton reading, though."

"No, but they're the same granules as the ones in the lab."

Janey joined him and crouched. She blinked a few times to zoom in more. The crystalline granules contrasted with the rounded shape of the surrounding dirt. The reflective, diamond-like structures sparkled at this magnification. Beautiful, like microscopic diamonds.

With a hand scanner the size of a pen, she took footage of the spot, both stills and video, then crouched to gather the granules into a sani-bag.

"How did you spot these?" she asked. "The bio-photon readings were high, yet I couldn't pinpoint an exact location."

"I configured the scan to Soren's chemical specifications."

"Right. Good move." The rich warm earthy smell and the gentle lap of the pond on the grassy shore lulled Janey into a calm. Fans hidden in the walls and ceiling generated a gentle wind. She inhaled to bring it all in. "Where did they come from? How did they get here?"

"Someone brought them in. Maybe one of our intruders came in to take a swim." She sighed. She'd have to talk to Madge about the vids at the entrance.

"You know we make a good team," Orlando said, his voice soft, and he bumped his knee against hers. His gaze invited, his maleness beckoned. He leaned closer to her.

"I know." She stood. She needed some cooler air. "I have to talk to Madge again. She's not going to like this."

Orlando stood too. "Need me to come along?"

"No, it will go better if you're not there." Her cheeks reddened. "She knows things about us—"

"Oh, she's that kind of friend." Orlando picked a leaf out of her hair.

They were close, noses almost touching. She swayed back toward the water, losing her footing on the soft ground. He grabbed her arms and drew her against his chest. Solid, warm, his heart beating next to hers.

She held on for a moment too long, eyed his lips. So close. Ready for her. He sighed and leaned in.

Janey gripped his shoulders for leverage, danced

around him, and pivoted out of his arms. She stepped back on the path.

"Tease. You have too much self-control, McCallister." Orlando followed her, his deep voice rumbling through her.

"We're working, Valdez," she threw over her shoulder. Then she glanced at him. "Would you mind taking these samples to Soren?"

"Yes, ma'am." He gave her a short jaunty salute.

"Oh, and let him know I'm sending him the footage I took."

"What am I, your messenger?"

She waved a hand at him to show she heard and made her way toward Madge's shed.

Maybe the microscopic crystals would help them find the thieves. She needed a break in this case.

TEN

Janey knocked on the gardener's shed door. The wooden door swung open at her touch. "Madge?" She entered the shed, twice as big as her small quarters. The space smelled of rich organic soil and dampness. Empty ceramic and spindly potted plants littered the entrance.

"What do you want?" Madge shouted from somewhere in the back, behind a wall of tall plants in full greenery.

"I'm sorry for upsetting you," Janey said.

"Go away. I have work to do."

"I know you're mad."

"No one likes to be spied on."

"Madge—this is serious." Janey picked her way through the stacks of pots, bags of soil, and tall ferns.

Madge bent over tiny seedlings on a table. "What do you want?" She transferred the little seedlings to bigger containers and didn't look up from her work.

"I have just a few questions."

"Want to take me to interrogation?"

"No. Now you're pissing me off."

"Why? You have no right—"

"Madge, you know what my job entails."

"And you know where I come from? What I had to deal with?" She spat into the dirt on the floor. "Goddamn Overwatch."

"I do." Janey rubbed dirt between her fingers.

Originally named Magdalena Juarez Gomez Takahashi, Madge came from the profit city-state of San Diego—a hard city to live in despite the great weather. Madge had grown up mostly fending for herself on the Mexican half of the city-state of ten million, her parents migrant farmworkers. They'd managed to get her to school. Madge's hard work had done the rest with scholarships and grants and lots of part-time jobs.

But when Madge was fourteen, her parents had been tagged by drones after trying to travel north into the Granton region of Los Angeles. They'd been arrested and deported to Mexico, even though they were originally from the Japan Zone. Madge had escaped the Overwatch drones, changed her name, and lived on her own for a few years until a full-ride to the Granton college in Boston.

Janey blew out a breath. "Schoeneman had Kim and Milano install the security when the station first opened. I wasn't here yet. I wasn't part of that decision."

"Must you spy on your friends?" Madge squinted at her.

"Only when we have to. Only when we have good reason." Janey picked up a delicate seedling in its paper pod, reaching up through the dirt and toward the heat lamps. "You know what happened today?"

Madge grabbed the seedling out of her hand. "Ed killed and Kosi in critical care in a heist."

"Does everybody know what's going on?"

"We know better than to get in your way when you're on the hunt, but yah, I'd say we know."

"We have to keep L'Étoile running... business as usual."

"I know, and I know the station's on lockdown. You're on the job, and the hottie Orlando Valdez is here too, helping you." Madge speared her with an intense look and harrumphed. The warmth of the shed pressed on her, and the brown walls covered in a wandering vine plant seemed to glower at her. "You two are a thing now, aren't you? Has he proposed yet?"

"Yes, we're together. And no, he hasn't proposed. Besides, that's an outmoded tradition."

"It's never outmoded when a man professes his undying love for his lady love." Madge wiggled her eyebrows at her, her anger apparently dissipated. She blew hot and quick but always came back to steadfast balance.

"You watch too many Tele-novellas." Janey crossed her arms over her chest.

"My favorite, mi corazon. Watashi no shin'ainaru yūjin."

"I know. Now, let's get back to the case. We found these granules beside the pond at the foot of the Japanese maple." Janey showed her the holo screen of a high magnification view of the crystalline structure.

Madge took a long look, then shook her head. "What are they?"

"Soren's not sure, but here's the chemical composition." Janey flicked the screen to get to the chemical equation.

Madge studied it. "Carbon, in a salt structure complex, minerals found in quartz. Amino acid structures, some form of bio-matter." She looked up at Janey. "Strange. Never seen this combination before."

"Could it come from an engineered plant?"

"Possibly. But it's odd."

"How so?"

"It's as if someone put an organic compound in a crystal structure or the other way around."

"That's odd?"

"Well, if I remember correctly from my O-chem class, that's the setup for living computers."

"Organic bots have been outlawed. Only mechanical ones are allowed."

"Since when did that stop anyone?" Madge looked straight at Janey's right eye, the one with the ocular implant, which was now illegal but had been legal for a time when Janey was a teenager.

"I'm human with an enhancement. Not the same."

After a hobby project exploded on her when she was thirteen, Janey had lost her right eye. She'd been lucky she hadn't lost both eyes.

"I know, dear." Madge patted her arm. "You think there was one of the o-bots in my garden?"

"Possibly. We could be looking for an organic bot that doesn't show up on our sensors." Janey scuffed her boot in the fine dirt covering the shed flooring—and the kind of people who could program and/or run such a bot.

"What did the security footage of the vault area tell you?"

"Nothing. It was shorted out before the crime. Or shut down." Janey shoved her hands into her jacket pockets. "I need to get back to the search." She came around the table to Madge's side. "Thank you for your help."

"I know the vids aren't your fault." Madge wiped her

forehead with a cloth. "Schoeneman's a real piece of work, isn't he?"

"But you knew that coming in. Like we all did."

"Well, actually Carl Linden, the first station engineer, hired me. Before your time. He was the one to design the living wall in the casino I installed a few months back. He was so happy I was here. He retired the following month." Madge transplanted another seedling, tapping the dirt down carefully.

"Old guy, really tall? I saw his file in the old employee records," Janey said. "Speaking of Carl, he had a lab here, right? Would he know what this compound was? Could he verify the organic bot theory?"

"Shouldn't Soren be able to help you with that?" Madge transferred the last two seedlings into pots and wiped her hands on her apron.

"He is. It's just that something Carl said before leaving. Just remembered it. In his exit interview with Kim, he said that soon his job and yours would be done by happy garden bots. He laughed like it was the greatest thing."

"What are you doing listening to old exit interviews?" Madge asked. "Wait. I don't want to know all the ins and outs of your job." She regarded Janey strangely as if she were an unwanted bug on one of her precious plants.

"I wasn't spying on you or this department," Janey said. "Milano asked me to archive old staff exit interviews, and I was curious. So, I listened to a bunch of them. Some of our past cases involved staff. I was looking for patterns." Janey felt like she was over-explaining, even apologizing, so she stopped talking.

Madge made a considering noise and moved to another table, this one full of delicate ferns almost too big for their containers.

Janey remained fixed to her spot, rubbing the grit between her fingers. Carl had retired, but a few of the files she'd archived were of employees who'd been fired.

Janey punched one fist in the other. "That's a lead! Retired staff. Fired staff." She rushed over to Madge and kissed her on her dirt-smudged cheek. "Thanks, Madge."

"You're welcome?"

She smiled and hustled out of the garden shed, past the arboretum, and into the green corridor.

She had a new line of inquiry that could fit the puzzle of what had happened this morning. Finally, only five hours after the crime. Not horrible. Not great either. They still hadn't caught anyone, but she finally had a suspect pool to examine.

Retired staff would know the location of the vault, how to disable the vids, and could have the ability to pressure the L'Étoile staff to help them.

She was in the elevator heading back down to ops when her comm vibrated against her wrist. It was Kim.

"I'm heading your way," Janey said. "And I have leads." She couldn't keep the excitement out of her voice.

"Schoeneman's missing," Kim clipped, her voice cool.

"What do you mean he's missing?" The flutter of panic beat in her gut. The man had the run of the place. He could be squirreled away in one of his executive suites or meeting rooms.

"As in missing. Ms. Zasada just called it in. Meilani and Antonia are up again and are there to take charge of the scene."

Janey left the service elevator and hurried toward ops. "I'll be there in ten seconds."

"Where?" Kim asked, but in the next moment, Janey commed off and entered the ops center.

The place was humming with a frenetic energy she'd never felt. The hotel-casino owner was missing.

The hair on the back of her neck stood on edge. Security staff stared at their screens like their lives depended on it. It did. At least, their jobs did. Staff rushed in and out of the ops center. People still had to work their stations in the machine shop and the casino, the two sensitive areas they oversaw, even while this newest crisis loomed.

Kim stood in the middle of ops, an earpiece in one ear. Three large holo screens extended up from the table.

"Where is Ms. Zasada?" Janey asked.

"In Schoeneman's suite." Kim waved over one holo screen, moving icons around.

"And the film crew?"

"They went there to interview Schoeneman, but Ms. Zasada couldn't find him. That's when she called it in."

"Is someone with them, keeping them contained on-site?"

"I sent Anahi, the rookie, to secure the scene."

"Good job. Any footage of suspicious activity in or outside the suite?"

Kim frowned. "The corridor vid shorted out ninety seconds after the journalist and her crew arrived at Schoeneman's suite. No other traffic in the corridor since you and Orlando left the suite an hour ago."

"Who knows how to do that kind of hack?" Janey asked.

"Besides you, me, Milano, and Schoeneman? No one, except Orlando."

"He was just with me, said he was heading to Soren's lab." Janey eyed Kim's screens, trying to make sense of all the dots and codes below each one.

Kim checked the screen. "He's still there."

"Could the vid feed be hacked by staff no longer on the station?" White dots in Schoeneman's suite corresponded to the film crew and Ms. Zasada. No other white dots anywhere on L'Étoile. She'd finally mapped every inch of this station, and he was nowhere on it.

Kim's eyes widened, and she paled. "Not possible. My algorithm changes the security system passwords every twelve hours. Binomial algorithms and combinatorics. Quite hard to crack."

"What about the hardware side of things? Could someone hack the cameras that way? Who had or has access to that?" Janey drummed her fingers on her leg. "Why hadn't I thought about that before?"

"Probably the machine shop engineers. They built this station." Kim's wrist holo flickered, her comm pinged, and one of the large screens flashed a pop-up message. "Status reports. Janey, I need to get these."

"Go," Janey said.

Kim responded to each hail in sequence, putting two on hold and taking the comm message.

Chief Milano spoke through Kim's comm, and Janey stepped closer. He reported that he was keeping an eye on things in the casino and needed an update on Schoeneman. From the sound of pots clanging, he was in the kitchen. No doubt Kim had called him right before calling her.

"Nothing yet, sir, but Janey is on it. She is on her way to the scene now."

"I want an update every thirty minutes from her—and from you," Chief Milano said.

"Yes, sir," Kim and Janey said in unison.

Kim commed off.

"Any ransom note?" Janey stared at the holo screens without seeing them.

"No."

"Any unauthorized escape pods, shuttles, or space jets leaving?" Janey checked the logs as she spoke.

"None."

The logs verified that. She headed for the exit. "I'm on my way to Schoeneman's suite. Tell Meilani and Antonia."

"Will do."

Janey commed Orlando on her way to the elevator. "Meet me at Schoeneman's suite. He's missing."

"Missing? As in not on the station?

"Yes, as in we can't find him in the whole place."

"Think it's connected?"

"Most likely. Anything new from Soren or the Doc?"

"No. Doc is running tests. Something's highly abnormal, but she won't say anything yet, Soren says."

"Nothing about this case is normal. We may be out of work tomorrow." Janey picked up her pace to a run.

What could be gained by taking Schoeneman? Who took him? And where the hell was he?

ELEVEN

Two minutes later, Janey rushed into Schoeneman's suite, Orlando right behind her. The housekeeper Ms. Zasada greeted them with a wringing of her hands. Worry lines crowded her forehead. She led them through the entryway to the sitting room where Janey had been only an hour previous. The film crew was there, seated on the plush red couch and chairs. The journalist, Ladipo, conferred quietly with her team, two camerawomen, and a man with what looked like sound equipment. A third woman nodded at Ladipo and signed into a wide wrist screen, presumably documenting for their media presentations. Security Agent Larissa Ferreira stood at the edge of the huddle, legs akimbo, watching the film crew with a sharp gaze. The film crew didn't seem to notice her.

Ladipo threw her a questioning look and glanced at Orlando as if he was the answer. Ignoring the ping of jealousy restricting her breath—she knew she could trust Orlando—Janey focused on releasing a long breath and lifted a finger for the journalist to wait. Ladipo went back into her huddle.

From behind her, Ms. Zasada said in a whisper, "You have to find him."

"We will," Janey said, though she really shouldn't be promising anything. "You didn't see him leave?"

"No. Like I told opps, he'd have to pass me. And he didn't."

"I understand. I need to take a look around." Janey moved down the hall where the kitchen came off the right side. On the left was an open living room, complete with wallscreens, couches and pillows, done in browns and golds. Tall ferns dotted the corners. The wall screens displayed an aerial view of a jungle and a wide river.

Ms. Zasada followed her. "Mr. Schoeneman would not like you nosing around. His lawyer told me not to let you." She pursed her lips.

From the hallway, Orlando asked. "You called his lawyer?"

"When Mr. Schoeneman didn't come when I paged him, I thought of Mr. Bennett immediately. His primary attorney. Those two men are always on comm or vid with each other. And today, almost constantly." She wrung her hands. "You must find him."

"We will, ma'am," Orlando said. "Can I get you something? A glass of water?"

"Oh, no. It's my job to serve you."

"Why don't you get some tea or coffee for the journalist and her people?" Janey said, then gestured with her chin for Meilani to come over.

"I was in the middle of that when this all began." Ms. Zasada sniffed and scurried off to the kitchen.

"Meilani, comm Schoeneman's lawyer to get permission to search the suite. Let me know as soon as you do," Janey said.

"What if he doesn't give permission?"

"On top of the disasters of today, his boss is missing. I think he will," Janey said. "If not, remind him that the station's charter is granted by the Sol and can be revoked."

"Yes, ma'am." Meilani grinned, quickly smoothed her expression to serious, and then took a few steps away to make the call.

Orlando opened the door across the small sitting room. It was a small washroom. He ran his scanner over the tiny space, a bathroom for guests. "Just checking for … anything. Nothing out of the ordinary here."

"Scan this whole area," Janey said. "Entry, sitting room"—she stepped closer—"the kitchen and further, discreetly."

"Of course."

Janey went farther down the hallway and entered the kitchen.

"Investigator, you shouldn't be in here." Ms. Zasada bustled around the kitchen, filling a tray with a tea and coffee service. She added silver boxes filled with cookies and biscuits, a creamer, and small bowls and spoons.

"I came to get your statement."

Ms. Zasada handed her a glass of water, and Janey nodded her thanks.

"I already told your investigators everything I know."

"I know." Janey tapped her holo to bring up Meilani's report. "The journalist and her crew arrived at 11:40."

"Yes. They were early." Ms. Zasada rearranged the cups and saucers, so they fit on the tray like a completed puzzle. "I made them wait while I finished in the kitchen. And—"

"What were you finishing in the kitchen?" Janey interrupted.

"What?" Ms. Zasada paused nimbly stuffing more cookies into another silver container.

"What were you doing in the kitchen before you called Mr. Schoeneman and while you were making the news crew wait?" Janey asked.

"The usual." The housekeeper reached for more cookies, but Janey caught a glimpse of the woman's pale face and a fast flutter in her carotid artery. Either she was uncomfortable, scared, she was hiding something, or all of the above.

"Since I don't know your routine, perhaps you can let me know what you did once you left the crew. Did you call Schoeneman?"

"Mr. Schoeneman," Ms. Zasada corrected.

"Yes, Mr. Schoeneman. Did you call him to let him know that they were here?"

Ms. Zasada huffed and busied herself with straightening the carafes on another tray. "I didn't. I knew he was in a call. The news crew was early. I"—she shrugged —"did what I always do."

"And what's that?"

Ms. Zasada stared at Janey for a long second. "I made them wait."

"Like you did to us earlier today? But we were on time."

"Twenty minutes. It's a policy."

"You categorically make people wait twenty minutes? Like in a manual?" Janey asked.

Ms. Zasada surveyed the trays. "Yes."

"You did nothing for twenty minutes and—"

"No, I didn't do *nothing*." Ms. Zasada wrinkled her

nose as if she'd just smelled the worst kind of cheese. "I prepared the service, at a leisurely pace."

"But you're doing it now." Janey gestured at the two silver trays on the middle island of the kitchen.

"I'm refreshing it. There's a difference."

"Then what happened when you called Mr. Schoeneman? Show me how you call him."

Ms. Zasada nodded. "You're thorough. Your investigators didn't ask me such detailed questions."

"Good to know. They're in training. Show me how you call him."

"I use the intercom in the suite." Ms. Zasada waved to a panel that blended in with the cream-painted wall.

"Can you show me how it works?" Janey had a good idea, but she wanted to recreate the moment to see it for herself. Most people just used wrist comms, even for calling between rooms. Intercoms were an antiquated technology. Ms. Zasada wasn't wearing a wrist comm.

Ms. Zasada pressed a black dot on the panel and released it. The panel transformed into a vid screen. "Normally, Mr. Schoeneman replies. I don't need to say anything at first."

"And then when he replies, you—" Janey prompted.

"I tell him that his guests are here. But I didn't, not this time. Because he didn't reply. He usually replies right away."

"Then what did you do next?"

Ms. Zasada gestured toward the hallway that led farther into the suite. Three doors led off the hallway, probably to bedrooms. At the far end of the hallway, ornate double doors dominated the space.

Janey hurried toward the doors.

Ms. Zasada followed, calling after her, panic in her voice, "You can't go in there."

Janey stopped before the doors. "What did you do once Mr. Schoeneman didn't answer?"

Ms. Zasada glared at her. "I am not supposed to go in there if he's not here."

"But we don't know where he is, and perhaps you're impeding this investigation, Ms. Zasada. Shall we take you in for questioning?"

"But the lawyers…"

"We can't wait. Time is of the essence."

Ms. Zasada frowned but pushed the doors inward.

"You came in here and? …" Janey prompted.

"He wasn't here." She looked guilty. "I searched." She stepped in, circled the massive hardwood desk, clear of any items, and pointed to a door. "I checked in here." She opened the door to reveal another washroom.

"And then?"

"I left the office, took his plate, and checked the master bedroom and guest rooms."

"Show me." Janey followed Ms. Zasada out of the office. The housekeeper opened the two guest bedroom doors, stepping in and opening doors to the ensuite bathrooms. She paused before the third door, presumably to the master bedroom. She opened her mouth to speak, to demand Ms. Zasada open the door, but the housekeeper finally opened the door.

Janey took readings the whole time. Both guest rooms were neat and clean as if no one lived there. In Schoeneman's master bedroom, she picked up his bio-readings, but no one else's. No odd bio-photon readings in any of the bedrooms.

Ms. Zasada returned to the kitchen. Janey followed.

"Where do you sleep, Ms. Zasada?"

"Next door."

"You have your own suite?" This floor had mostly

large suites for the high rollers. Made sense that Schoeneman stayed in one when he was visiting the station.

"He treats his employees well."

"Thank you for showing me this, Ms. Zasada."

"I'd like to serve the news crew now if you don't mind. If you don't have any further questions, that is. I told you everything."

"A few more items. I need to see the vid for the interior of the suite."

"What? No. Recording is absolutely not allowed inside this suite or any other in the hotel." Ms. Zasada bobbled the carafe she was holding, glared at Janey.

Janey nodded.

"When did you call the lawyer, and where?"

"In the kitchen. I have a vid station there." Ms. Zasada opened a cabinet. A vid screen and other equipment were normally hidden from view.

"Then you called security."

"Yes, I called Ms. Iona." She glanced at the doorway. "And then you arrived about three minutes later."

"When was the last time you saw Mr. Schoeneman?"

"I brought his mid-morning coffee at 10:30 a.m., and then I made him a sandwich and brought it to him at 11:30 a.m."

"You saw him?"

"Yes, of course. Why don't you believe me?" Her cheeks reddened.

"I believe you." Was the housekeeper hiding something? "What kind of sandwich did you make him?"

"It's a special kind, I don't know the name officially. He calls it his vegetable sandwich."

"What's in it?"

"Tomatoes, cucumbers, avocado, and romaine lettuce. Lots of spicy mustard." She opened the refrigerator and waved at the ingredients she mentioned, in plain view on the middle shelf. "See for yourself."

"Thank you, Ms. Zasada."

"May I serve my guests now? Would you and your investigators like something too?" she said, without a smile, finally glancing at Janey.

"Please serve them. And no, we don't need anything."

Ms. Zasada carried the tea service into the sitting room, a suppressed air of displeasure following in her wake. Probably to mask her worry for Schoeneman.

Orlando was in the step-down entertainment room. Janey joined him.

"Check this out." Orlando scanned one of the wall screens behind one of the couches. "There's something behind the screen. A door."

"His safe?" Janey checked her holo and corrected her guess. "Venus Hells. A tunnel. I've never seen anything like this on the station maps. Have you?"

"No. Whoa. The tunnel is at least eight feet long." He stared at his holo screen. "There's no trace of anything being disturbed here."

"Maybe the house recently cleaned here," Janey said. The couches, table, and rug held no traces of anything, not even Schoeneman.

"If there is a tunnel off this room..." Orlando said.

"There could be other tunnels, in other rooms." Janey hurried down the hall, bypassing the guest bedrooms, Orlando behind her. "The last place Ms. Zasada saw him."

She shoved open the gilt-edged double doors and moved into the spacious office, taking it in. She scanned for the spaces behind the walls. Nothing behind the desk. That wall was decorated with small framed holos of Schoeneman with other people, some she recognized, some she didn't—media moguls, heads of government, and glamorous movie stars.

Nothing odd on the right wall. Just lots of gilt-framed diplomas.

The washroom was just a bathroom, albeit a big one, at least twice as big as her small quarters.

The final wall. There was something behind the bright cheerful large painting done in reds, greens, and blues, full of grid lines. An original from the looks of the thick brush marks on the canvas. The only piece of real art in the whole suite.

She lifted the painting off the wall or tried to. The thick gold-painted wooden frame was at least six feet long, four feet tall, and heavy. Orlando helped her heave it off its hooks.

"Mierda." Orlando whistled and stared.

"Venus Hells." Janey sucked in a breath.

A tunnel led into the bowels of the space station— dark and musty, and wide enough for an adult to crawl through.

TWELVE

Ms. Zasada gasped behind them.

Janey spun. The film crew crowded in the hallway, bustling in their direction. She had to contain the situation. And fast. Meilani and Antonia were calling them back into the sitting room, but they weren't listening to her.

"Ms. Zasada, go back to the film crew. Shut the door."

Ms. Zasada stared at her, her mouth agape, frozen.

Over the housekeeper's shoulder, Janey saw one of the crew heft the professional camera to her shoulder in a swift move. Janey pushed the stunned Ms. Zasada out of the office and shut the door, ignoring the older woman's sputtering objections.

Janey commed Meilani and Antonia.

"Investigator?" Worry laced Antonia's voice.

"Contain the situation," Janey said.

"How?"

"You'll think of something. Lock the door. Just keep them away from this room."

"But I want to help," Meilani chimed in. "We both do."

"Coordinate with Kim," Janey replied.

"Will do. What will you do?"

"Gonna take this tunnel we found. Get a map of this warren and send it to me."

"How?" Antonia asked.

"You'll figure it out."

"Yes, ma'am." Antonia commed off, determination in her voice.

Janey eyed the tunnel that led straight into shadow and waved her arm back and forth in the tunnel's wide opening. No bio-photons showing that anybody passed this way. No human DNA either. No traces that she could spot as if the area had been wiped clean. Venus Hells.

Maybe the tunnel had been built by and for a mainte-nance crew in the early days of station construction and then covered over. But she had no knowledge of these tunnels, and she'd been all over the station, although never inside the guts of it. She hadn't known it had such guts. A flush of fiery anger pulsed through her. Did Milano know of these tunnels? Did they extend only from Schoeneman's suite? Or was there a warren of them throughout the whole station?

A security hazard waiting to happen.

Maybe it already had and that was where their crimi-nals were hiding. Right under their noses.

"They have up to a ninety-minute lead," Orlando said. "My sensors show no one up ahead."

"They must have some way to mask their bio-photons," Janey said.

"Cloaking," they said at the same time.

Orlando stepped closer to her. "Could be dangerous."

"I know." She held his gaze, drinking in his concern and banked excitement.

"Come on." She peered in without touching the metal. After a few feet darkness overtook the tunnel. "We have to go in."

She blinked to adjust her implant, allowing in more light from the room, and saw nothing of note. Only the smooth metal tube, extending into the distance straight for fifty feet. Then it hit a T-junction and split left and right.

"Why don't you send in Larissa or someone else?" Orlando said.

"What? And miss all the fun?" She placed a palm on his chest. "You scared?"

He moved closer still, his warmth a comfort. "No."

"Then what?" She eyed his lips. "You aren't one for caution."

He eyed her lips. "You're going in blind. They're cloaked. You don't have a map of the ducts."

"Not yet. I don't have a map, yet." She moved closer until only an inch of air separated them. "But I can see in the dark."

"What's this? You're making up for all those lonely nights?" He whispered in her ear.

"Just making sure you and I can manage in tight spaces." She leaned in for a kiss. She'd been wanting to get her hands on him since he'd arrived. Their lips touched, soft and welcoming. He tasted so good. She pressed against him and dove into heat, into fire, and combusted into a kiss. Time stopped.

Then her comm pinged. She ignored it. It pinged again.

She came up for air, a little disoriented. "Yes, Kim."

Orlando leaned his forehead against hers, panting.

"You okay?" Kim asked.

"Yes. Orlando is here too," Janey said. Orlando's heat enveloped her. "What's up?"

"Hi, Orlando. Thought you'd like to know what I uncovered in the search of hate mail," Kim said.

"Yes, I would." She pulled away. Orlando followed her, as in a dance step, palms on her shoulders.

"I've flagged two people or parties. I've sent you the short and skinny."

"Give me the highlights," Janey said.

"There was a series of hate mail from a person or group calling themselves Kurskaya, advocating the overthrow of the Russian oligarchy and claiming that Schoeneman is bankrolling the Russian Underground."

Kurskaya, named after a Moscow metro stop, was the moniker of the Russian Underground, controlled by a brutal leader who kept to the shadows and was not afraid to order violence if it served his purposes.

She heard the first claim before on a previous case but not the second about Schoeneman. "Why do they stand out?"

"Their video messages threaten robbing Schoeneman and stripping him of all his wealth."

"That's a new spin on well, everything," Janey said. "What's the second source of hate mail?"

"The Rhombium Collective. Heard of them? I couldn't find them anywhere," Kim said.

"No," Janey said. Orlando shook his head. "Neither has Orlando. What is their claim to hate?"

"Theirs are short untraceable messages threatening life and limb to Schoeneman and all his holdings, including his asteroid mining claims. They were encoded by one of our in-house coding algorithms."

"In-house?" Janey asked. "I don't like it." Another link toward an inside job.

"Me neither. They show up nowhere else. I mean nowhere, not even in the shadow net," Kim whispered. "I don't like that they're using our algorithm."

"Have you checked the public Sol Security Office database?" Orlando asked.

"I did," Kim said. "But maybe your clearance takes you where I can't go."

"I'll check." Orlando waved away on his holo.

"While he's doing that, Kim, do you have a map of these tunnels? Maybe you got Antonia's request." Janey paced the large office.

"I did, and I don't have a map yet. I have a call in to engineering, specifically Laura Hidalgo on unofficial channels. Normally, a map should have been logged in the archives. But where it should be, it's not, as if it was filed, then deleted. Hidalgo was the last known user of the schematics map, six months ago."

Laura Hidalgo was Chief Milano's wife and one of the chief engineers in the station's machine shop.

"Not good." Janey adjusted the settings on her holo and blinked to adjust her ocular implant to the micro-scope setting. "Let me know—"

"As soon as I have the map. Will do. I'll send Larissa to talk to Hidalgo."

"Good idea." Janey commed off and studied the lower edges of the tunnel at the smallest scale she could, one thirty-second of an inch at a time, for anything she missed in her earlier scans. If someone climbed into the tunnel, they would have scraped the bottom edge with their clothing or their shoes.

The tunnel's edges were beveled smooth—a high-caliber job. Nothing out of the ordinary so far. She kept scanning. There were occasional microfractures in the edging where a thread or dirt could have lodged. She might get lucky. Janey stayed with the painstakingly slow scan, finding nothing on the bottom half, so moving upward.

They worked in silence for a few minutes, him on his holo, and her on scanning the tunnel's edges.

Finally, Orlando exhaled heavily. "Kim was right. There's nothing on the Rhombium Collective anywhere."

"So, a dead-end," Janey said, craning her neck to view the upper parts of the tunnel opening.

"Si, Mierda."

Janey sucked in a breath. "I have something here." Using the high magnification setting on her ocular implant, she imaged the spot, at the three o'clock position, then with the tweezers from her belt kit, she reached up and plucked a micro thread off the edge of the tunnel.

"How did it get there?" Orlando held out a small tube.

"Luck." She dropped the trace into a small tube. "We need Soren here to search for more of whatever this is."

"Whoever they are, they're careful." Orlando labeled the tube.

"Definitely pros. They've probably been planning this for some time." Janey motioned to the trace. "Leave it here. One of my people will take it to Soren. We need to take the tunnel."

"Without a map?"

"Since when are you the cautious one?"

"I put a lot of preparation into my ops, despite appearances." Orlando left the tube on Schoeneman's empty desk.

Janey sent a message to Kim about the evidence,

stowed her tweezers, and checked the rest of the contents of her belt pouch. "I have water, snacks, and my multi-tool. Flares, tracers, beacons, and evidence kit. What do you have?" She gestured to his slim backpack.

"Same. Plus, a head-lamp." He donned it but didn't flip it on, studied his holo, and scratched his scruffy day-old beard.

"What is it?"

"On a whim, I ran a search in the database for the rhombus or rhomboid shape. It's a common enough shape—essentially a parallelogram with uneven sides and non-right angles." He gestured with his hands as if he was holding a fat sandwich.

"What did you find?" Janey resettled her pack and tightened the straps.

He scratched his chin, staring at his holo.

She scrambled up into the tunnel. "Can you share and hustle at the same time? We need to go."

He eyed her.

"Coming, Orlando?" Janey threw the words over her shoulder and crawled forward on her hands and knees.

"Yes, right behind you." His boots scuffled against the metal. "Smells funny in here."

"Like what?" Janey sniffed the dry air.

"Not sure. Dust, stale air, something metallic."

"Didn't notice but makes sense." She shuffled onward on all-fours and was halfway to the T-junction when she said, "You were going to share what you found."

"It's nothing."

"What do you mean?"

"Like what Kim saw, no mention of Rhombium, rhomboid, rhombuses. Nada."

Janey swore. "As if all mention had been erased. Has to be an inside job, maybe even from inside the Sol."

"Or just excellent hackers who know how to cover their tracks."

"Or hackers who are working with people on the inside."

"Or..." Orlando trailed off.

"What?"

"Nothing."

Janey commed Kim. When Kim answered, she asked, "Can you see us?"

"I can. And Laura is in the middle of a job and will get back to me as soon as she's done."

"But this is urgent. I thought Larissa was going to see her. Have her turn off the damn fabricator and help us. I need whatever map of the tunnels she can find. Who knows where these tunnels lead? I want to know what we're heading into."

"Larissa is waiting at the machine shop, nearby. What Laura is doing is urgent too."

"What could be more urgent than getting a map of the station tunnels?"

"She's building a replacement Meal Maker for a guest, who accidentally bust his last night during a party. You know we can't keep the guests waiting." Kim huffed out a breath.

"I know. Did you investigate the guest?"

"Larissa was there this morning taking an accident report."

"Anything fishy?" Janey hadn't had time to go over the morning reports. Too busy trying to catch a murderer and thief.

"Not at first glance. Why? You want me to dig deeper?"

"Yes." Janey arrived at the T-junction and stopped.

"We'll look into it," Kim said.

"I'm at our first junction."

"Use your bio-photon tracer beacons as buoys, and I'll trace your path as you go," Kim said.

"Comms will do the rest." Janey smiled. "Good idea, Kim. McCallister out."

"Not sure why you need me," Orlando said. "You and Kim make a good team."

"Of course, but we're in the field, and she's in ops." Janey studied her holo and then her ocular implant for a clue as to which way to go at the junction. No differences in either straightaway. Just more wide tunnels to crawl through. "We're not splitting up, though. Changed my mind."

"What changed it?"

"I have to keep you out of trouble, Orlando." She smiled.

"I'll do the same." Orlando nodded. "I have your back, McCallister."

"Thanks. We're going left. Schoeneman is somewhere in this mess of tunnels, and we have to find him." Janey scanned the junction up ahead.

"Whoever is behind the heist could be behind the kidnapping too," Orlando said from behind her.

"Assuming it is a kidnapping." Janey frowned. "Have to consider all possibilities."

"What else could it be?" Orlando asked.

"I don't know. My boss has gone—"

"Loco?"

"Maybe Schoeneman has gone crazy. Maybe the heist was staged for insurance fraud."

THIRTEEN

JANEY CHOSE THE LEFT TUNNEL. AFTER crawling for eight feet, she came to another junction and paused. "Setting the beacons?"

"Yes, ma'am," Orlando said. "But I'll run out before too long."

"I have ten."

"I have eight more. I'm leaving them one per length. We've taken five junctions so far." He glanced about, studied his holo, and frowned. "Where do you think we are?"

"The temperature is just a few degrees hotter than the standard sixty-nine degrees. So, we can't be too far from the heating ducts."

"But where are we?" He scratched his chin. "Which level?"

"I don't know. Between two suites maybe."

"There's that much space between suites?"

"On this level. Probably." Janey hated not knowing. Then she got an idea and commed Kim.

Kim didn't reply.

Janey hit her wrist comm, again and again. No answer.

"What's wrong?" Orlando asked.

"I can't reach Kim." Janey waved on her comm and sent a message to Kim to call her. The wrist comm honked a disgruntled sound. The message didn't go through.

"Can you send a message?" Janey asked.

"I'll try." Orlando tapped on his wrist holo. The holo image flickered, didn't resolve, and then fizzled to nothing.

The stone in her gut came back.

"No, no reception." He glanced at her. "We should go back. We really are flying blind now."

"No, we have to go forward."

"Janey, you know no one can track us."

"I know."

"Just checking. The beacon idea won't work if we can't send or receive messages."

"I know. But if we don't go forward now—" Janey blew out a breath and fiddled with her pack straps. "We'll lose time." Even her words sounded weak to her ears.

"We could go back. Regroup," Orlando said, but he didn't sound serious.

"Since when are you one to back down from an adventure?"

"Oh, I'm not backing down. Just making sure, you're sure." He scratched both sides of his chin, his face mostly in shadow from his headlamp.

"We have to keep going." At the junction, Janey looked both ways down the tunnel. "There must be some kind of cloaking. Maybe a Faraday cage. Or someone could be jamming our signals."

"Which way then?"

"Let's go to the right." She blew out a breath.

"Why?"

"That leads toward the edge of the station."

"Whoever took Schoeneman could have taken him the other direction or back that way."

"You have a point, but I need to pick, so I pick this way," Janey said. "Edge of the station means egress. If I were kidnapping Schoeneman, I'd want to get him off the station."

"Okay. Good idea. Lead on." Orlando said, determination in the set of his jaw.

Janey went right and crawled another eight feet before they hit another T-junction. Both directions faded into blackness beyond a few feet. Even with her ocular opened to let in all the light it could, she could only see the grey outlines of the tunnel's edges in front of them.

"The right one is decidedly colder. Let's go left," she said.

"I thought you wanted to head to the edges."

"I thought I did, but if it gets too cold—"

"We will freeze to death." Orlando finished quietly. "I left my spacesuit in my other backpack."

"Me too," Janey said. No one wanted to get caught in a no-oxygen high radiation environment unprotected. She peered in both directions again, first left, then right. "Yes, left, for sure. I don't think whoever took Schoeneman would want to kill him. Otherwise, they would have killed him in his office. We saw no signs of any struggle. He went willingly." Janey crawled into the left tunnel, hands and head-first, on all fours.

After a few feet, past the region she'd been about to see, the tunnel made a sharp right. She shuffled forward on all fours. Then wished she hadn't. It sloped abruptly downward, had to be at least a thirty-degree angle.

Venus Hells.

She reached out, but the walls were slick. There was nothing to grab onto. She slid head-first, fast.

"Orlando!" she yelled.

Arms out in front of her, Janey tightened her center mass to stay steady and breathed out. She had this. She was military trained, Space Wing, hardcore. She focused on her breath and blinked to adjust her ocular implant to let in more light.

But only blackness was ahead. Cold heavy blackness. There was no light to let in.

Janey gulped and rocketed farther down the metal tube. She pressed her boot soles against the walls but that didn't slow her down. She had to arrive somewhere soon. Right?

Her breathing came short. It was so black. Her breath rattled in and out. Sound closed in around her. Blood rushed to her head.

Orlando called after her, his voice strong, with a wobble. He was afraid too. "Janey, hold on! I'm right behind you."

That helped. She could focus on the here and the now. This wasn't weightlessness, the void of space she most feared, but it was a close second. Falling. In the cold. With an unknown destination.

Getting colder. Her vision narrowed. She was panting.

"Janey!"

His words, his concern, snapped her out of the cold black descending upon her. She yelled back, "No, stay. There's nothing to hold on to." But she could hear him close behind, his boots sliding against the metal.

Her vision cleared to normal, even as her eyes teared

up at the cold air hitting her face. She blinked rapidly to clear the wet and to flip through the spectrum. Even with infrared, whatever was ahead of her and below her looked like a dark pool, absorbing all light. Not even Orlando's headlight could penetrate it.

Venus Hells and Jupiter's balls.

The whooshing sound of her descent dampened as whatever *it* was rapidly approached. Finally some action, possibly clues that could lead to answers. That she could handle.

She protected her head, curled into a ball, and landed with her body thudding against a wall. It and the floor were freezing. On all fours, she scrambled out of the way, just in time as Orlando crashed beside her.

The room wasn't lit, but now with her infrared vision, she could see clearly. Her heart rate slowed to normal, and her panic receded. Thank the stars.

A noise like a muffled cry sounded nearby.

"Shh. Did you hear that?" Janey spun on her knees, her heart jack rabbiting again. She breathed out.

Focus.

She had this. She was going to be okay.

"No." Orlando rubbed his back and sat up. "I can't see a damn thing. Headlamp's busted." He waved his hands in front of his face.

A calm descended over her. She had something to do. She called up her version of the station map she had on her holo and studied it. At least that was working.

Orlando pawed through his sack, retrieved a glow stick, and shook it to activate. "Let there be light."

Janey blinked to adjust her eyes to normal light, covered her eyes, and waited for the glow stick to flare white.

"I did want you all to myself, but in much better

accommodations," Orlando grumbled. "This is a bit dreary."

She opened her eyes. The space was stark. Empty of any furniture or light fixtures, the ten-by-ten-foot room with a twenty-foot ceiling had black painted walls. The floor was clean faux tile, painted black, a light-absorbing black. No visible door.

"A holding cell? An old storage room?" Janey brushed her hands against the cold floor and walls where she was sitting. The place was cold and smelled of metal.

"The decorators did their job well, then. Where are we in relation to the rest of the station?" Orlando knocked on the walls. A dull thud barely reverberated in the small space.

"Don't know." Janey scrambled to her feet, then paced, waving over her comm. Some of its functions had to work. They weren't all reliant on the station's network. "We started at Schoeneman's suite, headed away from it, so we were probably behind the next suite. Then we zig-zagged some left, right, lefts—all sloping gently downward. Now that I think about it."

"Yes, down. And five times."

"Right, five times. Then down the slope to this small room." She calculated the rate of speed of her descent. "About forty feet in a diagonal direction, then downward about twenty feet, then a big drop."

"Sounds about right to me." He stretched the light stick above his head. The ceiling was painted the light-absorbing black too. "Ceiling's out of reach."

She smoothed her hand against the wall, rapping her knuckles against it too, and watched her comm.

"Anything?"

"Nothing. You?"

"Same. So far." He frowned at his holo, waved it a few times, and went back to pounding the wall.

She hit her wrist comm to call Kim. Nothing. She spoke a message to Kim and ordered it sent. Her comm honked an error message.

What area of the station blocked the comms?

Perhaps someone had gone to great lengths to block the signals. This room could be surrounded by a Faraday cage or intentionally jammed. Like the tunnels were. But since her comm didn't work, she couldn't discern anything.

Orlando swore.

"What?"

"She's muzzled."

"She who?"

"My holo gal interface."

"I know how you feel." Janey frowned and waved over her wrist comm glowing faintly.

"Just say it, McCallister. It's okay. You don't know where we are."

"I don't, but I'll find out." Janey pounded the wall, hard. "And it's not okay that I don't know where we are. That I didn't know about these tunnels, that we've had a robbery-murder, and that Schoeneman's missing, kidnapped maybe. Or worse."

"What's that?"

"What?" Janey stilled.

There it was again, a muffled sound.

"A yell, maybe." Orlando pounded on the wall, moving quickly around the small room.

Janey joined him. "There's got to be a door here somewhere. Or a panel. Something where the wall is thinner."

They pounded hard on the walls, going around the

room. Flat thuds as if building cement was behind them, the base material of the entire space station.

They heard the muffled yell at the same time.

"Could be Schoeneman," Orlando said and then yelled, "Hey!"

Janey shouted too.

They stopped shouting, but there was no reply.

"Strange," Orlando said. "How can we hear them, and they not hear us?"

Janey pounded more of the walls, territory they'd already covered. This time more methodically. There was a flat thud across the first wall, the second also. The third was the same. Halfway across the fourth wall, there was a more resonant thud.

"A door?" She pounded the wall down and across and traced the faint edges of a door. She kicked it. The wall didn't budge. "Filled in with cement."

Orlando kicked it. A loud hit, but still no movement. "Mierda."

In the moment of quiet, a yell sounded, this time with the distinct words of "Anyone there?" in a deep voice.

It sure sounded like Schoeneman. Maybe their kicking and pounding had loosened something inside the walls to allow the sound to travel.

"Yes, Janey McCallister and Orlando Valdez!" Janey shouted.

"Where are you?" Schoeneman asked.

"In a small room? You?"

"The same. I think. It's dark."

"Who took you, sir?"

"What?"

Janey repeated herself, louder.

"I don't know," Schoeneman replied, his voice raised a notch.

"What happened? How did you get here?" Janey yelled.

"Someone came out of my washroom, masked, dressed in black, held me at gunpoint. A second person too. They dragged me to the Mondrian. A third person moved it. I was pushed into the tunnel. Forced." Schoeneman paused. Maybe to catch his breath. Then he yelled, his voice pitched high, panic driving him. "Do you know where we are?"

FOURTEEN

Beside the door, Janey glanced at Orlando and blew out a breath. She had to answer Schoeneman, but she'd never felt so helpless.

"No, sir, I don't know where we are exactly," she huffed out as loud as she could. "I was never informed about these tunnels. They aren't on any map."

Schoeneman said nothing.

She blinked repeatedly to switch her ocular implant to infrared. There had to be some detail she missed that could tell them where they were.

A pain kicked up in her temple. She groaned and covered her eyes, blinking furiously to reset.

"What is it?" Orlando strode to her and enveloped her in a hug, his strength surrounding her.

Knots in her shoulders loosened a little. She let herself rest there for a few moments. She didn't need to always know.

"Too fast. I went through the frequencies too fast."

Water hissed somewhere. A distant metallic clang. A low hum reverberated through her boots.

"Maybe we're near the machine shop." Her face was buried against Orlando's neck. He smelled so good, of a spice all his own. She felt him nod. He nuzzled her at the sweet spot below her ear. She sighed, letting the tension unspool a bit more. He held her gently without demand, a comforting strength in his quiet presence.

Renewed, she stepped out of his warmth. In a loud voice, she told Schoeneman where she thought they were, near the machine shop.

Schoeneman said nothing.

"Sir?"

"You need to find a way out of here, Investigator McCallister. Do your job." His voice had an edge of anger, the high-pitched panic gone.

"Yes, sir. I'm doing my best." Janey cleared her throat against the dryness of yelling so much. "How long have you been here?"

"Forty-two minutes."

That was precise. He must be manically checking the time.

"How long from your kidnapping to landing in the room?"

"About five to ten minutes. I wasn't counting."

"What does your room look like?"

"I don't know. I can't see much. My holo keeps flickering on and off."

Maybe Schoeneman didn't have an eye implant, after all.

"Where are you standing now? By a wall?"

"Yes."

"Pound on it."

A dull thud sounded from the adjacent wall. In three strides Orlando was there and pounded back.

"I hear that," Schoeneman said.

"We're right next to you, Mr. Schoeneman," Orlando said.

Janey joined Orlando at the wall and scanned it, hoping against hope. A door would be nice. Nothing still. The comm didn't even pick up their bio-photons, let alone Schoeneman's on the other side of the wall.

All these high-powered communication tools and none of them were working.

How were they going to get out of here?

"Sir?" Janey called out. "Measure the room. Count your steps. Keep your hand on the wall and walk to the corner. Then walk that wall."

Schoeneman said nothing. Janey leaned against the wall to wait. Schoeneman was a smart man. He'd do as she asked. People reacted differently under stressful conditions. Some were the take-action type and others were the freeze-and-freak-out types.

What kind of man was Schoeneman under pressure with no way out, after unknown perpetrators robbed the hotel, and he'd been kidnapped in his own hotel-space station?

Orlando pulled her into another hug.

"We're working," Janey protested weakly but didn't pull away. "Schoeneman sure is taking his time."

"He's probably double-checking. And we're waiting," he corrected. "Rest here for a moment. Let me indulge. And relax. Three months is too long, Janey," he whispered that last bit under his breath. He massaged her shoulders and said louder, "You're tense. You hide it so well, McCallister."

"We don't have any signal, Valdez, no ability to send a message or receive one. No one knows where we are. How are we going to get out of here?" She snuggled against his muscled chest and let herself relax under his competent, strong hands kneading her shoulder muscles.

"Hey, just turn it off for one minute. Take a breath."

"I am breathing." She let herself have another minute of bliss. Then stepped away and paced the room again, eyeing the floor, the ceiling, anything but the man in the room, who was radiating warmth toward her. "I got us into this mess. I have to get us out of it."

Janey eyed the corner of the room. Orlando followed her gaze. "It's worth a shot." He kept his tone neutral. She knew their chances were slim. But she had to try something.

"Hoist me onto your shoulders."

He positioned himself under the hole that had dumped them in the black room. Janey clambered up, one foot on his thigh, then his shoulder. She reached up, balancing stretching her arms. "I can't get a grip." She growled and hopped down to the floor.

"I have a pickaxe."

"Why didn't you say?"

"I'm saying now." Orlando hauled out a foldable pickaxe and opened it up. What was about the size of her forearm was now twice that and sturdy looking, the pointy edge dull with the patina of use. What had he last used it for?

"Not sure this will work. Lost its sharp edge."

"Worth a try."

"Okay. Hand it to me once I'm up there." Janey climbed up on his shoulders again. He passed up the pickaxe, handle first. "Hold steady."

She whacked the pickaxe into the metal tunnel as hard as she could. A vibration surged up her arm, but the axe didn't grip. Orlando wobbled a little below her. She tried, again and again, but the axe couldn't get a grip. "Blast it. Let me down."

"Hand me the axe first."

Janey gripped the metal head and delivered the axe to him. Then she jumped down and slapped the wall. "Jupiter's balls. How are we getting out of here?"

"We'll find a way."

She stomped away from him and kicked the black wall.

"Janey, you're not alone in this. I'm right here."

"I know." She spun to face him. "But for how long? Then you'll leave again. We'll be apart until the next vacation months from now."

"I'm here, Janey. On long-term assignment." He looked like he was going to say more, but Janey jumped in.

"But after that? You'll go back, and I'll be—" She huffed out a breath. "Silly, I know. The work—"

"We talked about this, back in Las Cruces. I'm yours, carina." He reached out a hand. "What's really going on?"

Janey paced. "This morning—I wasn't really mad at you."

"I know."

"The calls, for my mom. Looking for a new treatment."

"I know."

She paced some more and glared at the black floor—black like the ball of fear in her throat.

"Janey," Orlando said in a soothing voice.

She glanced up. His hand was still outstretched. She reached for him.

Schoeneman pounded on the wall, interrupting their

moment. "Three point zero one meters square," he shouted.

"Thank you," Janey yelled back and dropped her hand. "We're the same." She eyed where the wall and the ceiling met the wide duct that slid them into the room. "What if? ..."

"You want to try and climb up that?" Orlando followed her gaze, understanding the direction of her thoughts.

"How would I hold on?" She mused aloud. "It's a steep thirty-degree angle at least."

"Suction cups," Orlando said. "Or a pulley system or ladder."

"We have none of those things."

"Ideas are better than dwelling in hopelessness." Orlando rubbed his shoulders and neck.

He must have been feeling the pressure too, and they'd only been in the room thirty minutes. Who knew what the bad guys were doing? Maybe taking one of the docked space jets hostage to escape.

How were they going to find them, let alone catch them?

Maybe it was too late.

She had to do something, anything, to beat back the darkness from overtaking her. "Sir, Mr. Schoeneman, do you know why they took you? Did they say anything? Request anything? Any detail could be useful."

"Nothing. I asked them about the heist, demanded to know. They shoved me, prodded me through the dark tunnels, but didn't speak."

"That's it? Anything else?"

"One of them chuckled. Self-satisfied bastard."

"A man?"

"Yes, all three were men." Schoeneman had some relief in his voice, maybe at being able to offer something.

"Good. What else? Height? Weight?"

"Slight build, maybe five-eight, five-nine."

Schoeneman was at least six foot three.

"Good. Skin tone? Voice quality?"

"I told you, Investigator, they were masked. Completely. Some kind of black military-grade uniforms. Light-absorbing black."

"That's useful," Janey said. "Anything else? Someone could have slipped up. You were in the tunnels with them for a while. Your unconscious mind may have noticed something your conscious mind passed over. We generalize and can miss details that way. Smells? Sounds? Every little bit helps."

"We're stuck here!" he yelled, his voice sharp with rage. "Someone has all the station's money and access to *all* my other holdings. I'm ruined."

Janey lifted an eyebrow at Orlando. "All?" she repeated in a low tone. She hadn't had time to dig into the list of stolen items. "We'll get you out of here. Sir."

"How? You're trapped. Same as me." Schoeneman pounded on the wall as if he were beating a punch bag.

"Save your strength! We'll think of something!" Janey yelled. "We have to," she said in a quiet tone.

The pounding stopped.

"Do your job, McCallister!" Schoeneman shouted before giving the wall one last punch. "And make sure that Sol agent helps you."

"We got this," Orlando said and rubbed her arm.

"He doesn't like you much," Janey said.

Orlando shrugged, his expression closed for a

moment. "He has everything at stake and is now locked in a box," Orlando said and rubbed a spot on the floor with his boot as if scratching at a stain.

"It's so strange to hear him break down like that. But I get it." Janey shook her head. "He's a multi-trillion-dollar industrialist, usually so in control."

"These are strange times. I get where he's coming from, though—even if these are strange times indeed."

"I'm surprised you have compassion for him," Janey said.

"I know, me too"—he sat against a wall—"but we're stuck here too, for the moment."

Janey sat beside him, her knees touching his, and then she glanced at him.

"Run through?"

"Yes." Out of habit, she waved over her comm as she spoke, entering the notes in for the record. Helped her feel like she was doing, something. "They are professionals. Pros. They planned the heist. And the kidnapping. Quite elaborate. Maybe there are two teams involved. The mastermind, probably an engineer. And the technicians, the doers."

"At least. Someone with knowledge of the safe's contents. That'd be someone with insider knowledge," he said.

"Especially to know our security protocols and the vault location and codes," Janey added.

"They knew the station layout—these tunnels," Orlando said. "Maybe one of the original builders of the hotel."

"Maybe they'd kept the original schematics..." she said. "What's their motive for stowing Schoeneman here?"

"Good question. I have another. What about us? I bet they didn't plan on us coming after Schoeneman," Orlando said. "And do all the tunnels lead to slides that shove people into these black boxes? Okay, that's two questions."

"But what if they did plan on us coming after Schoeneman?"

"And they want to take us out of the game too." Orlando stood. It was his turn to pace, frenetic long strides, two in one direction, spin, two more back toward the other black all that looked exactly like all the other walls.

"Any smart ideas, McCallister, for getting us out of here?" Schoeneman shouted.

"Any tics or off gestures?" Orlando asked loudly and studied his holo as he walked back and forth.

"Why do you ask? No, never mind," Schoeneman said angrily.

"What are you getting at?" Janey edged closer to Orlando. "What are you doing?"

"Just checking my personal files." He stopped and glanced at her. "Thief stuff."

"You come by your skills of deception honestly."

"Thank you," Orlando said. "Some thieves have favorite tools, gestures, or stances. Not everyone has studied disguises and taking on other personas like I have. To mask our sneaking nature."

In the time she'd known him, Janey had seen him don at least four other identities, all in service of his job. Five, if she counted his official work as Sol Special Investigator. But in his stint on the station so far, since this morning, she'd only seen him as his professional self. And a little bit of his personal self. But he oozed sex appeal all the time. Even other women picked up on it.

How was she going to hold on to him, when women flocked to him?

A vibration jiggled under her feet, accompanied by a deep rumble almost out of hearing, but it lodged in her body like a primordial thunder in the distance.

She sucked in a breath. "Did you feel that?"

She'd thought they were near the machine shop, but the noise triggered a new orientation. And the map of the station snapped in her mind's eye. "We're near the space jet hangers."

"Why do you say that?" Orlando asked.

"The rumble. That low noise."

"At one hundred forty decibels," Orlando said, staring at his holo.

"That's a space jet. But none should be arriving or leaving," Janey said. "How are you measuring the sound?"

"I have a simple sound meter. You don't have one?"

"I have a fancy one. They're not working. You're so low tech."

"My low tech may save our asses."

"How so?"

"What was that?" Schoeneman shouted.

"I think we're near the hangers, sir!" Janey shouted.

Think. Think. What did she know about this part of the station?

Schoeneman said nothing.

Orlando circumnavigated the room once more, slowly this time, staring at his holo.

"What are you doing?" Janey asked.

"I'm using sound to map what's below us and around us."

"Echolocation!" Janey switched some settings on her comm. "Feed me your readings. I'll overlay them on the station map I have." Excitement bloomed in her like spring flowers in her mom's garden. "We could have used that tool to map the tunnels."

Orlando studied his holo and moved to the center of the room. "I checked, but sounds were coming from multiple directions and not making any sense. What do you have?"

"A major duct is under us, and the hanger is directly below that. How is it that we haven't spotted a door? I'm guessing this was a storage area of some kind. You need a door for that." Janey stared at the map. The answers to getting out of this room were here. She knew it.

Schoeneman pounded on the wall. "Update, Investigator."

Wow. The man was bossy in his tight spot. At least he'd gotten over his panic.

"We're working on it!" Janey shouted.

"We are?" Orlando said in a normal voice.

"Yes." A plan was formulating, but it depended on her team and Kim looking for them, which they certainly were. They had to be. She'd trained them well, and Kim was capable of managing them.

"We're going to send a message, sir," Janey said loudly to Schoeneman. "Stand by."

"How are you going to do that? None of the comms are transmitting." Anger and panic were back in Schoeneman's voice.

"His Zen didn't last very long," Orlando said.

"A powerful man utterly powerless. Relying on two people in another black box of a room to get him out of his tight spot." Janey leaned against a wall. "I guess I understand him too. It's hard to feel out of control."

Orlando leaned against the wall beside her and

crossed his arms, understanding in his gaze. "What's your idea?"

"Morse code."

"Tell me more."

"The team is looking for us, but they can't find us on any sensors. So we have to use an approach that doesn't use those sensors and uses what we all have: our natural senses. So, old-fashioned Morse code."

"Do you know it?" Orlando asked.

"Just the basics. I learned in low-tech survival training at the academy. You don't know it?"

"Sorry to say that I didn't. What do we say?"

"How about 'we're here.' Or 'SOS.' That's the most basic."

"Let's do it. How?"

Janey dug through her pack, but the right tool wasn't there. "What do you have in your pack that will have a good resonance when hitting the floor? Something metal?"

Orlando pawed through his pack.

"Mr. Schoeneman?" Janey called out.

"What?" He growled out his words.

He still sounded pissed. He was probably scared, and that was how he expressed it.

"We're going to use Morse code to send a message. An SOS."

Schoeneman said nothing. Finally, Janey heard, "Good job, Investigator."

"Thank you, sir."

"Orlando, your pickaxe would come in handy just about now." He passed it to her. She hefted it, finding its center of mass, and beat out on the floor three quick taps, then three more taps spaced apart, followed by three quick taps again.

She continued the rhythm for a while—three short taps, three spaced apart, then three more quick—spelling SOS. Hopefully, someone on the team had studied Morse code too. She hadn't included it in her training program, but if she got out of this and still had her job after today, she'd include it. Low tech and high tech needed to work hand-in-hand.

The tapping put her into a meditative trance where time seemed to slow and pull apart. Orlando leaned against the wall, watching her but not with his eyes, more with his whole body.

She was aware of his gaze on her, of the tapping she was creating, of the resonance of sound in her body, through the floor and out into the huge hanger below.

Over one thousand feet long and five hundred feet wide and high, the hanger could land two space jets at the same time, each carrying one hundred passengers plus crew.

Schoeneman said something, and Orlando replied, but she didn't hear the words. She kept the tapping up with her right hand, then switched hands. At some point, Orlando put his hand over hers and took over, a seamless handoff like the baton on a track relay team in high school. She'd been good, she'd been fast, and she'd loved learning the finesse of gripping the baton and passing it off.

Janey leaned on the wall and shook out her arms, releasing the buzz throughout her body. She hadn't felt the buzz until she stopped. Then she paced the ten-by-ten-foot room to get her circulation moving.

Schoeneman was quiet. She replayed what she heard but hadn't digested of Schoeneman and Orlando's conversation. Something about tics and mannerisms. Even in replay, she couldn't make sense of it.

In the quiet, her ears buzzed an SOS echo, a high-pitched ghost of a sound.

"Why did you stop?' She rushed to Orlando.

"I heard a reply," he said, peering up at her, hope filling in his eyes.

FIFTEEN

JANEY HELD HER BREATH AND WATCHED Orlando absorb the incoming Morse code. He closed his eyes and tapped his fingers against his leg as if to let it sink into his bones.

The pinging of metal against metal was faint but steady. One of her team was communicating with them. Three rapid pings, followed by a pause, a ping, and another short pause and another ping. A longer pause and then the pattern repeated, again and again. Three rapid ones, pause, ping, pause, a last ping.

Then all was quiet.

"I got it," Orlando said. "What does it mean?"

"Thank the stars," Janey said. "It's shorthand for 'understood.' Or 'received.'" Her team received and understood their SOS message. A flood of relief had her legs trembling from an adrenaline surge. She took a few deep breaths to find her center.

"Got it. I'll reply with the same message," Orlando said and tapped out the same pattern, repeated it a few times. Then jumped up and did a few jumping jacks, letting off steam too, then he paced, posting his knees high like a footballer high-stepping it across the pitch.

"What was that?" Schoeneman shouted.

"The security team knows we're here. We need to be patient, sir. They're coming." Janey coughed, her voice raw from all the shouting.

Orlando stopped in the center of the small black room and stared at her.

"What?"

"You sure?" he asked softly.

"Sure about what?"

"That they're coming." Orlando's expression was neutral.

"Do you doubt my team?"

"Actually, I don't." Orlando scratched his chin. His five o'clock shadow was getting an early start. It was only 1 p.m.

"Then what, Orlando?" She sat cross-legged on the floor, energy drained from her legs suddenly. Ever since they'd arrived in this small room, she'd been trapped as if in a lab experiment gone wrong. She knew what that was like. Last time that happened she'd lost an eye.

"Nothing." He stared at the floor. The chase and being trapped must be wearing on him too. "Forget it. Chalk it up to stress talking."

"Okay, I will." But she saw the shadows in his gaze when he glanced at her. There was something else going on, some inner struggle perhaps. "When this is over, you will tell me. Yes?"

He made a noncommittal sound.

Fatigue washed over her. She lay down and put an arm over her eyes to block out the glow from the light stick, still bright and white. The thing would last a lot longer than they would if the rescue attempt took too long.

"Taking a nap?" Orlando spoke in a soft tone.

"May as well. I just need to shut it off for a few minutes. Can you take watch?"

"I got your back, McCallister. Always." His voice was low and rumbled through her.

Janey sighed, smiling at that last word.

He'd said it softly, intimately.

Would they ever get a chance to be two normal regular people together without a case rushing them about, without the tension, risks, and pressures of work? Probably not.

She could always give up this post and find a different way to earn a living to support her mother. Several years ago, Dana McCallister had been diagnosed with Myasthenia Gravis, a rare neuromuscular degenerative illness that attacked the immune and digestive systems, making it harder to move and absorb food. Janey had had high hopes for this latest round of experimental drugs, but that trial was ending soon, and her mom was looking worse.

Mom. Blissfully unaware of her current situation and of the other dangerous situations she'd faced on the station. But Mom knew her job had risks.

"Seize life by the throat and don't look back," Mom used to say, and then she'd salute her drink, usually tomato juice with a touch of something stronger. These days it was just tomato juice, enhanced with whatever herbs her friends could concoct that wouldn't interfere with the strong meds.

Mom was grateful for the financial support that paid for her daily medical and home care and allowed her to stay in her home, in her hometown, with her friends and social routine. She said gracias all the time. She knew how tough Janey's job was and sent her cute vid messages about her daily card games and friends' stories.

Lately though, those daily messages had become more disjointed and meandering. Her mom's doctors said her mother was no longer responding to the experimental treatment Janey had been funding, and there was no other treatment on the horizon. They'd tried them all for her rare illness. She had maybe six months to a year left—if that.

Janey didn't want to believe it, but the reality was sinking in.

Mom knew but didn't talk about the doctors' predictions. She only wanted to play cards with her friends and vid with Janey daily. Her mom wanted a regular life to the end.

And Janey should be there when the time came. Whenever that was.

Even though you couldn't predict death's timing, only that it would come.

What the L was she doing still 22,000 miles away?

But Mom had repeatedly said, "Stay. Live your life." Mom wanted her to do what she loved, and Janey would go crazy at home—with nothing to do, no justice to serve.

Janey had plenty of credits set aside for Mom's last year. Mom could live with her and play cards with her friends—the aunties. Women who'd known Janey since she was scampering about the neighborhood in a jumper and pigtails, playing her favorite hide-and-seek game–Ollie Ollie Oxen Free—with the other kids.

If she lived with her mom, then her mom wouldn't have to worry about her dangerous job.

If she blew it and couldn't catch these thieves and

murders and recover the casino funds, the choice would be made for her, and they'd all be out of a job. Or worse. That would suck.

Venus Hells.

She had to catch them. And her team had to pull through for them.

The floor rumbled again.

Janey jumped to her feet, her heart in her throat. "Shit! Is a jet arriving?" She glanced about wildly as if she could see it.

"You zoned out, McCallister," Orlando said. "It's your team. They're here."

The sound sharpened into a high-pitch whine. A buzz saw. That was it. On the floor, off-center, someone was cutting a wide hole. The arc glowed red.

After a few tense moments, metals scratched against metal, red flared bright neon, and a circle in the floor fell away. A loud bang sounded as the metal circle crashed below them. Thank the stars for power tools.

A few minutes later, Soren popped his head through the manhole-sized circle. "Are you guys okay?" He gazed about, his eyes wide. "I never knew this was here."

"We're good. Schoeneman is next door to us." Janey pointed to the wall.

"We were wondering," he said before disappearing and yelling to someone about Schoeneman. A few minutes later, he popped back up like a gopher in Janey's mother's garden. "You two come down, and we'll come up and cut through the wall to get Schoeneman." He glanced at her. "Sounds good?"

"Yes, fine," she managed to croak out, but Soren looked at her funny, so maybe she wasn't speaking loudly enough.

She said it again louder, coughing again, and then she

shouted for Schoeneman's benefit. "Mr. Schoeneman, our team's here and will get you out soon. Step back from the wall."

"Understood!" he yelled back, his voice firm, back in control.

"We have to go," she added.

"Get those bastards, McCallister. No time to waste," Schoeneman said.

"Yes, sir."

Soren scrambled up with the power saw in hand, eyed the room, and frowned. "How did you get here?"

She pointed to the duct high on the wall. "Tunnels. We couldn't send you anything. Data send-and-receive sucks here. Get Schoeneman down. Then we'll debrief."

Soren studied the dark tunnel. "Kim has Laura Hidalgo in the conference room. Turns out Milano's wife knows this station better than anyone. She helped build it. She should have the maps of these tunnels. But I can send in my bug drones to start mapping."

"You have bug drones?"

"It's a hobby," Soren said.

"Good, do it. But we'll still need you in the lab."

"Of course."

"But—" Soren started.

"What?"

"Ms. Hidalgo's not talking. Chief's there," Soren said and bent to work. The jolting high-pitched buzz of the saw filled the small space, ending any more conversation.

Not talking? What could Laura Hidalgo have to hide?

Larissa popped up and pulled herself over the lip of the hole, gawking, wide-eyed. "Hi, boss. Whoa. Never knew these were here."

Janey gave her a look to get to the point.

"Right. We have an old blueprint of the station and a

list of old employees who could have knowledge of these tunnels."

Janey nodded her thanks and made her way down the ladder, a sturdy vertical affair. In six steps she was on a platform. Then another ladder. Two more platforms and she was on the floor of the hanger, Orlando soon at her side. Medics rushed to them, made them sit on hover stretchers, and ran their sensors over them.

Kim oversaw the engineers hauling up equipment and taking readings. Then she slipped through the hovering medics to them.

"What's Hidalgo—" Janey stood, despite her rubbery legs. Must be the adrenaline aftermath.

Kim hugged her, cutting her off, and whispered, "I was worried about you. Glad you're all right. Beyond strange about those rooms, the tunnels."

"How did you find us?" Orlando asked Kim as a medical assistant fussed over him.

"The SOS." Kim stepped back and eyed her up and down. "Good job using your Space Wing training. Now with the maps and Soren's bugs, we should be able to find the vault contents."

"Hope so. What's this I hear about Hidalgo not being helpful? Makes her look guilty," Janey said, ignoring the medic telling her to sit back down.

"It does. I know." Kim studied her comm. "Can I see your comm? Maybe I can find out why we couldn't get any messages from you."

The medical assistant hovering over Janey frowned and said, "I need to get you to the med bay."

"I'm fine." Janey held out her arm for Kim to scoop out the data from her wrist comm. This immense corner of the hangar was filled with a dozen-plus personnel, all busy with equipment for their rescue. "Where's Schoeneman?"

"He asked for Tseng. I don't see them. Maybe they went to his suite." Kim frowned at her comm. She said to the medic, "Are you done?"

"Yes, but I don't like some of these readings," he replied, then said to Janey. "You're to report to the med bay as soon as you can."

"Okay. What's wrong?"

"Some readings that don't make sense."

"Just send them to my doctor Earthside. They're probably normal for me."

The medic handed her an energy drink and scurried away, finally leaving her be. She didn't realize how dehydrated she was until she guzzled down the berry-tasting drink.

The medic scanning Orlando released him with a "Drink this. You're in good health."

"Ready?" Kim said.

"Yes, stars yes," Janey said. "Kim, what happened with Laura? Did she come in willingly?" They crossed the hanger to the staff elevators that would take them back to the security level and stepped in, Orlando with her.

"She did, but once she got there"—Kim pursed her lips—"she clammed up."

"I wonder what she's hiding. Who is she protecting?"

"My thoughts exactly."

"And the chief?" Janey asked.

"He's distraught. Hidalgo furious. I had to break up their shouting match a few times. I didn't understand a word. It was in Italian and Turkish, I think. It wasn't pretty."

"He's probably feeling betrayed. He dotes on his wife. Does she know about the tunnels?"

"She won't say." Kim motioned for Orlando to show her his wrist comm so she could grab all his data too. Then she studied her holo screen, now full of Janey's and Orlando's data from the tunnels and the black room.

She finally glanced at Janey. "That's odd."

"What is it?" Janey asked, something constricting her breathing.

"While you were in the tunnels, your frequencies were being intentionally jammed."

"I thought so," Orlando said. "Maybe a Faraday cage?" Faraday cages could be used to block electromagnetic fields, in their case signal transmissions, and could be embedded into structures.

"Possibly," Kim said. "But I think it was more intentional than that."

They arrived at the security wing and exited the elevator. "How can you tell?" Janey asked.

"See for yourself." In the corridor, Kim stopped at a wall screen and waved over it to activate the screen and transfer her data.

Janey studied the data on the screen. Kim was right. There it was—a jamming frequency specifically tuned to their comms. Someone had intentionally blocked all comms inside of the tunnels and in the small black rooms.

"So not a Faraday cage. Sabotage," Orlando said.

"But why? What would they have to gain?" Jane asked, her breathing catching in her throat. She willed herself to relax and take a deep breath. They had to catch these bastards.

"To distract us, delay us," Orlando said.

"Delayed us on our end too, once we knew you were missing and started looking for you," Kim said.

"Kim, can you trace its source?" Janey asked. "That might help locate them. They've got to be on the station, in one of the tunnels most likely, since they're shielded."

"I'll get on it," Kim said.

"So, Laura Hidalgo... Bring me up to speed on her background. I need something when we talk to her," Janey said. "I need to know what makes her tick."

"Want me to go in there with you?" Orlando said. He was a good judge of character and could see when people were hiding something.

"Yes, thanks," Janey said. "And prep is key."

"Always," Orlando said.

"Let's get you up to speed right now. Here." Kim waved over the wall screen and read out loud from it. "Laura Madeleine Hidalgo is from the Palm Springs region, within the zone of San Diego, so she grew up in a 'free zone.' This one's by the SunAg conglomerate. Her parents worked for their vast agricultural holdings, mostly in the factories. Laura left for trade school at sixteen and never returned to the area."

"She met Daniel Milano on the job in the Turkish Domain fifteen years ago," Kim continued, "when he worked for Silverstein Insurance as an investigator, and she was an engineer at the Ankara/Istanbul subsidiary of Terrium—a manufacturer that worked closely with Silverstein Insurance to provide custom food crafters to their clients. Her record doesn't state how the two met."

"It wouldn't," Janey said. She didn't want to dig into Chief Milano's records or even question him just yet. Unless she had to. "It's a sticky situation. Any priors?"

"None. She's squeaky clean," Kim replied. "I sent you the rest. Plus, her recent work logs and HR file."

"Thanks." Janey blinked to bring the new information to her ocular implant, the quickest way to access it. She read at double most people's normal speed and smiled. Gotcha.

"What did you find?" Kim asked.

"Circumstantial evidence," Janey replied, a flutter of excitement hitting her in her belly. An inroad to answers and to recovery of the casino's money and the truth, possibly.

"I can run her name through our databases," Orlando said.

"Yes, please. Do it." Janey strode to the conference room door and then paused to smooth down her jacket, ready to face what was in front of her. She couldn't do anything about what had just happened—the tunnels, Schoeneman's kidnapping, and the blocking of their comm channels. She'd process it later. For now, she needed to catch these bastards. And Laura could be the key.

She'd lifted a hand to have it scan the door and open it when Kim stopped her with a hand on her arm.

"You might want to clean up first."

Janey checked her appearance. There were dust patches on her knees and chest, her palms were sooty, and there were small tears in her jacket. Like an added layer on her skin, the grime and sweat caked her face. When did that happen? "Right. I'll use the washroom in my office."

She headed across the hall, unlocked the door with a wrist scan, and let them in. Orlando followed, studying his holo in the middle of the room.

"Anything?" Janey asked as she stepped into her office's tiny washroom. She scrubbed her hands, washed her face, and did her best to brush the dust from her clothes.

Orlando rubbed a cheek, rearranging the dirt there.

"You could do with a wash." She watched him through the mirror.

He hadn't left her side since this morning. He looked good, even with the smudge of dirt along the side of his face. She wet a cloth and approached him.

He didn't look up at her until she was wiping his jaw. He stilled her hand with his.

"Thanks, I got it." He held out his wrist for her. "Read what I found."

Janey handed him the washcloth. He washed with his free hand, and she read his holo screen.

It was a Sol Special Investigations report dated fifteen years ago.

"Rhombium Consortium claimed responsibility for the bomb that killed four at the Russian embassy this morning in Ankara/Istanbul Turkey. All communications in or out of the embassy have been jammed so we have no further information at this point."

There was a note under the report, updated a week after filing. An investigator had speculated that a machine shop engineer or two were involved in the blast, along with a communications expert and some extremely advanced tech like that used in mining operations in the asteroid belt. The investigator also noted that many things had been taken from the embassy, including records, precious metals, and a quarter of the digital currency on hand—seventy thousand credits.

Janey whistled and regarded him. Smudge gone, Orlando had a clean face and looked refreshed. He still needed a shave, but she liked him a bit scruffy.

"Could be Laura Hidalgo was involved," Janey said. "But this is circumstantial at best. We only know she was based there at the time. But combined with what I know—"

"Do you think she's capable?"

"I don't know. All the times I've played cards with her or had dinner as a group, she's been mostly quiet. Not cagey, just unobtrusive, an observer." Janey headed for the office exit. "Anything is possible. I've seen that plenty since working here."

Guests came to L'Étoile to have an exotic getaway. Staff often came to start or restart their lives, like she did. A few people probably came to escape from their previous lives too.

Orlando followed her out of her office.

At the conference room door, Janey paused again. How did she want to play this?

Orlando stood close to her, reading his holo.

"Find anything else?" Janey eyed his screen.

"I've been checking and cross-referencing the Rhombium Consortium with the Rhombium Collective."

"The Consortium claimed responsibility for the Russian Embassy bombing in Istanbul, and the Collective sent threats to Schoeneman. Right?"

"Right."

"So anything?"

"Nothing." Orlando shook his head. "And that's fishy."

"Why?"

"There's not even a follow-up file from the embassy attack."

"Could it have been deleted?" she asked.

"It could have."

"Before you run it up the chain of command, let's talk to Laura and not tip our hand," Janey said. "Okay?"

"The searches could have alerted this Rhombium group," Orlando said.

"Even though your systems are secure?"

Orlando closed the distance between them and put a hand on her cheek. "Anything's possible."

"True." She leaned into his caress for a second, then pulled back out of their private warmth and breathed a sigh. "Let's do this?"

She unlocked the door with her palm and strode into the room.

The chief was standing behind his wife, hand on her chair. Laura sat slumped, staring straight ahead, her expression defiant, closed. Her arms were crossed. The room felt tense, full of static.

Larissa stood by the coffee pot and watched the couple over a steaming cup. She nodded at Janey. "Investigator." She set down her cup, pushed off from the counter, and headed for the door. "I'll go help—"

"Stay. Learn." Janey waved her hand over the table, activating the room recording, and sat.

Orlando took up a post, leaning on the counter. Larissa set a steaming cup of coffee in front of Janey and handed one to Orlando, which he accepted before taking a seat at the far end of the table near the windows. Larissa took a seat to Janey's left, two seats down.

"Investigator McCallister, do you need me here?" Chief Milano said, respect in his voice. He knew the regs, that family members should not be present during an interrogation—unless that family member was a minor.

"Has your wife asked for counsel?" Janey asked him and then said to Laura, "Have you?"

Laura peered at her, jaw tight, defiance in her gaze. Then she shook her head, no.

"I'll be in my office if you need me," the chief said

and peered at his wife, who sat stony-faced. She made no move to acknowledge him. With a pained expression, Chief Milano sighed and left the conference room.

Janey sent a thought command to her ocular implant to scan for frequencies outside the norm. The check started. She'd know in a few minutes if Laura was sending or receiving, or both, working with others on L'Étoile. She didn't want to use the unknown frequencies herself, in case she alerted anyone scanning them. If the frequencies were in use, she'd know soon enough.

"How are you, Laura?" Janey asked.

Laura gave her a stony-eyed glare.

Janey waited, letting the silence stretch.

Laura looked away, at the walls, the floor, not at any of them.

Janey said to Larissa, "Have you read her her rights under the Geneva Convention?"

"Just the Basic Sol rights of representation, protection, and court use." Larissa lifted an eyebrow, asking Janey what she was up to.

Janey waved over her holo, bringing up what she needed. She read from the screen. "You have the right to representation under the Geneva Convention for crimes against humanity."

"What are you talking about?" Hidalgo straightened, and her voice pitched to a near-hysterical. "Crimes against humanity?"

"For killing four people at the Russian embassy."

"What?" Laura stared at her with wide eyes.

"Fifteen years ago."

"I thought you wanted to talk to me about the tunnels in the station."

"I do. What do you know?" Janey watched Hidalgo dart a glance about the room as if looking for an escape route or for the chief. "What have you been hiding from your husband and from all of us?"

Laura's eyes widened further, no denial on her lips, and her pupils dilated a micro-fraction. But that was all that changed.

SIXTEEN

Janey read off her holo. "This morning you went on shift at 8 a.m. and reported to your station, Extruder Machine Number Sixteen. Made cross-beam components." She glanced up at Hidalgo. "What are they for?"

Hidalgo blinked as if taken off-guard and spoke in a flat voice. "Chairs. New chairs for the party next week."

"Do you plan to be here for that?"

"What?"

Janey scanned her holo, though she'd already read the information. "I see you've requested time off-station, indefinite vacation leave, starting tomorrow."

Laura nodded, staring off into space.

Janey lowered her voice and wheeled her chair closer to Hidalgo. "Laura, may I call you that?"

Laura shrugged, her expression impassive.

Janey touched her arm and leaned in conspiratorially, then took a breath, about to speak.

Laura leaned back. A frown flashed and was replaced by a neutral expression.

That was a response.

Her guess? Hidalgo didn't respond to the girlfriend approach. That was fine with her. She was flexible. Janey scooted her chair back. Her ocular implant screen lit up with the results of her scan. The evidence she needed. She had Laura. She waved a message to Larissa.

"Laura Hidalgo, you are under arrest for harboring criminals aboard the Bijoux de L'Étoile Hotel-Casino and space station. Sol Security will be coming to bring you to holding. Your trial will be held under Security Crimes Order Number 179. Not even your husband will be allowed to be there."

Orlando rustled at the other end of the table, hopefully placing her request to his people at the Sol Unified Planets Police Investigative Services. She didn't want to look at him.

Hidalgo sucked in a breath. "When?"

"When what?"

"When will the Sol security police be here?"

"Soon. Tell me where your accomplices are." Janey slapped the table. "Now."

Hidalgo, startled, blinked at her as if she didn't understand Janey's request.

Janey said to Larissa, "Jamming frequencies on?"

"Yes, ma'am."

Janey turned back to Hidalgo. "We know you're communicating with them somehow, so we jammed all communications in and out of this room."

Hidalgo paled. Orlando knew better than to say anything. She didn't know if he got the message out to his people before Larissa set up the block.

"But we have been able to locate the frequency you're using. The ELFs. Or Extremely Low Frequencies. Perfect for the enclosed space of the station."

Hidalgo shook her head. "But I said nothing."

"You didn't need to. I scanned you and saw you have an enhancement."

"Not even my husband knows," Hidalgo whispered and stared unseeing at the far wall.

"Now that we know what to look for, we'll catch your friends." Janey nodded at Larissa. "Take all the agents you need." Larissa nodded and headed for the door.

"They're not my friends," Hidalgo said.

"Who are they then?" Janey asked.

"I owe them." Hidalgo looked at Janey, pain and betrayal in her gaze.

"What? What do you owe them?" Janey signaled to Larissa to wait a moment. The young investigator stopped at the door.

"Everything." Hidalgo slumped back in her chair again, folding in on herself.

"Tell me," Janey said. "It often helps to tell the story."

"Doesn't matter now."

"Why?"

Hidalgo shook her head. "You don't understand, Investigator."

"Explain it to me."

Hidalgo stared at the floor.

"We can protect you."

"Me? The one who's harboring murderers and thieves?" She barked a bitter laugh.

"We've protected people on the station before."

"I can't— This can't go on—"

"Then tell us," Janey said. "Your accomplices have to have a complete and accurate map of the place. You gave it to them. Give it to us."

Hidalgo hugged her arms around herself and rocked.

There had to be a way to get her to talk. Time was

running out. At any moment, a space jet, whether it was the Sol Special Investigator's, a private citizen's, or Schoeneman's would dock, and the criminals would have a chance to escape. Schoeneman was probably arranging for private transport for himself right now, even though the chief counseled against it until the criminals were caught.

Janey scanned Hidalgo with her ocular implant again, as she'd been doing since she'd walked into the room. A form of spying, but well within her rights given the situation. The woman's electromagnetic frequencies had been most active in the low frequencies, but since Larissa had activated the shield on the room, Hidalgo's EM frequencies had diminished. What remained was medium-range and some high-range. Random. How odd. What kind of implants did she have?

Janey said to Larissa, "Please have Doc come here."

Larissa nodded. "Anything else?"

Janey glanced at Hidalgo. "I need your permission to access your medical file."

"Why? I thought you didn't need my permission now that I'm under arrest."

"You do still have basic rights. This is one of them."

"Whatever. Yes. Access it." Hidalgo moaned a little and stifled a sob as if the weight of it all was crashing down on her. In a whisper, she said, "I just want it over."

Janey said to Larissa, "Have Tseng look at the medical record and report anything unusual. Point out the ELF transmitter, if she doesn't spot it."

"It's not a transmitter," Hidalgo said.

"No? Then what is it?" Janey snapped her gaze back to Hidalgo.

Orlando stood, shoving his chair back so hard it banged against the wall. "What are you doing wasting time with this woman? We haven't learned anything useful."

"What are you talking about?" Janey said. "You're disrupting my interview."

"That's right. It's an interview, not an interrogation. You're being way too soft on her." He stormed out of the conference room, leaving agitation in his wake.

Janey hoped he did that for a reason, but she couldn't fathom what it was. Nor where he was going.

Larissa was still at the door. "Anything else, Investigator?" She hadn't even moved when Orlando had stormed past her to exit the conference room. She was pretty unflappable. Good for her. Had to be in this job.

"No, thanks, Larissa. Get going. The sooner we find these accomplices the better. And be careful. Reconnaissance only. Do not approach. Extract their data only."

"You're not going to extract anything." Hidalgo flew to her feet to pace the length of the room, back and forth.

Larissa nodded and left.

It was just Janey and Hidalgo now.

"Sit down, Laura. We're not done yet," Janey said.

"I'm done." Hidalgo paced, long steps for her short stature.

Finally, the woman sat, her machine shop grey engineer coat wrinkled and smudged.

Janey scanned the coat with her comm. It was coated with the same particles that she'd found in the tunnels and the small room.

"You've been in the tunnels," Janey said with certainty.

Hidalgo shrugged.

"Where are they? We're going to catch them anyway."

"Why should I help you?"

"Don't you want to make things right?"

"That's what I was trying to do—by helping them."

"The Rhombium Consortium."

"How did you know?"

"What do they have on you? Why do you owe them?"

Hidalgo collapsed in her chair.

"Look, Laura," Janey said calmly. "There's no one in here except you and me. This room is completely shielded. And"—Janey hit the control on her comm—"the door is locked. We can't be disturbed by anyone, not your husband, not Mr. Schoeneman. So, you may as well be straight with me. Or it can come out in the trial and go on your permanent record. Then your husband will find out. And anyone looking for you. Like the Rhombium Consortium."

At Schoeneman's name, Hidalgo curled her lip into a sneer, then quickly straightened her expression.

"I don't like him either," Janey said.

Hidalgo snapped her gaze to Janey. "But you work for him."

"So do you."

Hidalgo shook her head.

"What do you mean? You're not on the payroll here?"

"No, I am." She sighed. "It's complicated."

Janey waited a beat, but Hidalgo said nothing, staring at the table in a zoned-out state. Janey was wasting her time. She had no leverage on the woman, it seemed. She'd be better off spending her time sweeping the station for the ELFs with Larissa.

A knock sounded on the door.

"Who is it?" Janey called out.

"Doc. Unlock the damn door."

From her comm, Janey unlocked the door. Doc strode

in, all six feet of her intimidating self, dressed in a colorful jacket, beads swinging from her hair. Her clean white lab coat was open, revealing a heavy turquoise necklace over her long smock.

"Did you know that Ed died a horrible death?" Doc stopped next to Hidalgo and peered down at the woman. "All his organs aged in an instant. He was in horrible pain before he died."

Hidalgo glanced at Doc as if mesmerized by the giant of a woman. "I—I didn't know he would kill anyone."

Doc harrumphed and stalked away, toward the coffee.

"He, who?" Janey asked.

Hidalgo tightened her lips.

"Doc, I need you to scan her for an implant of some kind and take it out," Janey said.

Doc poured herself a cup of coffee.

Hidalgo popped out of her chair again. "You can't do that. That's against all prisoner protocols."

Doc sipped her coffee. "I can do that. I have the instruments right here." She set the coffee down and dug into her lab coat pockets. She drew out a silver tube with a needle-like point on one end and a screw top on the other. Janey knew it was a device Doc used in her autopsies to extract body fluids, not something used on the brain—where surely Hidalgo had her ELF transmitter or whatever it was. But it looked scary enough.

Hidalgo waved her hands in front of her. "No, no, get that thing away from me. I hate needles."

Finally, something she was afraid of.

Janey shook her head. "I really don't want to have to do this, Hidalgo. But we need the information you have in your head. And if you don't tell us…"

"You're lying. You're just trying to intimidate me."

Doc stood at Janey's shoulder and made some adjustments to the device, making it click a few times.

Hidalgo paled and backed up against the wall screen, which flickered to life at her touch, revealing the murder board.

Janey got up and waved onto the board under "Prime Suspect": Laura Hidalgo. She faced her suspect. Hidalgo was shaking, eyeing Doc's device and then glancing at Janey.

Doc advanced on Hidalgo.

Hidalgo glanced at her. "You—you can't do this. I have rights."

"You've been hiding a possibly illegal enhancement," Janey said.

Hidalgo looked up at Doc. Doc was eyeing her like a specimen, neutrally.

"No, wait. Stop," Hidalgo said.

Doc took another step.

"Stop!" Hidalgo yelled.

"Where are they?" Janey said calmly.

"At tunnel junction T-9, opposite where they rescued you." Hidalgo slid to the floor, shaking. "Near Hanger B."

Doc stopped her advance toward the engineer.

Janey hit her comm. "Got that?"

"Yes, ma'am," Larissa said over the comm.

"Wait for me outside the tunnel. I'll be there soon."

"Yes, sir," Larissa said.

"But you said the comm was blocked," Hidalgo said.

"It's complicated," Janey said and smiled without mirth.

SEVENTEEN

Staring at Hidalgo, who glared back, Janey waved her wrist comm again and called for Chief Medical Officer Tseng to come to the conference room right away. "Engineer Hidalgo needs your care," Janey said.

"On my way." Tseng commed off.

"It was all an act," Hidalgo said, her voice shaky.

"Not all of it." Janey held out her hand. "Come on, take a seat. I'll call the Chief—Daniel."

Hidalgo shook her head, grabbed Janey's hand, and wobbled to her feet. She narrowed her eyes at Doc. Doc sipped her coffee, ignoring Hidalgo's nervous glances.

She had a few minutes before Tseng arrived. Janey studied her comm to see what Larissa was able to uncover as the young agent scanned the hangar area for ELFs. They had shielded the conference room, but every time the door had opened, Janey scooped up Larissa's data.

Now that she knew for sure Hidalgo was involved in the crime, Janey had full right to do a deep dive into her personal files. Since Hidalgo wouldn't give the map of the tunnels to them, they had to be somewhere in her digital files.

But before she had a chance to dig, someone knocked. Janey unlocked the door to Tseng and one of her assistants. That was fast.

Tseng hurried to Hidalgo and scanned her. She frowned at Janey. "I need to get her back to Medical to run more tests. She has an acute case of *summa metum*."

Extreme fear. Right. Janey had studied a bit of Latin. A fake medical term if she ever heard one. What was Tseng up to? Was she overprotective of Hidalgo? Tseng had been on the station for almost as long as the engineer. Or, and this thought seemed unlikely but had to be entertained, was Tseng somehow connected to the case?

"You can treat her there." Janey pointed to the small room behind the murder board. "Doc, please oversee them." Better to be safe and monitor the situation. Security should be with a prisoner at all times.

Tseng scrutinized her but didn't protest. Doc frowned and followed the chief medical officer and Janey's suspect into the small break room.

Janey needed one more person here, just in case. She didn't like the way Tseng eyed her. Could be nothing, but no sense in taking chances. Not today.

Dropping the comm shield, Janey commed Kim. "Can you send someone to watch the conference room?"

"Yes, on it. Have you spoken to Larissa? I have a question for her. I commed her, but she's not answering."

"Weird. I told her to wait for me if she found something," Janey said.

"Well, I've lost her on the station vids," Kim said, sounding worried. "And her bio-tracker is not showing either. Checking another sensor. One sec."

"Thanks," Janey said. While she waited, she waved a

message to Doc to not let Hidalgo out of her sight and to supervise Tseng closely, and there'd be security officers at the door if she needed them.

"Janey?" Kim said.

"Still here."

"Larissa's last known location is Hanger B?" Kim said.

"Yes. You picked up her signal? How long ago?" Janey asked.

"It disappeared three minutes ago."

"What the regolith!" Janey dashed for the door. "Have Orlando meet me there and any other security we can spare."

"On it." Kim commed off.

Janey stopped at the door. It hadn't opened on her approach. Of course. She unlocked it, rushed through, and waved the manual lock back on. She broke out into a run through the corridor, to the service elevator, and, inside, she waved at it for the hanger level.

"Come on, come on." The elevator zoomed, and the door swooshed open. She headed for the side stairwell, taking the steps up two at a time, landing on quiet footfalls. No sense in alerting who might be hiding in the tunnels behind the walls.

The landing led to a service walk—a thin catwalk that overlooked the hanger from fifty feet. Her guards were arriving on the hanger, searching for her. She muted her comm, so incoming messages wouldn't give away her position. She thought-messaged to their comms about her position. She watched them read the message and then glance up at her. She gave them the stay signal with a palm up. They nodded.

She advanced on the catwalk, looking for something that would let her know a tunnel was there. Duh. She used her comm to scan for ELFs at the frequency Hidalgo was broadcasting.

There, twenty feet ahead. A short blast had registered here a few minutes ago—Larissa's transmission. Janey hurried to that location, but there was a blank wall. No doorway or any portal. How would she get in there?

The walls were thick, made from toughened syncrete, part of the original structure of the space station when it was just a space jet transit hub for miners on their way to the asteroid belt.

And where was Larissa?

Her comm vibrated her wrist. It was Orlando asking for her sitrep. Where did she want him?

She peered down at the hanger floor. He waved at her, then ran to confer with the security guards on the floor. Soren was there too with his power saw. They moved the huge ladder apparatus into position. Orlando grabbed the saw and climbed up.

She thought-sent her message for him to stay as quiet as he could, ignoring the burgeoning headache—the cost of using the thought commands too much.

There had to be a way to get to the other side of the wall at this location without alerting whoever was on the other side.

The frequency was still broadcasting. Was that where Larissa went? How?

Janey studied her map of the area. Hydroponics was on the other side of this wall, taking up almost the full length of the hanger. She tapped out a message to some of the guards on the hanger floor to go to the long corridor outside hydroponics to cut off possible escape routes.

But the suspect or suspects could take the tunnels to anywhere in the station.

She sent the ELF frequency to the rest of the team with the order to scan for it from this area, spiraling outward, and to cut off all escape routes. For all the good that would do if people were crawling through tunnels in the walls.

Orlando popped up and scrambled to his feet on the top of the ladder. He handed her the power saw and hopped over the railing, nimble and quick. He had a gleam in his eye, the sharpening of the hunt.

Her stomach was in knots. What if they were too late? Larissa could be in there. In danger. Wherever "there" was.

Orlando got into position, the power saw against the wall. Janey held up a hand for him to wait and scanned again. The ELFs were still coming from the other side of the syn-crete walls. That was all she could detect. No bio-signs, no other frequencies on the EM band. Then the signal was gone.

She stared at the wall, blinking to send out an x-ray in a brief flash—all she could handle—just in case her ocular implant could detect something. A human skeleton, something. It didn't. She didn't have thermal imaging capabilities. Soren probably had a tool for that, but she didn't want to wait. She nodded at Orlando for the go-ahead to start the saw. Her head pounded at the x-ray use. She clenched her jaw, pulled out her gun from her back holster, and held it down at her side.

Orlando started at the twelve o'clock position and ran the power saw clockwise. The deafening jangly buzz surely alerted whoever was on the other side. Even so, Janey held herself flush against the wall behind him. When he sawed to the nine o'clock position, she stilled him with a hand on his shoulder. A muscular steady-as-a-rock shoulder.

He glanced at her. She made the "stop" motion, and he stilled the machine. In the blessed quiet, she nudged him. He edged to get out of the way and nodded at her.

Ready.

Janey kicked the wall in at the cut. He went high, gun at the ready. She crouched low, gun angled toward whatever was behind the wall.

EIGHTEEN

IN FRONT OF JANEY, THE SPACE WAS BLACK, AN absence of light. Probably why her x-ray vision didn't work. Janey adjusted her ocular implant, letting in as much light as possible. Still, it was completely dark. Must be a light-dampening field. Like the black room they'd been stuck in. Her chest constricted, breath coming short. Not again.

She had no time to figure out what kind of tech was blocking the light or her vision. She was here for Larissa. Where was the junior agent?

She blinked to switch to infrared.

There.

Two human figures glowed red. One lay on the floor, the other hovered over it, a gun-like shape in its hand. The gun shape glowed red in its center, radiating heat, so maybe it wasn't a gun. Or the gun had just been fired. Or the red glow was some kind of biologically active compound.

"Larissa?" Janey approached and stopped a foot away from the two figures. Was that Larissa on the floor or was she the one with the gun? Her gut clenched, knowing more than her conscious mind wanted to acknowledge.

Nobody moved.

"Boss, is that you?" Larissa spoke with a scratchy whisper from the floor.

Janey knelt beside her and put her hand on her shoulder.

"I'm here, Larissa," Janey glanced about for the other figure but didn't see it anymore. She didn't want to leave Larissa. Under her uniform, the young guard's body felt warm—too warm.

A hand on hers. A weak squeeze.

"I messed up, boss. I went in. I saw an opening and —" Larissa coughed, sputtering, a liquid cough.

Venus Hells.

"I understand. Who is here with you?" Janey asked, her voice calm. She had to keep her cool, for her agent.

"Don't know what hit me. Something's wrong, boss. Can't—breathe."

There was a slight noise, like a rustle of clothing, faint.

Janey pivoted and pointed her gun at the other figure. "Stop!"

The figure stilled—a red blob where the head should be and the rest of the body invisible.

She blinked and adjusted her implant to quadruple the number of cones, so she could see perfectly, although only in shades of black and white. Like an old-timey vid. She'd messed up and wasted precious seconds.

A man's face came into focus, his skin pockmarked and pale. He hovered over Larissa, a syringe in his hand. He was dressed in a black jumpsuit that absorbed all light. Even with her implant, he appeared to be only a face hovering above the floor, against the backdrop of the solid black walls in the ten-by-ten-foot room.

"Drop it!" Janey ordered. She blinked to call up the station personnel and guest database. This man was in neither.

"It's too late for her," he intoned in an accent she couldn't place.

Janey shouted, "Orlando, get Medical here. Larissa is down!" Hells. She should have called sooner.

Orlando relayed the message to the security agents on the hanger floor.

"Go get 'em, boss," Larissa croaked, her breathing heavy and crackling. Sounded like fluid in her lungs.

The man spun toward the far wall.

"Stop!" Janey commanded again. "Drop it."

Ignoring her, the man stepped toward the faint outlines of a door, barely visible even with her enhanced vision. Janey shot his leg. Or where she thought his leg should be.

The man dropped to the floor with a groan.

She needed him alive, to question him, to find out what he gave Larissa.

At the opening, Orlando shouted, "Medical is on their way. Two minutes."

Janey rushed to the man, cuffed him, and hauled him to his feet.

"Hey!" the man yelled. "You shot me."

"No kidding." She shook him. "What did you do to my agent?"

He laughed bitterly. "She's dead already."

"What is it? What did you give her?" She shouted in his face.

"Why do you care? She's dead."

"Am not," whispered Larissa.

"Save your strength, Larissa. Medical's on the way." Janey shook the man again. "What is it? What's the antidote?"

"Hey! That hurts."

"Well?" Janey shoved the man to the floor.

He moaned. "You can't do that. I have rights."

"You have nothing." He may have been the one who attacked Ed and Kosi. Kosi was critical but recovering. Ed was on the autopsy table in Doc's lab. She couldn't speak about the possibility of losing Larissa. "You're going away for the rest of your life," Janey spat out, anger getting the better of her.

Orlando hustled in with a torchlight and set it on the floor beside Larissa. The room brightened white, blinding her. Janey sucked in a breath at the pain at her temple and blinked to reset her implant to normal vision. She rubbed her temple.

Larissa's face was pale. She didn't look like she was breathing.

"No!" Janey released the man, rushed to Larissa, and knelt beside Orlando.

Janey felt on Larissa's neck for a pulse. She didn't have one. Janey bent over her friend, her protégée, and started CPR. Where were Medical and their specialized equipment?

"Come on, come on." Janey pumped Larissa's ribcage, puffed air into her lungs. "Come on, Larissa!"

Why would that man kill her?

She didn't know how many minutes later Orlando pulled her off the younger woman.

Janey fought him, pounding his chest, but Orlando was stronger than she was.

Orlando held her away from Larissa. "The doctor's here. Let her work."

Janey stopped struggling and peered wildly around the small room. The man was on the floor, pressing a hand to his bleeding leg. Janey rushed over to him, hauled him up by his shoulders, and slammed him against the wall. She yelled in his face. "Give me the antidote. Give it to me!"

He stared at her impassively.

"McCallister, she's gone," Tseng said quietly from behind her.

"What?" Janey dropped the man and spun.

Larissa's body was desiccated like Ed's had been. Old before her time.

There was no coming back from that.

"I am so sorry," Orlando said quietly from her side.

A medic stepped toward her.

"What?" Janey barked.

"Can I treat him?" The nurse gestured with her med kit toward the killer.

Janey stared at her.

"Let her." Orlando tugged on Janey's arm to move her out of the way.

Janey stalked over to the man while the medic patched up his leg. "Who are you working with?"

He said nothing.

"Who are you working for?" Orlando shouted.

The man winced as the nurse finished up the dressing and stepped away with the med kit.

Janey hauled the man up by his arm. "Move." She pushed him toward the sawed opening.

Natalia poked her head into the room and gasped at Larissa's body on the floor.

"Natalia, guard the space and coordinate the sweep of this room and beyond." Janey motioned to beyond the wall. "Everyone works in pairs, and no one goes into the walls or tunnels until they're mapped and cleared. Not safe. Others may be there. Understood?"

Pale, Natalia nodded and eyed Larissa again.

"Another thing"—Janey pushed the man onto the catwalk—"there're no signals in this room. I sent you the ELF frequency they seem to be communicating on, but we haven't cracked it or jammed it, except in locations we control."

"Morse code then," Natalia said.

"Yes, and sight-to-sight communication."

"Right," Natalia said.

One of the hanger security guards, Hannah Chadwick, rushed up. "Where do you want me?"

"With Natalia. She'll brief you. Stay sharp."

Chadwick nodded and blanched at the sight of Larissa's desiccated body being lifted onto a stretcher.

"Go." Janey pushed the murderer ahead of her down the catwalk.

He grunted and limped forward.

Orlando pushed past them and pivoted to snap an image of the man with his holo. "I'll run him through our database. I gather you couldn't find him in yours."

"I didn't. Thanks," Janey said, waving the man's image to Kim with a request for analysis and telling her they were on their way back.

Kim commed. "What happened?"

Janey's throat clenched as she told Kim about Larissa.

They moved down the narrow walkway to the bare stairwell. Orlando held his gun at his side. Hers was holstered at her back, within reach. They made it to the hanger floor without incident.

Security agent June Acosta approached. The older woman usually guarded the spa. "Need me, McCallister?"

"Follow us. Watch our backs," Janey said.

All four of them moved into the small service elevator.

Acosta took a wide stance and un-holstered her gun, ready for anything.

NINETEEN

As they approached the grey security corridor outside Interrogation Room One, Janey called out to Orlando in front of her, "Stop here."

"I recognize this place," he said over his shoulder.

Janey lifted an eyebrow. "Hold him while I unlock the door."

The man wriggled in Orlando's grip. Acosta glared at the man, her gun pointed at the middle of his back.

With a wave of her wrist over the door pad, Janey unlocked the interrogation room. The door swooshed open. She waved them in.

Orlando shoved the stocky man into the room. Janey cuffed the man's hands to the chair's back and his feet to the chair legs. The chair was bolted to the floor. She wasn't taking any chances.

Orlando leaned against the corner of the small room.

From the corridor, Acosta caught Janey's eye and lifted her eyebrows in a question. Janey gave her the stay gesture.

Acosta nodded and watched the corridor.

Janey shut the door and fiddled with the room settings to turn on the recordings and to jam any outgoing low-band ELFs. The man could have an implant broadcasting like Hidalgo did. She had to take every precaution she could.

She scanned the burly man with her wrist comm but detected no frequencies beyond the normal human biophotons everyone emitted. Kim hadn't sent her an ID yet.

Janey glanced over her shoulder at Orlando. "Pick up anything unusual?"

He peered up from studying his holo and shook his head.

Great. She was flying blind.

Janey sat and eyed the man a beat before speaking evenly, calmly. "Who are you?"

He glared at her and said nothing.

"I'll give you the rights warning now." She recited the Basic Sol rights of representation, protection, and court use. "Do you understand?"

He nodded.

"Speak for the record your understanding," Janey barked.

"Yes, I understand," he said without looking at her.

"Why did you kill my agent?" She swallowed at the surge of grief that rose in her throat.

He glanced away and shifted awkwardly in the chair. His bulky frame appeared torqued, one shoulder twisted forward more than the other. Maybe an old injury. His blacklight-absorbing catsuit stood out against the recyclo grey walls.

Her eyes ached at the glare, the contrast kicking up. Janey adjusted her ocular implant to compensate for it. "We'll find out soon enough."

He shrugged and winced at the pain of moving against the tight cuffs.

Janey crossed her arms and held the man's gaze.

He gulped.

"You thought you wouldn't get caught," she said.

He frowned, glanced away again, and breathed out longer than normal. He was looking down and to the right—the area of emotions. Disappointment?

"You let someone down?" Janey said, guessing.

He snapped his gaze to her. His pupils dilated. A sharp intake of breath followed.

She was right.

She gave him the once over and nodded. She knew his type from her days at the Space Wing Command patrolling the outer space stations. "You're a miner from the asteroid belt, used to hard work and uncomfortable situations. My guess is you injured your right shoulder in an accident, and it didn't heal properly. Hard to get good medical care in the Belt." She paused to see if he'd confirm or deny. He said nothing, not twitching at all. "You're a long way from that rough-and-tumble stretch."

"You'd never survive out there," he sneered and made a point of looking her up and down. "A thin one like you."

Janey nodded. "Maybe so. But at least I know your last known residence."

He shrugged and winced at the movement.

She needed more information and tapped out a message to Kim, asking for an update on the man's ID. There had to be a record of him somewhere. He was or had been employed by someone. One didn't mine asteroids as a privateer. You had backing from an investor. Asteroid mining was costly, and the rewards were astronomical.

Kim's response came back in less than a second.

Thank the stars.

Janey perused the man's record. Indeed, he was a miner on the Schneider mining freighter, employed by the Rhomboid Consortium. The actual owners were masked by privacy laws. No word yet on who ran the mysterious Rhomboid Consortium. His ident had been buried under layers of bureaucratic files, Kim noted. Someone had tried to hide him in a bureaucratic mess.

But there it was. His name was Kocak, Evrim Kocak, and he held a Turkish Domain passport.

She read aloud, summarizing.

"Mr. Evrim Kocak, born in Istanbul, did trade school on the lunar colony, worked in mining operations in the asteroid belt for over twenty years." Janey glanced at him. Kocak held her gaze and showed no emotion. She continued, "Travel visas for over two dozen major cities around the world over the last twenty years. Oh, what's this? Assault charges filed against you in seven of the twenty-eight cities you visited. All dropped. Lucky."

"Good lawyers," Orlando said behind her.

"You're in someone's pocket pretty deeply," Janey said, prodding, guessing. "Someone using you like the good little servant you are."

Kocak frowned.

"You don't like being in someone's debt, do you?" Janey leaned back. "Hurts just a little too much. You work so hard to be your own man, but no. They won't let you. You have to do their bidding at the drop of a hat."

He clenched his jaw. "You don't know me."

"Where are they? Your accomplices?"

Kocak barked a laugh. "If you haven't found them by now, you'll never find them."

"We found you, didn't we?"

He harrumphed and glanced away.

"Where are they?" She leaned forward. "Where's the money? Why did you kill my guards?"

He slouched, his sallow skin going even whiter. "You'll get nothing from me."

"But you have already given so much." Janey stood and headed for the door.

If she read him right, he was not the one in charge. One of the others hiding on this station was.

Janey swiped open the door and then slowed a second, waiting. When Kocak said nothing, she crossed the threshold, Orlando right behind her.

Acosta stood at attention.

"This isn't the academy, Acosta."

"Yes, ma'am." Acosta still didn't relax.

"At ease," Janey said. "Stay here. No one in or out, except me."

Acosta relaxed her spine a little.

Kim commed her. "Schoeneman wants an update. Chief Milano too."

"On my way," Janey said. "Send two more guards to Interrogation Room One and keep the recording running. McCallister out."

Three minutes later, Janey was back in the conference room, her gut churning with impatience. To Schoeneman and Chief Milano seated at the conference table, she gave her report, standing, Orlando at her side. She told them about her questioning Hidalgo, following the ELF lead, sending Larissa ahead, and the attack in the dark room. Larissa down. Kocak in custody.

"Kocak has more accomplices still hiding in the tunnels. One who's running the show. I have to ferret them out," she said. Orlando said nothing, but his warmth at her side was welcome.

"How exactly do you plan to do that?" Schoeneman said to her, ignoring Chief Milano's seniority.

Seated beside him, Chief Milano seemed to sink in his chair as if already relinquishing command.

"Chief?"

Chief stared at the table, unseeing.

"He's off the case," Schoeneman said, his smooth voice filling the room. "His wife is involved. Maybe he is too." He frowned at the chief.

Janey's gut churned even more. Her boss? "I don't think he's involved, Mr. Schoeneman. He was as shocked as we were about his wife's involvement."

Betrayed was more like it.

Schoeneman pointed his micro-diamond-encrusted pen-stylus at her. "You're acting Chief now, Investigator. Chief—McCallister." Schoeneman peered at her as if down his nose, even though he was seated, and she was standing.

Janey stared straight ahead. "Yes, sir." She clenched her jaw. "But I need to get back out there. I'm not sitting behind a desk."

"Run the Security Department as you see fit. That's why I hired you—your latent leadership talent."

Chief, former-Chief, Milano sucked in a breath. "You're firing me, sir?" he asked in a hurt voice.

Schoeneman stood, ignoring Milano, and lifted his chin at her as if daring her to fail. "You catch these killers. Or you're out of a job. And so is everyone else on this station. You have until the end of the day." He eyed his wrist holo. "Three hours. That's when the markets open in New York."

"What about your money—sir?" Janey said.

"Recover it. Before the markets open. And you can

drop the 'sir,' Chief McCallister. Just Frederick is fine."
He smiled wolfishly at her.

Her skin crawled. Only hours ago, she was dumb-
struck by his charisma. Not anymore. The time enclosed
in the black room and how he treated Milano changed
her view of him.

"Fine. I'll be an acting chief until this is over. Then
Chief Milano can have his job back," Janey said.

"Not your call. Clock's ticking." Schoeneman strode
to the door, bumping Orlando's shoulder in a show of
dominance. Then he stopped and glared down his nose
at Orlando, even though the two men were the same
height. "Agent Orlando, I want you off this station as
soon as this case is closed. In fact, I want you to bring
the perpetrators back to Sol Security Office yourself. And
don't come back. I'll speak to your boss directly and get
someone else from the Sol Special Operations assigned
to this station, for whatever top-secret case you're
working on."

"You were the one to approve my post here," Orlando
said coolly.

"So? I only agreed because the premier asked me, as a
personal favor to her." He shrugged as if it were no big
deal to be friends with the Sol premier.

"You changed your mind based on? ..." Orlando lifted
an eyebrow.

"Because I can," Schoeneman said.

Orlando's wrist comm buzzed low, and he answered a
call. "Yes?" He headed to the window and spoke too low
for Janey to make out the conversation.

Schoeneman strode toward the door and then faced
Janey. "I want an update in one hour."

Janey cleared her throat. "Mr.—Frederick, I suggest

you take two guards with you. It's not safe. They came after you once. They could again."

Schoeneman nodded. "Make it happen. But make it fast. I have affairs to attend to." He left the room without waiting for Janey to get him protection.

She swore under her breath and commed Kim. "Please have two guards catch up to Schoeneman. He needs permanent protection until we get this case closed."

"On it."

"Thanks. Then I need you in the conference room." Janey commed off.

Chief Milano stood. "You can use my office."

"I could, but I won't. It's yours." Janey went to the wallscreen murder board, and with a wave, she brushed aside a lot of the data to call up the map of the station and its inhabitants. "I see your wife is in Medical."

"She was hysterical," Milano said. "Tseng wanted to sedate her and keep her under observation. In case of harm to herself, she said."

"Tseng or Laura said that?"

"Tseng. Laura won't talk to me."

Janey pursed her lips. Understandable. She commed the Doc.

Doc answered with a grunt, her characteristically curt reply.

"Have you finished Ed's autopsy?" Janey asked.

"No."

"Complications? It's been hours."

"I know how long it's been."

"What's going on?"

"I can't culture whatever killed him," Doc said, frustration lacing her voice. "And now Larissa." She sighed.

"Can Soren help? Shall we find others to help? I'm

sure some of the engineers are qualified," Janey said. "We need an antidote. Something. Reverse engineer what stopped Kosi from dying."

"I'm still sorting through the data."

"Sort faster."

"You're not my boss, McCallister," Doc growled.

"Actually, Schoeneman just promoted me to acting Chief."

"What happened to Chief Milano?"

"He's fine, just on administrative leave. Long story having to do with his wife's actions."

"Related to this case?"

"Oh, yes," Janey said. "So, please hurry up with the data analysis. Recruit whoever you need."

"Yes, ma'am," Doc said.

"Good. Thanks. Go to Medical, if you have to, and get the samples from Kosi. This is urgent. And be careful. We still have hostiles in hiding. No telling if they have this—"

"Poison," Doc jumped in. "The good news is that it's only an injectable. Can't be aerosolized."

"As long as we don't stumble upon them, we can shoot them," Janey said.

"I highly recommend it." Doc commed off.

"She always was the cheery sort," Milano said, frowning.

Janey's comm pinged softly. A message from Natalia. The scene where Larissa was killed was secured and guarded, and she was bringing evidence to Soren to analyze.

Janey commed Soren and told him Natalia was on her way. "Anything new?" Janey asked.

"No," Soren said glumly. "I heard about Larissa. I am so sorry. What can I do?"

"Create an antidote with Doc as fast as you can," Janey said, "with whatever additional personnel you need. I want to be prepared in case they strike again,"

"On it, Chief," Soren said and commed off. Doc must have told him her promotion news.

Janey sighed.

"You would make a great chief," Milano said, eyeing her murder board. "Very thorough."

"Not thorough enough." She chewed her lip. "I need a map of the tunnels, and I need it now." She waved on the board to open Hidalgo's private files, but they were password protected. Kim didn't have the time to crunch this. Janey crossed her arms and said to Milano, "I know Schoeneman wants you off this case, but I need everyone."

"What do you need?" Milano crossed his arms too and nodded at the board.

"You know her password?"

"I don't." He frowned. "But I can get it for you."

"Great. Do it. The sooner we get a map to those tunnels the better."

"What will you do?"

"Kim and I will find a way to detect them. They're using an ELF. I have the amplitude of the frequency but not the specific hertz."

"You could talk to another machine shop engineer for the specs used to build all the interior walls," Milano said.

"Good idea," Janey said, her eyebrows raised at him.

"Don't look so surprised. I used to work in the field."

"It's just that you've been so hands-off since I've been here..." Janey said. "We never really talked... about non-case-related things."

"I took this job because of her." Milano stared out the window.

"What do you mean?"

"Laura is my everything." His shoulders drooped. "She was hired to build the station with the first crew. And she did such a great job—on time and under budget —that Schoeneman wanted her to stay on as part of the maintenance engineering group. I came on as soon as the station was operational and set up the security teams with the hangar chief." He eyed her. "That was a decade ago. I'm ready to retire, McCallister, and let a young one like you take over."

"I didn't come here to become chief. I never intended to stay in the profession forever. Four years, that was all I needed to secure my mother's future."

"But what about your own?" Milano asked.

Janey shrugged. She'd had her nose to the ground for so long, since learning of her mother's illness, that'd she'd had eyes only for the next step and then the next step. First, the Space Wing Command, then her rookie job as an MP struggling to make ends meet, then her applying for and getting this investigator job—all to pay for her mom's expensive and experimental treatments. Whatever it took.

"Once this work grabs you, it doesn't let you go," he said softly and left the conference room.

"He's right, you know," Orlando said, at the table, his call finished.

Janey stared at the board. "Maybe."

Kim entered the conference room. "Why does Chief Milano look so sad? Just passed him in the hall hustling out of here."

"Because Schoeneman kicked him off the case, put him on administrative leave, and promoted me to chief."

Kim widened her eyes in surprise. "When? I didn't get the forms."

"Just now. A verbal order."

"You put him to work?"

"I asked him to interrogate his wife, so we can get into her password-protected files," Janey said. "Enough to make any man sad, I suppose, to grill his beloved wife." She was sweating. Was the stress of the promotion getting to her already? It was this case. All on the line, for all of them.

Janey wiped a hand over her face and took the glass of water Orlando handed her. She sipped it and sighed, renewed.

"Poor Larissa," Kim said.

"Yes." Janey swallowed past the painful lump in her throat. "Let's crack their frequency. We need to find these guys before the reserves run out and the guests go crazy. And before the bad guys figure out a way off the station."

"And before anyone else dies," Orlando added.

"Yes, Chief." Kim sniffed and cleaned the counter with a stray napkin, though the counter was spotless. Janey didn't know what to do, then she wised up and pulled her friend into a hug.

"First Ed, now her. Our jobs." Kim sniffled into her shoulder.

"I know," Janey said.

"You have to catch these bastards. All of them." Kim stepped away and wiped her wet cheeks.

"We have two in custody." Janey glanced at Orlando.

"A few more to go—" he said.

"Let's hope that's all"—Janey clenched her fists—"or this will be our last day on L'Étoile."

TWENTY

TEN MINUTES AND A CUP OF HOT SOUP LATER, Janey stepped back from her analysis on the board. "We've run the numbers five times, and still, the hertz we settled on doesn't give us anything when we scan." She tapped the stylus against her palm. "What are we doing wrong?"

Kim scratched her scalp with both hands, messing up her already messy long, braided black hair, the bright red hibiscus flower drooping over one ear. "What are we missing? I threw it all the number-crunching tricks I know."

"What if they changed frequencies?" Orlando asked from his seat at the table, pouring over several table screens and extra comms, crumbs of food at his elbow.

"I scanned each frequency in the ELF band," Janey said.

"Either they're not using the ELF band and they're using another band altogether, or they've stopped broadcasting," Kim said.

"Well, we have Hidalgo in a Faraday room in Medical.

We've got the interrogation room jammed where Kocak is." Janey tapped the stylus faster against her palm. "I've run a scan on all radio and shortwave frequencies, but I'm guessing they're off all comm channels." Janey sighed. "They know we're looking for them."

Her comm vibrated against her wrist. It was a message from Soren. With a flick of her hand, she threw the message up on the board. The list of zero-g labs that could have manufactured the algae found on the scene.

"Anything we can use?" Orlando asked.

"We need to run down the owners, find connections to Kocak if there are any."

"I have the databases for that. Setting up the search now."

"Thanks," Janey said. "How long?"

"Not sure," Orlando said. "What happened to the bot angle? What signals would they emit? Doesn't every robot have its ID signature on a certain frequency?"

Janey spun to him with a hop. "Oh! I could kiss you."

Orlando smiled. "Well, come over here then."

Janey snorted and strode to the murder board. "How could I have forgotten about the robot residue?" She scribbled on the board as fast as she could. The list appeared on the board.

"—Metallic residue at crime scene.

—Guests' bots all accounted for."

Stylus tapping in palm, she asked, "What am I missing?" She stared at her list and sucked in a breath. "The film crew. Did we scan them? I mean after the crime, not before coming on station. I know we did that."

Beside her, Kim inputted into her comm, fingers flying. "Eyes on them now. They're still in Schoeneman's suite."

"This whole time? Who was with them? It was

Antonia and Meilani, then who else?" Janey frowned.

"Checking," Kim said.

She paced the room, her adrenaline kicking high, making it hard to think. She ended up at the counter and wolfed down a sandwich.

"Antonia and Meilani are still there," Kim announced.

She licked the crumbs off her fingers. Much better. "Good. Thanks. Stay off the comms, get a sitrep from them, and perform a scan of the journalist and her film crew for the metallic residue," Janey said.

"On it," Kim said.

"Oh! And just for kicks, have them scan for the low ELF bands and any other comm signatures. Schoeneman's suite may be shielded." Where was he anyway? He'd bounced back from his ordeal as if it hadn't even happened.

Kim sent the message.

Janey checked the feed of the interrogation room. Kocak had his eyes closed, his chest rising and falling. Getting some shut-eye. Glad things were quiet on that front, but she still couldn't trust it.

"You want me to ask him about the bot?" Orlando offered, waving at the live feed of Kocak.

Janey shook her head. "Not yet. You scanned him. Me too. Look at those scans. We were looking for ELFs and other frequencies. Not the metallic residue. But my device picks it all up, whether I set it to or not. Universal sweep. Checking."

"Mine too. Checking too." Orlando bent to his work. He had a smudge on his cheek. She wanted to point it out, clean it off. She sighed and glanced away, out the window at the moonrise.

Now they were both in black work jumpsuits— sweaty, grimy, and full of the day's upsets and wear and tear. And he still wanted to kiss her. That said something about the man.

Janey scanned herself with her comm, moving her wrist up and down her upper body.

"What are you doing?" Orlando asked.

"Scanning for residue. Just in case the universal scan missed anything." She ran the comm an inch away from her legs, her torso.

Orlando stood and was in front of her in a flash. "I'll help. I can reach the back of you."

She reached for his wrist, gripped his forearm, and typed the scan frequency into his holo screen.

He lifted an eyebrow and ran the comm over her front. "You missed a spot."

"Did I?" she said with a straight face.

He moved to stand behind her and scan. She felt his heat.

She cleared her throat and continued her train of thought before his proximity derailed her. "We were in the dark room with Kocak. What was he doing there? I don't know. But we picked up residue from the room too. Scan yourself and add the data to the rest."

"Mmm," Orlando said behind her.

"Mmm, what?" She spun.

"You're the pro on frequencies." He smirked.

"I am." She stilled.

The way he was looking at her, brown eyes full of warmth. Like he was a pro at adoring her.

"I came back here for you," he said softly.

"I thought it was for your case."

"It was. Is. Also."

"If we don't catch these guys..." Janey studied the screen and frowned. She swore. "Trimethylamine."

"Same as the first crime scene." Orlando scanned his

body. "I've got only trace, two parts per million. Other chemicals I can't identify."

"Same."

Kim spoke up. "Antonia reports that some of the film crew's equipment scans match the trace metals we're looking for."

"Have her and Meilani escort them here with all their stuff, saying I'm ready for my interview, and set up their shoot in the conference room." Janey approached the board and examined it for the nth time. She was missing something. "If they're in on the heist, I don't want to tip our hand."

A moment later, Kim said, "They're on their way." She stepped closer to Janey, eyeing the board as if she were examining it. "Sure you two don't need a room?"

"Stop. No." Janey glanced over her shoulder and sighed. Orlando scratched his day-old stubble and studied his comms.

Kim snorted. "Yah, right."

Janey examined the board and tapped her stylus on the station map. "*Where* are they?"

"We'll catch them." Kim put a soothing hand on her arm.

"We'd better." She spun and looked around the room. It was a mess, and so was she. "The film crew will be here soon. Kim, can you clean up in here? I'm going to change. Orlando, you too."

"You want me to come change with you?" He quirked a small smile.

"You were assigned quarters."

"Next to yours."

"Your doing, Kim?" Janey asked her friend and trusted colleague.

Kim smiled and hustled around the room, picking up

stray cups and plates and moving chairs back into place around the large table.

Janey touched the murder board and it went opaque. She thought better of it and adjusted it to show an aerial view of the last remaining rainforest in Amazonia. She grabbed her coffee cup from the table.

"Leave it. Go change. I got this, Janey," Kim said. "They'll be here in a few minutes. Go, so you can make an entrance, Chief."

Janey set down the mug with a clack. Orlando gathered his extra comms and stuffed them in his pockets. "After you, Chief," he said and winked at her.

Back in her quarters, a fast eight minutes later, Janey stared at herself in the mirror. She did look refreshed, though she felt hollowed out. Now she'd had a few minutes away from work, Larissa's death weighed on her. She could see it in her eyes, that despairing look as if there would never be a sunny day again. She'd felt that way when her best friend was killed a decade ago. Even though Larissa worked for her, Janey had felt a kinship and a connection of friendship. That had been cut short.

And even though Larissa hadn't waited for her and had walked into danger, she'd been Janey's responsibility.

Her despair burned into anger, a fire that steeled her spine and sharpened her mind.

She had to catch the rest of the group behind the murders and make sure Kocak and his accomplices would never see the light of day.

She spun, checking all her angles in the full-length mirror, and took a few calming deep breaths to center, to ground into the here and now. At least she looked presentable in her black pants, shimmery aquamarine top, and flowing black jacket. Practicality mixed with a few feminine touches—the choker necklace her mother had given her, fabricated mother-of-pearl earring studs, and light makeup drawing attention to her eyes and lips. And her hair was brushed and up, softening her normally ship-shape look.

"Janey, the analysis you sent me," Rhea, her personal AI, started in a smooth, friendly voice.

"Yes?"

"There was a strange transmission at 06:59 this morning."

"Can you trace it?"

"Not yet, Janey."

"Keep on it, Rhea."

"Of course, Janey."

There was a double rap at her door and then, "McCallister?" It was Orlando.

"Coming. Don't break in!"

"I won't. This time."

She holstered her gun at the small of her back and pocketed an extra scanner she'd been fiddling with in her off-hours. It was experimental. Time to test it in the field.

She stepped out of her room and hummed. Orlando was chic, masculine, and huggable in a russet fine wool sweater that showed off his broad chest. Black trousers tucked into black polished Hessian boots completed the ensemble.

He kissed her cheek and looped his arm around hers.

"What was that for?" she asked, leaning against him for a moment, his strength and warmth welcome.

"You look lovely," he said softly.

"Thank you. So do you." She headed for the conference room, her cheeks hot, her center melting for him.

"Let's go suss these people out, shall we?" Orlando

matched her stride for stride.

She glanced at him. Should she tell him?

"What?" he asked softly.

She shook her head and stopped. He stopped and lifted her chin, so she had to gaze at him. His expression was full of warmth. "Tell me."

She breathed in his solid strength and heat. "Okay." She clenched her teeth, then told herself that the stress was natural, and she could channel it into action. "I may have a way to look inside their equipment without them knowing."

"I know. Your ocular implant." He frowned. "What's the big deal?"

They were at the conference room door.

"It's experimental." She gripped the LIDAR device in her pocket.

"Doesn't sound good."

"It's a risk. I may black out." Janey opened the door.

"Wait." He whispered and pulled her against him, in full view of the film crew and the journalist.

"Orlando," she whispered. "What are you doing?"

"Don't do anything stupid." He eyed her lips.

"I may. For the case."

"I'm the crazy risk-taker. Not you. Have me do it."

"You can't. It's my body. My tech."

"I know. It's just that..." He glanced away, then back at her. "You have someone to go home to."

"I'll be fine. You'll be there. To help me."

He bent to kiss her fiercely. She met him with her own heat, not caring about the audience.

"Yes, I will. I'm here." He stepped back, letting her enter the room first.

Time to put on a show. Set a trap. Catch the rest of the killers.

TWENTY-ONE

JANEY STRODE INTO THE CONFERENCE ROOM and stood at the head of the table, Orlando at her side. Around the table, the camera crew ignored her. Two of the crew adjusted controls behind their cameras hovering on drone pads. At the far end of the room, a sound tech bent over a box the size of a big dog and fiddled with knobs and switches.

The journalist, Veronica Ladipo, stood at the window, gazing at a starscape of the Andromeda Galaxy, its spiral arms speckled white, reaching for each other. As Janey approached the conference table, Veronica pivoted and asked in a voice that filled the room for such a petite woman, "Where would you like to be for the interview? Seated or standing?" She smoothed down her red silk suit jacket over her matching skirt.

The journalist's gaze hopped to Orlando, then back to Janey, likely making the connection they were together. If Veronica had seen them kissing in the open doorway, she pretended she hadn't or that it was of no significance.

"Actually, I had you come here to ask you questions, not the other way around," Janey said.

"Oh." Veronica wrinkled her nose. Her gaze lingered on Orlando, a subtle up and down perusal. She sniffed and gave a secret smile, more to herself than to him.

Beside her, Orlando straightened and smiled at the journalist. "I'm sure you don't mind, do you, Ms. Ladipo?"

"Well, I *was* hoping to do our interview." She smoothed her expression, yet her tone was warm and inviting. "Do you mind if we tape the interrogation instead? I've never been interrogated before. I'm always the one grilling my sources." She chuckled, unfazed, or perhaps not aware of the higher stakes.

"No recordings. And it's not an interrogation." Janey put more of a bark into her voice than she'd intended. The way the journalist was preening in front of Orlando, and the way he seemed to encourage her... She glared at Orlando.

"What?" he mouthed.

She shook her head at him and glanced back at Veronica, who was frowning and shaking her head to one of the camera women at the table, a young woman with a hard look to her as if she'd been a boxer or wrestler.

"During a routine scan, we found some unexplained metal trace in your equipment. We'd like to search it," Janey said to Veronica.

"What is this about?" the boxer-like woman asked, arms crossed.

Janey ignored the tech and asked Veronica. "May we?"

Veronica frowned. "On whose authority? Schoeneman invited us. You know that, right?"

"I do." Janey lifted her chin. "He made me Acting Chief. I have full authority to do as I see fit."

"A little too eagerly, too, from what I see," the camerawoman said.

Janey checked the hotel registry on her screen. The camerawoman's name was Stephanie K. James. What did the K stand for? Janey was about to address Stephanie when Veronica jumped in.

"Why? What happened that had you running out of Chief Milano's office this morning?" Veronica strolled around the table toward Janey and perched her hip against the edge, leaning forward, casual yet assured as if this was her boardroom. "The guests act like nothing is going on. The staff in the casino are acting a little funny but are clamming up when we ask questions." She pursed her lips, then nodded approvingly. "Well-trained staff."

"You didn't say anything, did you?" Janey asked. No one had reported the journalist and her crew asking nosy questions.

Veronica shrugged—a graceful move. "What was there to say?" She squinted at Janey. "Besides, I signed an NDA. We all did. We wouldn't say anything we shouldn't." Veronica glanced at her crew. They all nodded, even Stephanie, with a frown on her face.

"Non-disclosure agreements have been broken before. Sorry we have to inconvenience you..." Janey held her gaze, not at all sorry. "But we need to scan your equipment again."

"Will you tell me what's going on?" Ladipo asked. "I know something serious is happening. Schoeneman kept us waiting, still keeps us waiting. Where is he, by the way?"

"He's taking care of business," Janey said.

"When can we see him?" Ladipo asked.

Time to change the subject. She headed for the equipment at the other end of the table. "We need to do this now."

"You haven't agreed to tell me what's going on," Ladipo said.

"In due time, as the situation warrants," Orlando said and patted the air in an effort to placate the journalist. "We need to conduct our investigation and follow it where it leads."

"Did something lead you to us?" Veronica stood and followed Janey to the other end of the table. "You need to tell me what's going on."

"Let us scan your equipment and then I may tell you," Janey said.

"Not exactly a fair trade, but okay. You have my permission. I don't see why you haven't scanned already. You have the technology." The journalist nodded at Janey's wrist and gestured as if to say, have at it.

"We have to be in close proximity to get the best reading," Orlando explained, clipped, all business.

Janey went around the room and scanned with her wrist comm, holo screen up, the cameras, the sound box, and another box she didn't know the purpose of that rested on the floor between two camera people. Nothing unusual in most of the equipment, except for the box on the floor—a mysterious tall and narrow black box, hard black plastic on the outside, impenetrable to her scans on the inside.

It was three feet tall and about eighteen inches wide and was emitting gamma radiation—thank the stars, not in dangerous amounts, but suspicious just the same. Maybe it was a speaker or storage device. Yet, there was no door or opening that she could detect or see, even with her ocular implant at high-resolution.

She peered at Ladipo. "What does this do? Looks like a storage device."

"It is." Ladipo crossed her arms. "We store all the recordings here in a sort of Faraday box, so we can edit it later and make sure it hasn't been tampered with."

"I need to see inside it," Janey said. "Abnormal readings are coming from here."

"How can that be?" Ladipo's brows came together, and she rubbed her arms as if she were cold. She seemed genuinely surprised, and the comfortable room temperature hadn't shifted. "Shouldn't be happening. Nothing should be emitting from this box."

"It's not a true Faraday box then," Janey said.

"That's right. It's like a Faraday box, but not exactly. The tech is experimental."

"Well, whatever it is, it's leaking, or you have something stashed in there. We need to look inside." Janey knelt beside the three-foot-tall columned box. No way to open it, as far as she could tell.

What if a bomb was stashed in there? Her gut clenched.

"We can't do that," Ladipo said evenly, no bite to her voice, but her brows drew together. "I know my rights." She stalked to the far end of the table and peered at the Andromeda Galaxy swirling slowly.

Stephanie joined the journalist by the window. Soon the whole crew was gathered around her, whispering fiercely. What could they be debating? The crew seemed to be arguing with their boss.

Janey stood and waved up the recorder on her comm. Though she couldn't hear what they were saying, the device would pick it up, and it could be amplified later.

Technically, it was illegal what she was doing. But they'd all be out of a job if she didn't find the last culprits and recover the stolen credits.

Orlando moved to break up the conclave, but Janey held him back. "Wait. Let them discuss." She pointed to her wrist comm, picking up ambient sound. He nodded and crossed his arms, tapping his foot. He wanted action as much as she did.

A few minutes later, the group broke up and sat back down around the large conference table, and Veronica moved across the room toward her.

"What have you decided?" Janey asked.

"We need to talk to our lawyer," Ladipo said.

Ah, the request. Grinding her investigation to a halt.

"Why? Have you done something wrong?" Janey asked.

"No, it's just that we have our holo footage in there and can't let anyone have access to it without a warrant. And if you're going to serve us with one, I want to be prepared."

"This has happened to you before," Janey stated.

"Many times. I'm normally the investigator, sticking my nose in areas the offended parties don't want me to."

"You're on my turf now," Janey stated evenly.

"I recognize that," Ladipo said.

"Then you understand the need to go after the truth, no matter what."

"I do."

"Where was your crew at 6:45 a.m.?"

"In our suite. Getting ready to meet you. Why?"

"Can you corroborate that?"

"I assume you have checked the hotel records and cameras, even though you're not supposed to."

Janey gave her a look. "What do you know about our security?"

"I've been to every resort hotel-casino in every Earth orbit and the few off it. I know they have security systems, even though most guests don't know it. They want to be protected after all." She shrugged and then squinted. "You do have hidden hall cameras, don't you?"

"We'll verify your story." Janey sent the query to Kim.

It would take Kim all of five minutes to verify with the hospitality records, the hallway cams, and the body sensors linked to people's wrist IDs that the journalist didn't mention.

Janey let the silence extend in the room. Maybe someone would spill. Some of the film crew fidgeted. After a minute, she asked. "What got you into investigative work, Veronica?"

"An insatiable curiosity and a desire for justice and fair play. You?" Veronica crossed her arms.

"My best friend's murder." And a desire to see justice done, Janey thought but didn't say.

Veronica sucked in a breath. "I am so sorry."

"Me too," Janey said.

"Did they ever catch who did it?"

"No. But I may have found a motive."

"What is it?"

"Exploitation." Janey shook her head. "Or at least an attempt to exploit her. And when she refused, she was killed. Evidence shows she put up one hell of a fight." Janey stared at the whirling stars on the wallscreen.

"How horrible." Ladipo sounded genuinely sad.

"It is horrible when a more powerful person takes what they want without regard to the humanity of those they take from. The ultimate form of bullying."

The journalist tightened her hands into fists at her

sides. "I know. That's what I investigate. It makes me so mad."

"What specifically makes you so mad?" Janey asked.

"All of it. When the filthy rich take advantage of the desperately poor, who feel they have no choice."

"So why are you here? Doing a fluff piece on a place where people spend their money made off the backs of those desperate people?"

Veronica glared at her. "Is that what you think?"

Janey kept her face impassive.

Veronica nodded as if she were understanding or seeing something about Janey. "Not all their money was made that way. Many of today's extremely rich do good work in the world," the journalist said evenly, but her gaze darted to Stephanie, seated at the table, arms crossed on her chest, frowning.

"But still, you said your editor assigned you this piece. Why did you say yes?" Janey asked.

Veronica gazed about the room and said lightly, "To see how Schoeneman pulled it off. It is the Jewel of the Sky, or Starry Jewel, is it not?" She smiled, but her skin muscles were pulled tight. Not a true smile.

Janey's comm vibrated against her wrist. She glanced at the holo screen. Kim had confirmed her crews' alibis. Every single person was accounted for. At 6:45 am, the journalist had been in the chief's office with him, and the crew had been in their shared multi-bedroom suite.

Janey looked up at Veronica. "You're cleared."

"Cleared of what?"

"Homicide and grand larceny."

"Murder and theft. Heaven's no!" Veronica clapped her hands over her mouth. "Who? What?"

Janey eyed her. Veronica seemed sincere. "I'll tell you if you open your box."

"I can only open it in a protected room."

"Protected how?"

"Closed to all outside electromagnetic fields. All comms have to be off. Even your on-station comms."

Janey asked Orlando. "What's the risk to us?"

"We can't call out if something goes wrong," Orlando said soberly.

"What could go wrong? We just want to protect our footage." Veronica blew out a breath, frowning, glancing from her to Orlando and back, all traces of flirting gone.

"I'm just being cautious," Janey said. "These criminals already killed two of our staff and wounded a third."

Veronica sighed. "Understood. But there's nothing to see. It's all encoded. A box within a box."

Janey waved on her holo screen and set up the shield around the room. "Our devices are off." She nodded to Orlando. He worked his three extra comms, laying them out on the table for the film crew to inspect. The crew looked them over and nodded back to Veronica.

"How will you see what you need to see without your scanners?" Veronica asked.

Janey approached the box. "I'll be able to see what I need to with my ocular implant."

Veronica jerked back from her a smidge and gasped, then recovered, looking mildly curious. Janey was used to that reaction, but it still bothered her. Only one in ten thousand had ocular implants like she did. Rare enough.

"A well-traveled, worldly woman like yourself surely has met other enhanced people in her work," Janey said mildly. "Now open the box."

The woman nodded, contrite in her gaze, then waved her hand in front of the box. Janey blinked to switch to an infrared setting. Sure enough, Janey could see the flash of laser light that read Ladipo's wrist implant to open the device.

The box snicked open. Janey knelt, Orlando beside her. She switched her implant to scan through the light frequencies quickly. Small black boxes were stacked one upon the other in a sophisticated storage stack. Without accessing them directly, she couldn't tell if the crypto-currency was stored in there or if they just contained 3D and VR audio and video files, as Veronica said.

"How do you download the data from here?" Janey stood.

"Direct link to our main database or by secure frequency band," Veronica said.

Janey blinked through the wavelengths again. Whatever they'd picked up before wasn't sending anymore.

"You can close it up." Disappointed, Janey hovered a hand over her comm. "I'm turning everything on."

Veronica nodded to her team to close the box.

Janey switched the communications back on.

Her comm beeped loudly. It was a message from Kim asking if she was all right. Janey commed her. "Sorry. Everything's fine here. You okay?"

"Yes, what happened?" Kim said, worry lacing her voice.

"We had to close the room and switch off the devices to look inside their storage device," Janey said.

"Okay. I have a new update on the residue. I'll be right over," Kim said and commed off.

"What is she talking about? The residue?" Veronica asked.

"Do you have a robot assistant with you?" Janey asked.

"No, why?" Veronica replied.

"We may have found traces of one on the scene." Janey frowned.

"Like a robot bomb, to steal hard drive data?" the journalist asked.

"What do you know about that?" Janey crossed her arms over her chest.

"It happened to us once. That's why we have a strong box as our storage. We've been attacked a few times by people who didn't like us snooping about."

"Janey, can I confer with you?" Kim said as she strode into the room.

Janey said to the journalist and her crew. "Will you excuse me?"

She, Orlando, and Kim huddled next to the board displaying the rainforest. "What is it?"

Kim gave a quick smile. "Did you really turn off all the devices for those three minutes thirty seconds?"

"Yes, why?"

"You forgot to turn off the murder board," Kim said in a whisper.

"Did we destroy their data?"

"I doubt it. But I can hack the board to see inside their storage boxes that way."

"Why do we want to?" Janey asked. "We've cleared them."

"But maybe one of their crew isn't who she says she is," Kim said and gave her a knowing look.

"How do you know?"

"I don't. Just guessing."

"Good guess. I think I know who that could be," Janey said. "I'll hold her back for questioning."

Kim nodded.

"I can go with the rest of the crew to their quarters," Orlando said. "Take a look around."

"Take at least one guard with you," Janey agreed. She said to Kim, "Stay here to do research while I talk to the camerawoman."

"Will do."

Janey said to Veronica and her crew, "You're all free to go. Investigator Orlando will accompany you to your quarters. He just has a routine search to do."

"We have nothing to hide. We've cooperated. Why do you need to search our rooms?" Stephanie asked.

Janey blinked and read her ocular screen for more details on Stephanie K. James. Birthplace: Istanbul. Education: All over, including all the same cities Kocak had been arrested in. "Because I think you do have something to hide. I need you to stay behind for questioning, Ms. James."

"Why me?"

"You're a person of interest in this case."

Stephanie said to her boss, "Veronica, they can't do this to me. Stop them."

"We have to cooperate, Stephanie."

"But you know my story, where I come from. Don't let them do this to me."

"I'm sorry, Stephanie. You know the work I do. *'The truth will out.'*"

The motto of her publication.

"But, Veronica—"

Veronica shook her head. "I'll contact my lawyer, get her lined up for you, but if you did something wrong, you need to come clean. This investigator is as fierce as I am at hunting down the truth."

Stephanie jumped out of her chair and dashed for the door. Janey got there first. She spun and tackled Stephanie, then hauled the woman to her feet.

"Running always makes one look guilty, Ms. James,"

Janey puffed, her blood thrumming with adrenaline. "Come on, I'm taking you to interrogation."

Orlando caught her eye and motioned he was leaving. Janey nodded. He gestured that he'd call her. Despite the seriousness of the situation, she smiled and hustled Stephanie out of the room.

At the threshold, Stephanie wriggled in her arms. "You can't hold me."

Janey handcuffed the camerawoman, hands in front. "There's nowhere to go. Stop."

"Am I under arrest? Let me go. You have nothing on me."

TWENTY-TWO

ONE HAND ON STEPHANIE'S CUFFS AT HER BACK and another on her shoulder, Janey perp-walked the woman down the corridor to Interrogation Room Two. On the way, Janey halted Stephanie at the door of Interrogation Room One, so Stephanie could look through the small window at face height.

Stephanie gasped. "No."

Suspicion confirmed. Stephanie knew Kocak. Janey waited.

Kocak peered up and paled. He knew her. There was a resemblance in the chin and the eyes. Father and daughter? Janey would dig into the DNA details and know soon enough.

Janey gave Stephanie a nudge. A few doors down, she stopped her in front of another door with a small window on it. She waved her palm in front of the door pad, and the door unlocked. "Go." She moved Stephanie into the room. "Sit." She guided her to the seat, unlocked Stephanie's cuffs, and then reconnected them on the chair, one hand to each side.

"Hey!" Stephanie struggled against the restraints. "You have no right!"

Janey sat across from her and gave her a hard stare. She studied Stephanie's records on her holo screen, both the public ones and the ones she unlocked with her security clearance, nodding and glancing at Stephanie from time to time. To study her with this new information, and to see how she'd react.

"What?" Stephanie frowned.

"I think you know," Janey said. "Kocak is your father. DNA confirms it."

"So?" She frowned.

"He's going away for a very long time."

"So?" Stephanie said again.

What was she, two years old?

"Stephanie, you can help yourself by what you say here, and you can help your father. Reduce your sentence." Janey softened her tone. "You want to help him, don't you?"

Stephanie paled. "How?" she said glumly.

"Tell me where the other accomplices are."

Stephanie slumped in her chair a little, the restraints pulling against her shoulders, and she stared at the table, reminding her of someone else's body language. The way Laura Hidalgo sat in the conference room only a few hours earlier. The slope of her shoulders, of the older woman, and the younger woman. Could they be related? What were the chances?

"Well?"

Stephanie said nothing.

"Not even to help your father?"

Stephanie didn't move.

Janey slammed the table with her palm. "Where is your other accomplice? Where's the money?"

Stephanie straightened. "You'll never find it—or her." Stephanie held her gaze, and then after a long moment, she stole a glance toward the door.

"You expecting someone?"

Stephanie shrugged, pulling against the restraints.

Janey had a hunch. "I see your mother isn't listed in your records."

"I never knew my mother. My father said she died in childbirth."

"But you had an aunt who looked after you from time to time. A Laura Sincero." Cash deposits, a few holo images of vacations, linked the two. Janey recognized the older woman in the images, even though she was always obscured by a big sun hat as if she wanted her face to always be in shadow.

"Yah, so?"

"Is this her?" Janey showed her a current full-frontal image of Laura Hidalgo's face from the employee database.

Stephanie nodded. "Yah, so?"

"Then we already have her in custody."

"No, no, not possible. She's..." Stephanie stared at Hidalgo's image, her face pale, her eyes wide in fear as if she'd said too much.

"She's what?"

Stephanie turned her head away, slumping in her chair, her jaw tight.

Janey had to confirm. "This woman, your aunt, who you know as Laura Sincero, is this woman?" Janey tapped on the tablescreen image of Laura Hidalgo to make her point.

Stephanie looked at the image glumly.

"Thank you, Stephanie, for sharing that with me," Janey said and left the interrogation room to Stephanie's protest that she didn't reveal anything and how dare they hold her. They would pay. In the corridor she moved out of earshot even though the rooms were soundproof and commed Milano.

"Yes, McCallister?"

"How's Laura?" Janey asked.

"She's still sedated."

"I don't know how to tell you this—"

"What?"

"She's involved."

Milano sighed. "You sure?"

"Yes, unfortunately." Janey called up the images of Hidalgo, Kocak, and Stephanie. "We have a second suspect in custody. Laura is our third."

"No one else in the hidden tunnels?"

"I don't think so, but we need to sweep them to be sure. Need to map them first."

"What do you want me to do?" Milano asked.

"Find the vault contents. They're somewhere in the tunnels, I'm guessing. We need accurate tunnel maps," Janey said. "You need to get the passcode from Laura to access her personal files. We looked everywhere else and couldn't find the maps."

"I'll cuff her, just in case," he said softly. "I can't believe it. My beloved Laura."

"I'm so sorry, Chief," Janey said.

"Don't Chief me. I don't deserve it." He huffed a breath. "What don't you want to tell me?"

He knew her well.

"We have forty minutes to recover the money. Chief —Daniel, we need that passcode from Laura." Janey paused. "Maybe they stashed the money in a clean box in one of the tunnels. We need to find it. Kim says the money hasn't been transmitted off-station."

"I'll get the doctor to wake her."

"Thank you." And she meant it. "McCallister out."

She didn't want to tell Milano over the comm that Laura Hidalgo had a daughter he probably didn't know about—with Larissa's murderer in Interrogation Room One.

Janey peeked into Interrogation Room Two.

Stephanie was staring straight ahead at the blank wall.

Janey stepped into the room.

Stephanie glared at her. "I didn't do anything. You can't hold me." She rattled her cuffs and winced at the pain.

"Somehow you are involved. You know two of the accomplices. My guess is your father murdered my security agent in the vault. You somehow fooled our sensors and were the technician behind breaking in, wiping the data, and were also part of the murders."

"No. No. You have nothing. No evidence."

Janey leaned toward her. "Where's the money?"

Stephanie sat back. "What money?"

"You want to play the innocent act? Fine. We'll dig into your files, comb your personal items for evidence, and take apart your equipment piece by piece."

"Ladipo will never allow it."

"She will. She didn't support you in there. She's not a criminal like you are."

"I'm not a criminal. I'm a freedom fighter."

"Whose freedom?"

"All of ours."

Janey sat back. "Explain. I feel plenty free."

"Do you?" Stephanie said, smug. "I bet you took this job because you needed the money."

"Part of life," Janey replied.

"But why? Why does working for pay have to be a part of life? Why can't we pursue our artistic lives without prostituting ourselves for money?"

Janey understood that all too well, having grown up in a corporate zone, but she wasn't about to tell Stephanie that.

"Is that how you view your work for Ladipo?"

"She's not my boss."

"She's not?

"No, I'm freelance."

"Okay, let me get this straight. You're an independent business owner thinking it's okay to steal from another business owner. Did I get that right?"

"Schoeneman is—" Stephanie sneered with steely hatred in her eyes, then froze, her eyes wide. "Nope. You're making me talk. I'm not saying another word."

"I'm not making you do anything. You made all these choices yourself. You're in charge of your life. No one made you decide to become a freelance camera operator."

"I'm not a camera operator. I'm a filmmaker. I only took this job—" Stephanie paled.

"Yes," Janey said mildly. "Why did you take this job? It was for the money."

Stephanie glared at Janey. "Money," she spat. "We're taking all of it. To make him pay."

"Who?"

"That Frederick Schoeneman."

Figured.

"Did you know that someone piggybacked on your vault theft to siphon off all the onboard digital operating funds?"

"Good for them."

"Do you know anything about that?"

"Should I?" Her tone was defensive.

"Who else knew you were robbing the vault with Kocak?"

"No one."

"Not even the film crew."

Stephanie sniffed in disdain. "Dilettantes."

"So you opened the vault for revenge," Janey said. "You want to stick it to Schoeneman. For something he did to you?"

Stephanie held her gaze defiantly, didn't flinch.

"Then if not for something he did to you, then to your father."

A small muscle twitched around Stephanie's eyes, betraying her.

"Did Schoeneman fire your father from a job?" Janey asked. "Maybe before you came along. When he was young and hopeful. And he's been holding a grudge ever since."

"It's not a grudge, it's a revolution."

"What revolution?"

"Overthrow the corporate overlords."

"And then what?"

"Destruction of the old guard."

"You sound so sure of yourself."

Stephanie nodded.

"Tell me more. And then what?"

"No, you're mocking me." Stephanie stared at the wall, and her pulse kicked up a notch.

"I'll find how you emptied the vault."

"No, I don't think you will. I didn't touch a thing."

"Except for the door."

Stephanie shrugged.

"When you opened the vault, was there anything in there?"

Stephanie shrugged again.

"I need an answer, Stephanie."

"You have nothing on me."

"Why do you say that?"

Stephanie snorted. "You wouldn't be here interrogating me if you did."

"My team is tossing your things as we speak. And you've admitted to opening the vault door."

Stephanie gulped, her cheeks reddening.

"You didn't think we would catch you?"

Stephanie shrugged and winced.

"You're not the brains of the operation," Janey said. "I think it was Laura. Right under our very noses."

Stephanie cracked a small smile.

"You think that's funny. You aided in the murder of a station agent, the attempted murder of a second, the cold-blooded murder of a third."

"I didn't touch anyone! A third?" Her voice squeaked.

"Yes, your father killed one of my agents who surprised him in the room above the hangar. That wasn't supposed to happen?"

Stephanie said nothing. Then under her breath. "I didn't know. No one was supposed to die. He just…"

"What, Stephanie? He just what? Evrim? Your father?"

Stephanie stared at the table and spoke in a choked voice. "He said one of the guards recognized him, even though he was masked and in camo. He had to, he said. He had no choice."

"So you know how he killed my guard?"

Stephanie shook her head.

"You must really believe in your cause. Does it have a name?" Janey asked softly.

"Why does that matter?"

"It matters."

"I've already said too much. Don't I get a lawyer?" She glanced away.

"Yes, but I thought you said you weren't guilty."

"Guilty of being the daughter of a revolutionary. Guilty of fighting for what's right."

"By killing innocent people, stealing someone else's property."

"Those men aren't innocent. They worked for the fascist Schoeneman."

"Then I'm not innocent either," Janey said.

"No, you're not. The only way to fix the system is to break it first," Stephanie said.

"You ever try to make changes from the inside of a system?"

"It's rigged against us little people."

Janey checked the time. Thirty minutes left and still no closer to finding the money. "If you can't help me recover the money you stole, maybe you can tell me what you injected my people with." She had to ask again.

Stephanie stared over her right shoulder and said nothing.

"Fine." Janey stood and headed for the door. "I hear the lunar penal colony station is peachy this time of year. But you can lighten your sentence if you help us..."

Janey waited, but Stephanie said nothing. "You're going away for a very long time."

Stephanie stared at Janey, defiance masking sadness.

Back in her office, Janey washed her face in the small bathroom to give her brain a moment to reset and then commed Orlando. "Sitrep." She stood at the wallscreen and waved up live footage of the cameras facing the sun. The bright light of afternoon shone in, but soon it would slip into darkness.

"I was just about to call you."

Her heart jumped at the sound of his deep voice.

"I beat you to it. What have you got?"

"In her room, Stephanie has a second ID wristband with her stuff." He sounded excited.

"And?"

"It's under a different ID registered to someone else on the station," he continued.

"She must have switched IDs and slipped out unnoticed, to create an alibi. But how did she get her original ID to not signal when it wasn't attached to her?"

Wrist IDs were designed to work only if attached to a person. bioelectric fields powered it.

"I found a small—pet—in her things."

"How did it pass screening?"

No pets were allowed on the space station.

"That's your department. But I have an idea," Orlando said. "Check the board for—"

"Just tell me. Clock's ticking."

"Then stop interrupting, missy."

Janey blew out a breath. "You're right. I'm listening." She went across the corridor to the conference room, unlocked it, and rushed to the murder board. She waved it on and called up the biosignatures of the film crew's suite.

"You there?" Orlando asked.

"Yep. Listening. Looking at the board. At a map of the room."

"What do you see?" Orlando asked?

"Your signal, the two security agents' signals, four other signatures, belonging to the journalist and her crew."

"Anything else?"

"No."

"How about now?"

"Yep. One more biosignature coming from the room, belonging to"—Janey waved over the new icon to call up the ID—"a one Monica Farmingham. Checking hotel records." Was it the same one she'd met that morning in Milano's office?

"I'll check our databases too."

Janey made an assenting noise, and using the board as her console, she queried the hotel registry. There was only one Monica Farmingham on board, a guest who had checked in five days ago. The record's image matched that of the banker she met this morning in Milano's office.

"Orlando, I need you to bring her in. She's in the casino, at SkyBar. I sent you her image. You'll recognize her. We met her this morning. The journalist's business partner."

"There's no police record on her," he replied. "Why don't you come with me? Change of pace."

"I need to oversee the search for money."

"Have Kim do it. She's more than capable."

"No question. But—"

"I know you, Janey. A break is as good as a rest."

"I can't afford a break. Deadline is in"—she checked the time—"twenty minutes."

"You need to stretch your legs. And you love the view from SkyBar. With me. It's a win-win-win." His tone was light and relaxed, but his tone radiated readiness for action.

Janey eyed the board, watching Stephanie and Kocak via the room's cameras. Hidalgo was in Medical. She didn't have an eye on her, but Milano was there.

Three suspects. Two murders, and one attempted murder. Missing millions of credits, precious contracts, and asteroid lingots. Digital cryptocurrency, untraceable but still on the station, and the operating currency for the hotel-casino about to run out.

Wait a minute. If the station was a closed loop, no currency off the station, but guests pouring millions into the casino, then there was plenty to meet payroll and pay suppliers.

It wasn't that the station would run out of money. It was that there was a scheduled bank deposit at the end of the regular business day. Once that happened, the station would be cash poor. But that was remedied with the start of a new cash cycle. That couldn't be the problem.

The problem was if they let the day's profits get transferred to the bank, the criminals could use the same signal to piggyback the cryptocurrency off the station. They could siphon off all the day's profits—and what they'd stolen this morning, while the heist was happening.

Schoeneman wanted to make that transfer, and nothing she could do or say seemed to convince him to not run it. Pure foolishness on his part. But it was his money. Was the man purposefully crashing his own business? But that didn't make sense on the eve of the hotel-casino's ten-year anniversary.

She needed to check with Kim. What if Schoeneman didn't do his daily bank transfer? What were the consequences?

"Janey, you there? Coming to meet me at SkyBar?"

"Yes, sorry, distracted, thinking. I'll meet you there. Give me a minute. Need to check something. Don't approach. Just watch."

"Janey, don't give me that order. You know I will approach."

"Okay, but don't show your hand."

"Right. My thoughts exactly."

"McCallister out," Janey said and commed off. She called up Monica's public record. A banker from Allied Consortium. Never heard of them. She checked out the bank. A private bank for business, not much on content in the public record.

Janey commed Kim. "Can you dig into some bank records for me?"

"Of course. On my way." Kim commed off. One minute later she entered the conference room. "Which bank records?"

"Ours, I think. Who does the station bank with? Is it Allied Consortium? And can you dig into this and let me know if anything's suspicious? I need to meet Orlando at SkyBar to rustle up a possible suspect."

"On it." Kim's fingers waved over the board, dancing, conducting, scanning, and sifting through into Allied Consortium financial records.

"Are they our bank?" Janey asked.

"No. They're a private enterprise with hardly any footprint. Very suspicious."

"I already knew that part," Janey said.

"Let me work. Go on your date. You're dressed for the front of the house."

"It's not a date, Kim."

"I know, but you haven't left the back of the house all day. Get out of here and let me work. I'll comm you as soon as I have something."

"Clock's ticking."

Kim waved and swiped above the screen, her hands a blur, not looking at her. "I know, Janey, I know."

TWENTY-THREE

JANEY STRODE INTO THE CASINO. AT THE entrance the clanging and tinkling of the bright, colorful slot machines greeted her. She didn't feel like saying hello back. Never did. She tamped down on her irritation at the overly cheerful noise, wound her way past the gamblers, and aimed for SkyBar. The long mahogany bar was full of guests, crowded shoulder to shoulder in their sparkling finery. Orlando wasn't there. Neither was Monica.

She caught the eye of the bartender, her friend, Faizah, who headed over to her. "The usual?"

Janey shook her head. "Have you seen Orlando?"

"He was here a moment ago with a very well put together brunette. She ordered a Cabernet. He ordered a club soda with a twist." Faizah nodded.

Faizah got it that she was working and wouldn't broadcast it. Those were the rules. Security agents worked undercover in the casino all the time, per Schoeneman's orders. Even with the station under threat, Janey was going to hold up that order. It was a good one. Kept panic to zero.

Faizah pointed deeper into the casino. "That way. Good hunting."

"Thanks, Faizah," Janey said and wove through the rowdy crowd of young hotshots, new asteroid wealth, and old Earth capital.

They mingled, laughed, drank, and joked, letting their hard-earned—or not-so-hard-earned—currency flow through them into the casino. Oblivious of the danger. Oblivious of the murder perpetrated today on two of her people. Oblivious of the cash reserves gone.

The crowd thinned a little, but she still didn't see Orlando at the poker tables. She went farther in toward the specialized game tables. He wasn't at any of them. She circled them just to be sure, pausing a moment to gaze at the near floor-to-ceiling view of the starscape coming into view as the station rotated out of the sun's rays. Night was coming on. Dark ink and their sparkling constellations overtook the view. It took her breath away every time. She let her eyes de-focus. Just for a few seconds.

Looking at the stars calmed her, reminding her of her place in the grand scheme of things—insignificant, yet still mattering.

"We all come from the stars, baby," her mother would say when she tucked her in at night. Mom was dying. Her heart clenched. She had to get back to the case, so she could make the calls for her mom. So she could find just one more drug that would help her recover or at least feel better.

Out of the corner of her eye, she saw Orlando in the glass reflection. He was heading toward the restaurant set a few steps above the casino floor—small tables nestled amongst potted trees and ferns, dominated by a living verdant wall and low ceiling hung with fairy lights. Like being held in the palm of Mother Earth under an intimate sky.

Janey wove through the casino guests caught up in their games and approached the maître d'. It was Mai Chen.

Mai Chen smiled at her. "Janey! I haven't seen you all day! I thought for sure you'd swing by for your ten o'clock break."

"Busy day."

"What's wrong?" Mai stepped closer and said with a whisper, "A case?"

Janey nodded. "I need to know where Orlando is seated." The restaurant was a warren of tables hidden behind soundproof barriers in the form of strategically placed shrubbery, engineered to absorb most tones of human conversation. Seated, people were hidden from view.

Mai wiggled her eyebrows, teasing her. Mai knew all about Janey and Orlando.

Janey shook her head.

Mai caught the seriousness of the situation. "Sorry. Mr. Valdez is seated at the back left. Fig Tree table. Who is he with? She's—" Mai Chen caught the frown on Janey's face. "Never mind me." She put a hand on Janey's arm and lowered her voice even more. "Schoeneman is back at that table too."

"Oh?"

"He arrived a few minutes before they did."

What was going on?

"Thanks, Mai." Janey hustled into the restaurant before her friend could ask more nosy questions that Janey couldn't answer. Mai was used to hearing all about Janey's cases, but only after they were closed.

The restaurant was full, which was normal. It was a six-Michelin-starred restaurant, the only six-star establishment on- or off-planet. The pride and joy of Schoeneman and the chef who ran it with talent and flair.

Before rounding the last privacy tree-shrub, Janey held back. But she heard nothing coming from the table just beyond. State-of-the-art noise dampeners. Always impressive. She rounded the corner.

Schoeneman had his back to the wall, a glass of amber liquid in his hand. He leaned back, relaxed, a small smile. He gazed at the woman to his left, attentive in the way he studied her, in the way he caressed her with his eyes. Orlando too had his back to the wall. His club soda with a twist in front of him. He played with the garnish. This table was in the corner, so they each got a wall—the alpha position.

A brunette, presumably Monica, had her back to Janey, so she didn't see her approach until Janey slipped into the empty chair at the table. Monica had been speaking, waving her hands about.

"Hello," Janey said. "Mind if I join you?"

"Who are you?" Monica shifted away from her.

Janey held out her hand. "Acting Chief Janey McCallister, station security. Mind if I ask you a few questions?"

"Way to dive in!" Orlando said cheerily and winked at her.

Janey ignored him.

Monica looked between her and Orlando and finally peered at Schoeneman. "Frederick, am I being ambushed?"

"You catch on quickly, my dear." Schoeneman smiled, not at all kindly.

"But I thought we had a deal," Monica said, hands balled into fists beside her Cabernet.

"We did until I found out that you double-crossed me, with those...criminals," Schoeneman said.

How did Schoeneman find out, and why hadn't he told her?

"I—I did not," Monica sputtered, eyeing Janey and then glaring at Orlando. "I suppose you aren't who you say you are either."

"Oh, I used to be an insurance investigator. But now I work for the Sol Security Office, Special Investigation Unit."

"I feel ganged up on, and I did nothing wrong," Monica said.

"Sure." Janey leaned in. "That's what my suspect number two says."

Monica firmed her jaw. "I am a private citizen, on a much-needed and much-deserved vacation. This is harassment."

"If you want, we can make a scene and march you out of here in handcuffs," Janey said.

"I, for one, would like to see that scene." Orlando smirked.

"Cooperate with the investigators, Monica, and we can laugh over this when you get out in five to ten years. Let's not make a scene. Be a dear." Schoeneman sipped his whiskey.

"Mr. Schoeneman, it will be a lot longer than that," Janey said quietly, "There's been a third murder."

"Who?" Schoeneman asked, holding his gaze with Monica.

There was a history between these two. His pupils were dilated, his breathing sped up.

"Larissa Ferreira, one of my agents. Just turned nineteen." Janey firmed her lips and addressed Monica. "In fact, I can hold you as an accessory after the fact to two murders and one attempted murder."

"What? What are you talking about? I'm just a finance person." Monica paled.

"I know. You work for the Allied Consortium," Janey said. "What is that exactly? Who are your clients?"

"I can't divulge my client list."

"I can," Schoeneman said.

"You can?" Janey asked.

"Yes," Schoeneman said. "I used to be one of their clients until—"

"Until I broke up with you, you lying, stealing, sack of—" Monica's voice raised into a high soprano squeak.

"Now, now, I'm all for a good fight, but we do want to keep our voices down." Orlando patted the air.

"Let me get this straight," Janey said, but she paused as a waiter set a glass of sparkling water in front of her. Mai must have sent it over. Then she continued. "This whole thing—the theft, the murders—is because of a lover's quarrel?"

"No," Schoeneman said.

"Yes," Monica said.

"Which is it?" Janey asked. "Wait, no. Not the time. What we really need to do is one, prevent the transfer from happening in"—she checked the time—"thirteen minutes. And two, recover the cryptocurrency and contracts you stole."

"I didn't steal anything." Monica sipped her Cabernet. Her vitals showed she wasn't lying.

"Fine," Janey said. "Stop the transfer then."

Monica smirked at Schoeneman. "You don't want me to, do you? You want to crash your starry jewel in the sky, don't you? To prove me wrong?"

"Wrong about what?" Janey asked.

Monica said nothing.

"Mr. Schoeneman, what is she talking about?" Janey asked. "Catch me up to speed, and this time don't leave anything out."

Schoeneman downed his drink and waved for another. A waiter delivered another glass, two fingers of amber liquid. A whiskey neat, by the looks of it. Schoeneman sipped, staring at Monica but talking to Janey. "I pulled all my currency reserves from Allied Consortium and brought it to the station."

"I told him that was a foolish security risk." Monica sniffed and examined her manicure, done in hot pink to match her off-the-shoulder sparkly gown of the same color.

"So you hired some obscure revolutionaries to steal from the station to prove that his money wasn't safe here?" Janey said.

She lifted one shoulder in an elegant shrug. "I coordinated with them, without their knowledge." She gave a small smile.

"And the murders?"

"That's on them." Monica shrugged.

"You cold-hearted bitch." Schoeneman glared at her, his cheeks flushed. "McCallister, I can't stop the daily bank transfer. Monica has hijacked it."

"There's got to be a way," Janey said. "Some fail-safe. Some passcode." He knew all day, and he'd said nothing. What was his game?

"Kim could do it," Orlando said at the same time Janey did. He lifted an eyebrow. Janey commed Kim.

Kim answered without a hello and dove right in. "Allied Consortium used to be Schoeneman's bank."

"We know," Janey said. "I'm here with Mr. Schoeneman, Orlando, and Monica Farmingham, the mastermind behind the digital transfer hijack. She is going to siphon off the funds with the daily bank transfer unless we stop her. Can you?"

"I'll try. But I need some time."

"You have ten minutes," Janey said.

"Then I need the lockout codes for Allied," Kim said. "And I need them now."

Janey looked at Monica. "Well?"

Monica rubbed the inside of her wrist and then crossed her arms, presumably to stop from fidgeting.

Janey scanned Monica with her implant. She was normal. Just a wrist ID implant, like most people.

"What are you doing?" Monica asked.

"Checking to see if you have any enhancements?"

"I don't."

"What is the lockout code, Ms. Farmingham?" Janey asked.

Monica fiddled with the wine glass stem.

Janey had the experimental laser device in her pocket but didn't see how it could be used on Monica to get what she wanted.

"Did you check the wrist ID?" Orlando said.

"Looks normal to me," Janey said, studying the data.

"Look at the output," Orlando said.

"What output?" Monica asked. "It doesn't output."

"Everything does," Janey said. "Everything's emitting light frequencies all the time." She studied the data again. "What do you see, Orlando?"

On her screen popped up a message from him that read to knock Monica out with the experimental laser. No, she finger-waved back, glanced up at him, and shook her head. He tapped his wrist. What was he trying to say? Was that Morse code?

For the love of Minerva.

Janey pulled out the small laser device, no bigger than her palm, filled with enough voltage to knock out a horse. But it also had another feature, a fool-proof data scoop that specifically worked on biological material. She placed it in her left hand and rested her hand next to Monica's right hand, still fidgeting with the wine glass.

"Monica, I'll ask you one more time, what's the code to stop the transmission?" Janey asked.

"I don't have it here." Monica smiled and tapped her temple with her right forefinger, moving her hand out of range. "But soon I will."

"Thank you for that admission of theft." Janey stood up and said loudly, "Monica Farmingham, you are under arrest." Janey yanked the woman to her feet, restaurant guests gasping in horror, surprise, and some with delight.

TWENTY-FOUR

M ONICA PROTESTED AND JERKED IN J ANEY'S
grip.

"None of that." Janey slapped the cuffs on her.

"McCallister, discretion," Schoeneman said in a hard whisper, a warning in his voice.

Monica tried to head-butt Janey, throwing her head back.

Janey moved out of the way. "I'm sorry, sir." She then said to Orlando, "Hold her."

Orlando took her place, also out of the way of Monica's attempts at cracking her skull on his. A hand on her cuffs behind her, he held the banker in place.

Janey swiped the device from the table and held it above Monica's wrist. It chirped softly and repeatedly as it scooped up the data from a chip hidden behind Monica's wrist ID.

"Hey. That tingles." Monica wriggled in Orlando's grip but had no traction. "What are you doing to me?"

Janey said nothing. Numbers flashed on the cube's readout screen, the entire side of one cube. She brought the comm next to the cube, and the numbers jumped to there. With the wave, she sent the data to Kim and commed her.

"Did you get that?" Janey asked.

"Yes, inputting them now. How did you get these?" Kim said, awe in her voice.

"Later. Is it what you need?"

"Yes, but darn, it still needs a voice print," Kim said.

"Say your name," Janey ordered Monica.

"No, I will not," Monica said, struggling against Orlando.

"Keep struggling like that, and I'll say your name," Orlando said in a seductive tone.

"You will not!" Monica said haughtily. "You are most certainly not my type."

"Oh," Orlando said. "What type is that?" He grinned down at the petite brunette.

Janey glared at him, even though she knew he was trying to provoke the suspect into talking more, to help Kim get all the sound memes she needed.

"Young man, most inappropriate," Schoeneman said and stood, his torso puffed up like a cockerel.

"Frederick, I am not sorry." Monica lifted her chin and gazed at him with big eyes, a yearning in them.

"About what?" Schoeneman stepped toward her.

"Can we have this lover's quarrel another time?" Janey said. "We have a station to save." To Kim, she asked, "Do you have enough?"

"Almost. Get her to say 'farm and ham,'" Kim said, no humor in her voice.

"You're trying to get me to say my last name. Simpletons!" Monica said. "The voice print authorization doesn't work like that."

"You don't know our Kim," Janey said.

"Six minutes," Orlando warned.

"Stop this nonsense, Mon," Schoeneman pleaded, genuine remorse in his voice. "Please."

"You lying, stealing, cheating—" Monica spat, leaning over the table, knocking her wine over. It stained the white tablecloth a dark red.

"Framingham," Orlando said, yanking her to standing.

"Stop it," Monica hissed.

"Frimington," he said calmly.

"Stop."

"Framindon."

"It's Farmingham, you oaf," Monica said, then paled.

"I got it," Kim said, relief in her voice. "It's stopped. Thank the stars and outer rings. Transmission aborted. Monies recovered. I have to sit down. Glass of wine, maybe."

"You're a rock star, Kim." Janey let out a big breath. A huge weight lifted off her. "A full bottle of wine for you. I'm buying. We're on our way to you now. The suspect is in our custody." She commed off.

Monica stared at nothing, her breathing shallow. She was in shock.

Schoeneman swore, and Janey glanced at him. He checked his comm and shook his head.

"What is it, sir?" Janey asked, her heart beating in her ears. Had Kim failed?

"She did it. She actually did it."

"Did what, sir?"

He raised his glass high in a salute and then gulped down his whiskey. "Kim, you, him, you stopped her. Salute. You stopped the theft. I could kiss you right now." He came around the table and strode toward Janey, his intent clear.

She held out a hand to stop him. "I best be getting her to interrogation. Make sure everything's all squared away."

"Of course. You must do your job. You do it admirably so." He glanced about, grinning. "I must calm the horde." He strode off to talk to restaurant guests, some still standing and trying to get a look at the commotion in the back corner.

"Crisis averted," Orlando said, glaring at Schoeneman, who was now mingling in the restaurant, shaking hands and kissing cheeks.

Janey didn't know if he was talking about the case or about the way Schoeneman was about to make a pass at her. Maybe both.

Janey steered Monica through the restaurant and past the games tables, the bar, and the slot machines, and into the front hotel lobby. Without incident. All the while she had a napkin over the woman's cuffs. Orlando was right behind her.

Monica was quiet, subdued even, until they got her into the service elevator. She glanced up, panic in her eyes, but it was quickly masked with defiance.

"Where is that son of a—?" she spat, lunging toward the closing elevator door.

"Frederick?" Janey said mildly and yanked her back by the cuffs.

"He's such a liar. Cost me billions." Monica twitched, but Janey had a firm grip on her cuffs.

"Where do you think you're going?" Orlando said.

"I have to—get out of here. Claw his eyes out," Monica screeched. "The liar, cheater!"

"You're not going anywhere except lock up and then prison," Janey said and pulled Monica out of the elevator. "Lunar penal colony for you, Ms. Farmingham."

They marched down the corridor in silence. Janey stopped them outside Interrogation Room Three. She'd never used it in her almost one year on the station. She unlocked the door and shoved Monica in. The room smelled musty but clean of dust.

Monica spun, examining the small room. White walls, no visible mirror, a table, two chairs.

"Sit," Janey said and pointed.

Monica wrinkled her nose. "Smells in here. Like a cat died."

"I don't smell it," Orlando said and leaned against the wall.

Janey pressed down on Monica's shoulder at the chair. Monica resisted, then aimed her head at Janey's. Not this again.

Janey swiveled to get out of her way but took the brunt of Monica's head butt in her shoulder. She fell into the table. Breath whooshed out of her, but she was blocking Monica's exit to the door. Gulping, Janey straightened and reached for the woman but was too slow. Monica raced around the table. Right into Orlando. He had over a foot on her. She had nowhere to go.

"I'll do the honors," he said, grabbing Monica's cuffs and yanking her back around the table to the chair.

Janey gulped and nodded. Orlando shoved Monica into the chair and used the extra chains and cuffs there to anchor her.

Janey sat opposite and glared at the petite woman. She took a deep breath, rubbed her shoulder, waved over her comm, and spoke a little breathlessly, "Assault of a security officer." She glared up at Monica, who was returning the glare. "I've added that to your list of charges. To grand larceny and murder."

Monica said nothing.

"Hard to believe such a petite woman could have so much fight in her," Orlando said.

"Oh, I don't know," Janey said. "Besides that's an outdated sexist notion." Over her shoulder, Janey lifted an eyebrow at him. She said to Monica, "What surprises me is that such a moneyed woman would even know how to fight dirty."

"That just shows your bias." Monica sneered. "Only police and military can know how to fight? You know nothing about me."

"Clearly." Janey waved over her comm to open Monica Farmingham's records, using her security clearance.

This was unusual. There was little in her record. Just an address. No photos. No arrest record. No financial data. Not even a birthdate. No attempt to backstop her identity. This woman was a digital ghost.

Janey peered up at her. "Who are you? Monica Farmingham is clearly an alias."

Monica said nothing.

"We found your wrist ID with a suspect connected with a murderer and have evidence of the attempted data theft. A backup, I presume, since I see you have yours in your wrist."

"So?" Monica shrugged.

"The station's funds were being siphoned off to the bank you work at. Or maybe you run it. Maybe it's a front for the Russian Underground. Doesn't matter. Either way, we've caught you red-handed. We have the digital trace."

Monica glared at her but said nothing.

"We're done here." Janey stood and headed for the door. "Orlando, let's go."

"Where's Frederick? Get me Frederick!" Monica shrieked, coming to life.

Not replying or looking back, Janey exited the room with Orlando and headed for the conference room.

In the corridor, Orlando asked, "Where is Schoeneman?"

"Don't know."

Janey commed him, but Schoeneman didn't reply. She entered the conference room. There he was in an embrace with Veronica Ladipo, the journalist. How many women did this man date?

Janey cleared her throat. They broke apart but remained entwined in each other's arms.

Veronica opened her mouth to speak.

Janey put up a hand to stop her. "None of my business."

"That's right," Schoeneman said, a protective arm across Veronica's shoulder. He peered down hungrily at the journalist.

Janey suppressed a sigh and glanced at Orlando, so as to not have to look at her boss and the journalist using her work area for their tryst.

"Want some?" Orlando held up the coffee pot.

What she really wanted was for the case to be wrapped up, so she could have some alone time with him.

Janey nodded and said softly, "Sure." She spoke to Schoeneman. "Where's Kim?"

"I don't know. She wasn't here when I arrived to confer with Veronica." He rubbed the journalist's shoulder.

"I was trying to reach you too," Janey said.

"Oh. What about?" Schoeneman asked.

"I wanted to let you know that Ms. Farmingham is in

custody and to check with you about your funds, contracts, and other items taken from the vault. We still need to track down the contracts and gems." Janey rubbed her temples. Fatigue pressed on her shoulders. It was 6:20 p.m., and she'd been going nonstop all day on this crazy case.

"That would be good. By nine a.m. is fine." He gazed at Ladipo. "I'm busy tonight."

"I'd like to check the records myself. Make sure everything is in order." Janey strode to the board and tapped it to get access to the station's financials. But they were blocked to her. Password locked. Of course. "I need your clearance code, sir," Janey glanced at Schoeneman, who was kissing Ladipo.

Oh, for Minerva's sake.

She commed Kim.

"What? What time is it?" Kim replied, fatigue making her voice lethargic.

"Did I wake you? I'm so sorry," Janey said.

"I needed a little break. I'll be right there." Kim commed off, and a minute later, she entered from the small break room. She wrapped up her long black hair back into her bun and stuck a stylus through it. "Oh, hello, Mr. Schoeneman. We saved your station. I stopped the transmission—"

"I know. Thank you, my dear." He stepped away from Veronica and held out a hand. He grasped Kim's hand in both of his. "What would I do without you, and the rest of the team? You're a miracle worker." He kissed Kim's cheek and whispered something in her ear.

Kim pulled back, a look of shock in her gaze, then anger. She glanced at Veronica, back to Schoeneman, and blushed. She tugged her hand from his and hustled to retreat to the break nook.

"Mr. Schoeneman, what did you say to her?" Janey asked, neutrally. Didn't need to piss the man off. "She looks upset."

"That's between me and her."

Veronica headed for the door. "Frederick, when you're done with your games, you know where to find me." She left the conference room.

Schoeneman stared after her, stunned.

Janey glanced at Orlando, who'd been leaning against the counter sipping coffee and wolfing down a sandwich this whole time. He lifted an eyebrow at her as if to say that Schoeneman took womanizing to a whole new level.

Janey said to Schoeneman, "Sir, I need to check that everything has been returned and then proceed to file the report."

"Yes, okay." He went across the room to the cabinets and proceeded to open and close them.

Orlando watched him amused, not moving out of his way until Schoeneman was reaching above Orlando's head.

"Do you mind?" Schoeneman grunted.

"Not at all," Orlando said and moved to stand beside Janey next to the board.

Janey huffed and waved the lock screen to Schoeneman's financials. It honked at her. "Sir, I need your passcode to check."

"Of course." He found what he was looking for. He grinned and held up a bottle of scotch in one hand and three glasses in another. "Time to celebrate."

"Let's check the financials first, sir."

"I already checked. Everything is there." He poured.

"I'm just doing my job, sir," Janey said. "Crossing T's, dotting I's."

Schoeneman set down his booty on the counter,

strode over to the board, and waved in his code, said his full name for voice authorization, and placed his palm on the surface. He stood back with a grin, but the lock screen still remained, the red words "DENIED" flashing with several exclamation marks. Over the top. Almost as if it had been programmed that way just for Schoeneman.

"Sir?" Janey asked. "Are there any more security levels to pass?"

"No." Schoeneman frowned. "Something's wrong. It worked fine at the restaurant."

"Maybe apologize to Kim?" Janey guessed. "She does have access to this information too. But—"

"But what?" Schoeneman asked.

"You're not kidding. You really don't know," Janey said.

"Know about what? Speak your mind, McCallister. That's why I hired you."

"You upset Kim. Said something to piss her off. Apologize and she'll unlock this."

Kim was willing to piss off her boss and risk her job. She must be very upset. She didn't want to say all that to Schoeneman.

"You're sure it's her? Maybe it's another thief."

"Maybe. But she's the one who would know." She was explaining things to an emotional illiterate. Really? How could he have gone so far in business with such cavalier attitudes toward women?

Schoeneman had a puzzled look on his face but went around the board and knocked on the door. "Kim, I'm sorry. I shouldn't have said what I said. It was—" He paused.

"Inappropriate," Janey called out.

"Inappropriate," Schoeneman echoed.

For a moment, nothing, then the board beeped, and Schoeneman's financials scrolled on the screen.

"Sir, I have them," Janey said.

Schoeneman called to Kim again. "Please, Kim, come out. I'm sorry."

"Give it up, Schoeneman," Orlando said.

Janey studied the financials. "Not knowing what the totals were before, I can't say if anything is missing. Kim would know. But I do see the funds."

Schoeneman strode around the board and stared at the financial records. "Yes, it's all there. I'll have my accountant double-check."

"You're sure nothing is missing?" Janey asked. "Two people died because of this heist." She frowned at him. "We need to find the gems and contracts that are still missing. I'm not sure we've caught those thieves."

"I have every faith. We need to go back to business as usual. Lift the lockdown." He peered at her, then smiled as if to soften his order.

"I don't think that's a good idea, sir."

"No need to sir, me. You're no longer in the service," Schoeneman said, his voice buttery. "I'm truly sorry for your loss, McCallister. I know they were your friends." Without missing a beat, he turned to Orlando and snapped, "Call for transport and get these criminals off my station ASAP. I'm going to speak with my lawyers and prosecute to the fullest extent of the law." Now he was acting like a CEO and not a lovesick puppy. "And let the night flight dock. My customers are tired of taking the scenic route, and the captain is losing patience with their complaints."

"Sir, wait with that. I need to find the men that kidnapped you, and I need time to wrap up loose ends.

Make sure all the evidence will hold up in court," Janey said to Orlando.

Orlando nodded.

"McCallister, call me Frederick. I told you."

"I'd rather not," Janey said.

"All right. Schoeneman then." Schoeneman said to Orlando, again, "Send for transport."

Janey shook her head at Orlando.

"Do it," Schoeneman said. "Lift the lockdown. And find the ingrates who shoved me into the damn tunnels."

Janey strode to Schoeneman and put a hand on his arm. "Please...Frederick, I need more time. Doc is still looking for the compound that killed Ed and Larissa. I need to know so Medical can help Kosi. One of ours. And the missing items from the vault...Isn't it important to you?"

He peered down at her and smiled wolfishly before putting his hands on her shoulders.

"Janey," Orlando said, a warning in his voice.

"Frederick, please hold off on the transport," she said in a purring voice.

Orlando choked on something. She didn't look at him.

Schoeneman dropped his hands and stepped back. "You have ninety minutes to get what you need." And then he strode out of the room.

TWENTY-FIVE

Janey rounded on Orlando. "What was that about?"

"What?"

"The throat clearing."

He narrowed his eyes at her. "What was all that cooing about?"

"Just getting what I needed."

"Did you have to resort to tools of seduction?"

"Whatever it takes to close the case," Janey said.

"That's usually my line." He eyed her lips.

"Well, I used it this time." She stepped to him. "Borrowed it."

He stepped toward her. "Just this once."

She met him in the middle of the room. "I might need it again."

He brushed her cheek with his knuckles. "You can use it whenever you want."

She pulled him in. He fit just right. She gazed at his lips, his eyes, the strong column of his neck, back to his lips. "Thanks."

He kissed her, with passion and heat. She lost herself in the moment, hungry for him.

Sometime later someone chuckled softly. Janey looked up from the kiss, dazed, barely sated.

"Kim!" She smiled, sure it was lopsided.

Orlando held a firm arm around her waist. He was grinning.

"You two need a room?"

"We thought we had one," Orlando said.

"It's going to have to wait. I just received a request for a Sol security police jet to dock." Kim said, frowning at Orlando.

Janey glared at him.

"I didn't call it." Orlando raised his hands.

"Schoeneman," Janey said at the same time as Orlando and Kim did.

"Refuse docking," Orlando said.

"We can't do that," Janey said.

"Or can we?" Kim said to Janey, "Your orders, Chief?"

"Acting chief," Janey said to stall and consider her options. Her fight wasn't with the Sol Special Investigations Unit but with her suspects and making sure the threat was contained and the hotel and station secure. "Let them dock, but don't tell Schoeneman—yet. We don't need any more pressure from him. Alert the hangar chief and his team. Ask the captain and crew to stay aboard their jet and wait to hear from us about the four suspects."

Orlando moved away from her for a refill of coffee across the room, leaving a wake of cool air. Would he be leaving again, too? For how long?

Kim commed the docking chief and gave the order. She peered at Janey. "Next?"

"We tie up loose ends. Schoeneman doesn't seem

concerned but I am," Janey said. "Send someone to help the chief with Hidalgo. Strange we haven't heard from him lately. Maybe she isn't awake yet. We need the map of the station tunnels from her. We need to find the men who kidnaped Schoeneman and find the loot."

"You said loot," Orlando said in his coffee.

Janey glanced at him but refrained from sticking out her tongue at him. It would be unprofessional. It was the fatigue that had her wanting to act like a child.

"I'll contact Daniel," Kim said. "He and Laura trust me."

Janey nodded. "Thank you, but who will handle operations?"

"I'll get Madison Quincy on shift early."

"Two names now?" Janey asked, without enthusiasm.

"Yep. And 'they.' I know they're a bit of a tight-ass, but they can do the work."

"They can, but they like to question my every move. I don't need that." Janey needed to stay focused on the case, not on office politics. Stars above, she hated office politics. Another reason to hand the mantle of chief back to Milano or someone else as soon as this case was over.

"I'll say something, again," Kim replied and headed for the door. "I'll comm you when I get the map from Laura." She left.

In the quiet of the nearly empty conference room, Orlando spoke. "The robot used in the heist." He sipped his coffee.

"What about it?" Janey asked.

"We never determined how exactly it was involved, that metallic residue. Was it really from a robot? Or from something else?"

"True," Janey said.

Orlando held her gaze as if he wanted to say something more. So did she.

"What?" he finally said.

"Are you taking the suspects to NYC headquarters?" Janey asked.

"I—hadn't thought of that. They probably have an agent on the space jet. I've been given leave to work on my case…" His voice trailed off. "I wasn't planning on jetting back to headquarters so soon. I haven't even started in on it…" He swore. "I'll check in with them. Later. After."

"Thank you," Janey said. "I know you didn't have to help me."

"I was asked to. Besides we're a team."

"I know." Janey headed for the door, waved it open, and glanced behind her when Orlando didn't follow.

Orlando stood in the center of the conference room, gazing upward as if the ceiling held his answers.

"What?" Janey asked.

"Not sure. Just an idea. You trust me, right?"

She beckoned for him to join her in the corridor. Her heart sped up. "I do trust you."

Orlando followed her out into the corridor. "I want to question Stephanie again. Just follow my lead."

"Let's do it." Striding down the hall, Janey commed Soren.

When he picked up, she said, "Do you or Doc have an update on what killed Ed and Larissa?"

"Yes, I was just about to call you. Can you come down here?"

"No, we need to interrogate a suspect. Transport is here, waiting for prisoners. Schoeneman wants the case wrapped up in"—she checked the time—"eighty minutes. Just fill me in now."

251

"Comms are safe?"

"Yes." Janey eyed Orlando.

"We finally nailed the substance, a human-made crystal made from trimethylamine combined with organophosphates," Soren said. "It was a fast-acting poison, aging all the organs at an ever-accelerating rate."

"I saw." Janey stopped outside Interrogation Room Two. "I was there with Larissa. It was horrible." She sighed.

"Must have been. I'm so sorry," Soren said.

Janey closed her eyes. There would be time to grieve later. "How will that help us heal Kosi?"

"He's been taking iTR to help him stay young," Soren said.

"Thought that compound was banned."

"People can still get it," Orlando jumped in.

"The black market." Janey nodded. "So, we have a dealer on board." Another thing to address.

"That contraband saved Kosi's life," Soren said.

"I get it," Janey said. "So, can you make an antidote from the iTR to help Kosi?"

"Way ahead of you. Doc and I already started on it. That's what I wanted to call you about. We're almost ready to give him the antidote."

"Great job. Maybe there's a way to inoculate all of us against the poison," Janey said.

"Good point. Hadn't thought of that. We'll work on that too," Soren said.

"Anything else? From Doc?" Janey asked. "We'd come down to you, but—"

"Clock's always ticking," Soren paused. "Doc says 'nothing else'."

"Thanks, to both of you," Janey said.

Soren jumped in before she could comm off. "What's this I hear about you as the acting chief?"

"Long story. Thought you knew. Laura Hidalgo is in custody—one of our suspects. Schoeneman took Chief Milano off the case. It's just temporary." She hoped.

"You'd make a good chief," Soren said.

"Thanks, Soren. McCallister out." She frowned and commed off.

"You don't want to be chief?" Orlando flipped up his collar.

Janey gave him what she hoped was her what-do-you-think look. "I'm a hands-get-dirty type." She unlocked the door and entered the interrogation room.

"Why are you keeping me here? I've done nothing wrong!" Stephanie yelled.

"That's what everyone says in this room." Orlando leaned on the wall.

"Stephanie, we already have what we need to prose-cute you. We're here with just a few more questions." Janey glanced over her shoulder.

"Right, that's my cue," Orlando said and pushed off from his spot. "I was studying your files, Stephanie, and saw that you took a tech course from Blue Diamond."

"So?" Stephanie sat back and looked him up and down disdainfully.

"Well, that's a front for a Russian Underground recruiting center—specifically for tech geniuses."

Stephanie said nothing.

These details were news to Janey. Why hadn't he briefed her first? Right, no time. He'd asked her to trust him.

"You don't have to say anything," Orlando said. "I have a program scrubbing your files now. And you know what we'll find?"

More news to her. But Janey didn't want to interrupt Orlando. He was on a roll. His maverick ways had always helped her in the past.

Stephanie frowned. "You won't find anything." She said to Janey, "He's bluffing, right?"

Janey shrugged, sat back, and crossed her arms. "I don't really know." She peered at Orlando. "You could be bluffing."

"You know, I could be." He nodded to Janey. "But then again, maybe I'm not. I'm known as a loose cannon, you know. That's why my boss sent me here. Keep me out of the NYC office."

Janey lifted an eyebrow. That had to be a lie. His loose-cannon ways were highly cultivated and sanctioned.

Orlando leaned over the table, getting in Stephanie's face. "You're an agent for the Russian Underground, trained in robotics, and you're the one who designed the robots that unloaded the vault." He straightened. "That's what we'll find."

Stephanie stared daggers at him, her breathing rapid. "I am too smart for you to find any of that."

"Thanks for confirming," Orlando said.

"I didn't confirm anything."

Orlando glanced at Janey. "Catch that?"

"Why, yes I did. Increased heart rate and respiration. You certainly touched a nerve," Janey said. "Not that a jury would convict Stephanie on that alone."

"You're just messing with me. It won't work. You don't have anything. Why else would you be here, questioning me again?" Stephanie's voice rose to a squeak. "They said you would try that."

"They did, did they?" Janey said.

"Stop making fun of me!" Stephanie sounded like a child again. They'd definitely touched a nerve.

"I'm not," Janey said and glanced at Orlando. "Am I?"

"No, I don't think you are." Orlando's comm beeped a cheery short melody.

"What's that?" Stephanie asked, panic lacing her voice.

Orlando peered at his screen and then showed it to Janey. It was several lines of code.

"I can't read that," Janey said. "What does it say?"

Orlando glanced at it. "I'm no expert in the latest and greatest coding language, but I know enough." Orlando glanced at Stephanie.

She clamped her lips together and glared at him.

Orlando continued, "This code shows a backdoor into the station's safe and the encryption key to unlock it via the station's security system."

Stephanie's eyes widened. "She said that no one would be able to find that or read it."

"Well, that's a lie, isn't it? You've been lied to. Anyone who knows this coding language would be able to read this. As for finding it"–he shrugged—"I have my sources."

"But only a handful of people—" Stephanie sucked in a breath. "You're one of them!"

"One of who?" Orlando said casually, leaning against the wall again, his heart rate low and respiration long and even. His hiding stance.

"The Russian Underground." Stephanie stared at him, glanced at Janey, and back to Orlando. She leaned forward as much as her restraints would allow and whispered to him, "What are you doing here?" She gestured with her head to Janey. "Why are you working with her?"

"Trust me, Ms. James." Orlando moved back to stand

at the table, close enough to Janey so she could feel his body heat. He stood proud, his stance shifted. He puffed his chest out and frowned at Stephanie, looking different, more cocky, more virile, and a little mean.

Janey watched Stephanie. The young woman was mesmerized by Orlando, eating up his act.

Stephanie gaped at Orlando. "Sir, you have to get me out of here. There's been some mistake. I wasn't supposed to be caught. I had the perfect cover."

It was as if Stephanie had forgotten Janey was there, as if she thought Orlando was on her side and a superior officer in her cause.

"I was only supposed to open the safe. I didn't know Kocak would kill the guards. The guards weren't supposed to be there. She assured me..." Stephanie's voice trailed off. "We have a mole." She sucked in a breath. "You're the mole."

Orlando softened his stance, taking off the illusion. He leaned against the wall again. "No."

Stephanie blinked as if coming out of a trance. "You tricked me to confess!" She swore in Russian. Or maybe that was Turkish.

Janey stood and let out a breath she hadn't realized she'd been holding. "Got what you needed, Orlando?"

"Yes, Chief." He winked at her.

Pale, Stephanie stared at Janey, the realization that she'd confessed in her eyes.

Stephanie yelled racial slurs against all Latinos and then all male Latinos. In English.

Orlando marched out of the interrogation room, Janey right behind him. At the door to the conference room, Orlando clasped her shoulders and grinned. "You were great in there."

Janey narrowed her eyes at him. "Me? You're the one

who put on the show. What was that? How did you know?"

"I had a hunch."

"You bluffed."

"I did." Orlando gave her a quick kiss on the lips. "You trusted me. We make a great team." He gazed at her, his eyes twinkling. "What next, Chief?"

TWENTY-SIX

"WE NEED TO CHECK IN WITH MILANO AND HIS wife about the tunnels. And what else Hidalgo knows. Let's go to Medical," Janey said.

"You got it, boss," Orlando said.

Janey strode to the service elevator and said without glancing at him, "I am not your boss."

"Technically, you are. Chief Milano said. And that he's been removed from duty, doubly so," Orlando said, matching her stride for stride down the grey corridor.

"That's not a thing. Besides, he'll be back at his desk as soon as we close this case."

"I don't know about that," Orlando said. "You saw how Schoeneman treated you."

"Yes, and it was weird. Coming on to me one moment, treating me coolly the next. Think he was testing me? To see if I was immune to his charms?"

"You are." Orlando chuckled. "You told me he hired you because of your take-charge attitude. Bossy, was how you put it."

"I thought I was brought here to just take charge of

the investigative side of things. Milano's more of a report filer."

"You have to face the truth, McCallister." There was a hard edge in Orlando's voice.

"What truth is that?"

In a softer tone, he said, "That you are leadership material and made for a role like this." He held her gaze as if willing her to take him seriously.

Janey shook her head. "I'm made for being out in the field."

"And training new investigators."

"Yes, by doing. Not by filing reports to please Schoeneman." She crossed her arms on her chest.

"You already file reports." He matched her stance, gaze fixed on her, his broad shoulder touching hers.

"About the cases. What are we arguing about?" The way he was looking at her right now, with admiration, encouraging her to be more than she was. She stared at the grey elevator doors, so she wouldn't have to face him. She couldn't handle his attention just now. "You're leaving again, aren't you?"

"Stop that."

"What?" They stepped into the waiting elevator, and she spoke in the command for Medical.

"You're freezing me out." Orlando gently pivoted her to face him, but she didn't look up. The grey service turbo's recyclo flooring was grimy from the hectic day's traffic. "If you don't want to run things here, you could join me in NYC." Janey finally glanced at him.

"And do what? I couldn't work for the Sol Special Investigations Unit. I can't support my mother on that salary." Janey relented and caressed his cheek, loving the feel of the day-old stubble under her palm.

He kissed her palm. "We'll work it out."

"I can't leave L'Étoile. My mother is depending on me," Janey said, sadness weighing on her like a shroud.

The service elevator stopped. They exited and made their way down the service corridor to the public hall. She led them to Medical and entered the waiting area. It was empty, the clinic beyond too quiet. She pulled her gun out of her holster and hustled down a hallway, clearing each of the small examination rooms winging off to one side. Orlando searched the opposite wing.

"Clear," she said after each empty room. All six of them. Orlando echoed her.

There was a door with no window marked Supplies. She peeked in. The darkened room was filled with shelves full of supplies that stretched into the shadows. There was a curtained-off area in the back, with the edge of a cot showing. Perhaps where the staff took cat naps during quiet shifts.

She met Orlando back in the waiting room.

"Where is everyone?" Orlando said.

Janey shook her head, the hairs on the back of her neck standing up. The place was too quiet.

She advanced down a short corridor to the entrance of the main medical bay—a white door with a square window at face level. She backed against the wall, gun up. Orlando backed up against the other wall, his weapon at the ready. She nodded at him. He nodded back, ready for her to give the order. She nudged the door with her shoulder. It didn't budge. There was no locking pad. When she'd been here previously, it had always been open. Its controls must be on the other side.

She hustled back to the waiting area. Orlando frowned his displeasure but followed her. She hit her wrist comm, calling Kim. There was no answer. She tried again.

Suddenly, there was a loud bang on the other side of the door in the medical bay. The floor rumbled, and a metallic smell of blood permeated the air.

Kim replied with three quick clicks, three long ones, and then three short ones. SOS in Morse code.

Venus Hells. Kim was in the main medical room and in trouble.

Janey returned back the universal message "received" in Morse code and then closed the comm. Next, she commed Milano. He was in the medical too. There was no reply. She tried again. Again no reply. "We got to get in."

Orlando studied his comm. "It's one wide room on the other side."

Janey commed Quincy Madison.

He answered in his clipped New Englander tone.

"Quincy, can you unlock the door in Medical that leads to the main room?"

"Why? What's—"

"No time. Code black."

"Yes, ma'am, Chief," he said. "One moment. Stay on the comm."

"Of course." For once Quincy Madison didn't put on airs with her. When push came to shove, they could pull through. Good job.

"I've unlocked it, Chief McCallister," Quincy Madison said. "ID Link shows there are six people in there." He paused.

"Tell me who, Quincy Madison." Medical was specially shielded. Janey couldn't use her ocular implant to see through the walls.

"Former Chief Daniel Milano; Master Engineer Laura Hidalgo; Security Office Manager, Kim Iona; Chief Medical Officer Shu-chen Tseng; Medical Assistants

Grade 4 John Chivengali; and Grade 5 Alison Horsely."
So formal and lengthy, but now wasn't the time to teach
Quincy Madison tactical communications. Later though.

"Thanks. Do we have cameras in there?"

"Negative, ma'am. Privacy screens in place." Their
voice was more formal than usual.

"Everybody's got life signs?" Biophoton readings
weren't broadcasting beyond the shielded room either.

"Yes, ma'am. All green." On the security tracker,
wrist IDs flashed green for alive and red for dead.

"Thank goodness. Can you see anything on the EM
bands? Identify the source of the explosion?"

"Negative. It's just—" They paused.

"Out with it."

"There's an ELF coming from the room."

Electromagnetic Low Frequency emissions, like the
ones that jammed them in the tunnels.

"Thought you said there was nothing in the EM
bands."

"It's an Extremely Low Frequency that we don't scan
for on the standard sweep."

That had to change.

"What's the specific frequency? Could it have set off a
bomb?"

They gave her the frequency. "Anything's possible,
ma'am."

That was the same frequency Hidalgo had been
broadcasting on earlier. "I need your critical thinking, not
your obedience, Quincy Madison," Janey said, clipped.

They gulped. "Yes, ma'am, Chief, uh, it could be a
comm channel, so yes, it could have triggered a bomb."

Janey blew out a breath. "Thanks. Send Soren and
security personnel with bomb expertise our way. Orlando
and I are going in."

"Okay, should I alert Schoeneman too? Anything above a Code Orange, protocol demands that I alert him."

"Have you already?"

"Yes, ma'am, Chief."

"Then don't waste my time with asking." Janey huffed.

"Sorry, ma'am, I mean, Chief."

She commed off and grimaced. Glanced at Orlando. "Ready?"

"Hard fellow to communicate with," Orlando said.

"Hmmm." Quincy Madison was not the problem. She centered herself and headed for the door. Two feet away, the door slid open.

Her comm beeped, but she didn't check to see who it was from. Gun ahead of her, Janey stepped in and crouched low, sweeping her gun from the center point and then pivoting right. Orlando, behind her, swept left, covering the other half of the room.

Curtains were drawn over six medical bays. Spilled medical supplies were scattered across the room. Nobody visible. The lights were on, but low, as if for nap time.

"McCallister here!" Janey shouted. "With Orlando. Everyone okay? We heard an explosion."

"Over here!" It was Kim. Her voice was shaky but loud. "Two down."

"Bomb techs on their way," Janey said, "Who's down?"

"Hidalgo and Tseng," Kim said.

"We don't need bomb techs," Alison said, sadness in her voice.

Janey's comm beeped incessantly, repeating request-to-reply over and over again. Her holo screen flickered. She switched it off without looking at who was calling.

"Coming in." Janey pushed aside the curtain and froze.

Medical equipment whined a low sound, indicating someone had flatlined. On one side of the bed, Milano was sobbing quietly over a bloodied prone body. Hidalgo —her eyes stared unseeing.

One of the medical assistants, Alison Horsely, stood at Milano's shoulder, trying to get him to move. She had blood spatter all over her face.

On the other side of the bed, Chief Medical Officer Shu-chen Tseng was on the floor, her chest open, blood everywhere, her internal organs half in and half out of her body. Medical Assistant Chivengali knelt at her side, hopelessly trying to patch fragments of her skin over a bloodied chest. Near Tseng, Kim stood at the head of the bed, pale, blood all over her face and front.

"She blew herself up," Kim said.

"Who? Laura?" Janey asked.

"No, Shu-chen. She killed Laura and herself in the blast," Kim replied. "It happened so fast. One minute I was questioning Laura. Then boom." Kim swayed but stayed on her feet.

TWENTY-SEVEN

In a moment, Orlando was at Janey's side. "The rest of the room is clear."

"Thanks," Janey said, then spoke to Kim gently, "Can you come brief me?"

Kim nodded, stepped around Tseng's body, and headed toward Janey at the edge of the medical bay.

Orlando said, "I'll question him." He gestured to Milano.

"Yes, thank you," Janey replied.

Alison called out from beside Milano, "Ms. Iona, Kim, we need to check you. Make sure you're unharmed."

"Alison, I'm fine," Kim said.

"Chivengali, please check her," Horsely said. "You're closer."

"I'm on Tseng. Her pulse is thready. You do it," Chivengali said calmly from the floor, still patching Tseng's chest.

"Tseng's gone, John. You can stop. John, that's an order," Horsely said gently and stepped around Milano, who hadn't moved or acknowledged anyone.

Chivengali didn't stop his work. "Not giving up, yet."

"John," Alison said with a warning tone.

Chivengali laid one more skin patch, sighed, then sat back on his heels. "She's gone." He said louder, "Let the record show that Chief Medical Examiner Shu-chen Tseng is pronounced dead."

"So noted," Horsely said. Then she sobbed and slapped a bloodied forearm over her mouth.

"Alison, is Daniel injured?" Janey lifted her chin toward Milano.

Alison regained her composure, shook her head, and stepped in front of Kim, holding up a hand to stop the office manager from going farther. Kim stopped, staring at the far wall.

The medical assistant ran a medical comm up and down her body. "You're in shock, but other than that, you're okay." She gestured to Kim's face. "That's not your blood."

Kim wiped some blood off her cheek and stared at her fingertips.

"Sit down, Kim," Horsely said.

"I'm fine."

Alison led Kim by the elbow toward a sink between two curtained medical bays. "You're not fine. Let's get you cleaned up and get some electrolytes in you."

Janey followed and pulled out her comm to record and take notes. "Kim, what happened?"

Kim wiped her face with the wet serviette smelling of alcohol Horsely handed her. "I was questioning Laura. She was finally awake—groggy but awake. Daniel was holding her hand. I stood on the other side of the bed. She was telling me the tunnels were extensive and how to find them, when Tseng walked in and shoved me out of the way, shouted something I didn't understand—a code word maybe—and threw herself on Laura. Then the explosion."

Janey nodded. "Thank you." She addressed the medical assistant. "Alison, how about you? Where were you?"

"Here, drink this." Alison gave Kim a small juice box. To Janey, she said, "I was checking the monitors next to Laura's bed. She'd just woken up, and I was taking manual readings."

"As opposed to what?" Janey asked.

"I can get all the readings I need over there," Alison gestured to a monitor on a corner desk. "But when a patient wakes up we want to do a new baseline, and it's best if we do that on the instruments beside them. Better calibration." Alison wiped her bloodied face with a serviette.

"Did you notice any odd behavior the last twenty-four hours? Tseng acting any differently? Anything out of the ordinary?" Janey asked.

Alison paused in wiping her face and eyed Janey through the mirror. Then she spun. "Yes!" She tilted her head, remembering. "It was odd. She was holed up in her office for a while and then came and checked on Hidalgo every ten minutes."

"What's odd about that?"

"She usually had us checking on patients, always delegating. Liked giving orders. Wanted us to learn. Normally, we do the regular monitoring of patients." She rubbed her face harder. "Why?" She said that last bit to herself and shook her head.

"Why, what?" Janey asked.

"Why did she do it?"

"That's what we're going to find out." Janey waved

some notes into her comm. "So it was unusual Tseng being holed up in her office?"

Alison nodded. "She had her door closed."

"What's unusual about that?"

"Normally, the door was always open. Open door policy. She was always clear about that..." Alison glanced at Tseng's body and then called out to Chivengali. "John, come get cleaned up."

"Okay." He sounded defeated. A moment later, he approached the sink, Tseng's blood on his shirt and on his arms up to his elbows.

Alison stepped back to give him room. Kim moved to Janey's side.

"Alison, you were trying to revive Laura? Even after that severe of an injury?" Kim asked, more color to her cheeks.

"Sometimes, we can revive patients—about sixty percent of the time," Alison said. She stared at the body. Tseng's boots stuck out of the medical bay. "Why do you think she did it?" she asked again.

"We'll find out," Janey said.

Orlando came around the curtain. "Janey, Chief Milano—I mean, Milano—wants to talk to you. He won't leave her side."

"Did he say anything to you?" Janey asked.

"Just that he was at her side when the Tseng shoved him out of the way, threw herself on the missus, and then... both blew up." Orlando looked a little pale. "I've seen a lot of things, but I've never seen up-close destruction anything like this."

"McCallister," Milano called with some of his usual command voice.

Janey strode around the curtain, brushing past Orlando. He gave her shoulder a squeeze.

Milano stood beside his wife's body, the entire front of his shirt and jacket red with blood and body matter. "She was doing the right thing, confessing, and Tseng attacked. You have to find out why—and now." His eyes were bloodshot as if from crying.

"Yes, Chief. I'm on it." She kept her gaze on him.

"You and Orlando, did you catch the rest of the culprits?"

"We did."

"Good."

"The Sol Security Office space jet is here to take them to holding. I just wanted to get the map of the tunnels." Janey studied Hidalgo. Her chest was blown open, like Tseng's was. Some bio-metal fragments were embedded in her skin. "Some kind of bomb implanted there."

"Perhaps by her," Orlando said at Janey's side.

"By Laura? No!" Milano said. "She'd never do a thing like that."

"I'm afraid you didn't know her like you think you did," Janey said softly.

Milano glared at her. He knew she was right. "But she said..." He shook his head and covered his eyes, grief overcoming him.

"What, Chief, Daniel?'

He found his voice and peered up, his cheeks wet. He croaked out, "Our place, she said. Just before—"

"What place?"

Daniel shook his head, bleak.

"We'll talk later, Daniel." She held back the trite phrases: it'll be okay. We'll figure it out. All meaningless.

Orlando put his hand on Janey's arm. "Did you interview the other medical assistant? Do you want me to?"

"I'll do it in a bit." Janey gave him a tight smile, then to Milano said, "Let's clean you up."

Milano shook his head. "Not 'til Doc gets here."

"Right. I haven't called her. But Soren and the others should be here by now." Janey commed Doc.

Doc answered.

"Can you come to Medical?" Janey asked.

"I'm already here."

"Oh. How did you know?"

"Quincy Madison called me. They were watching the IDs and saw the two switch to red." Doc's voice came through double, both on the comm and from the hallway.

Janey closed the comm. In a long white lab coat covering her clothes, Doc strode into the room and surveyed the scene. She nodded to Janey and approached her and Milano.

"Chief," Doc said as a greeting.

"Doc," Milano said and did something that surprised Janey. He walked into Doc's waiting arms. They hugged for a long moment. Janey held her tongue about the transfer of biomatter onto Doc's lab coat.

"She's dancing with the ladies," Doc said, not saying anything about the breach in crime scene etiquette either.

Milano nodded and moved out of her embrace. "Thank you." He walked out of Medical.

Janey made to follow, but Doc put a hand on her arm. "Let him go."

"But—"

"He wants to be alone."

"How do you know?" Janey asked softly. "You two? …"

"We're friends. Let him be," Doc said.

"I'm worried he'll—"

"He won't do anything a good bottle of whiskey can't cure," Doc said softly.

"A man shouldn't drink alone. Not today." Orlando strode after him.

Janey shook off Doc's arm and followed.

She caught up with Orlando and Milano in the waiting room. The two sat on chairs, staring at the floor. Soren and two security guards were there.

"Doc told me to hold here until you or she called me," Soren said.

"You can go in. Collect what evidence you can. Though it's probably mostly in Tseng and Hidalgo. There may be residue on the surfaces of whatever caused the bomb. See if you can find the trigger. I'll work on the why of it."

Soren nodded and headed down the hallway for the medical room, tech kit in hand.

"Oh, Soren?" Janey said.

"Yes, Chief."

Milano didn't move or look up.

Janey said, "This is no ordinary case. Be more vigilant than ever."

He nodded grimly. "Aren't I always?" he said and continued on.

Janey's comm beeped. It was Quincy Madison. "McCallister here."

"Anything else you need?" they asked.

"Soon. I'll be sending you data to analyze."

"Okay. Schoeneman's been updated. Quincy Madison out."

Janey said to Orlando, seated beside Milano, "You'll watch him?"

Orlando nodded.

Janey went back into the medical bay. Kim wiped her

face again, though it was clean. Soren was taking samples from under the fingernails of Alison and John. He had bloody washcloths in evidence bags.

"Kim, are you up to talking?" Janey asked. "I still need the tunnel maps."

"Laura was about to tell me when—I can get the data from Tseng's computer."

"You don't have to work now. Not after—what happened."

"I want to," Kim said. "Quincy Madison isn't as good as I am in data analysis."

"They would be if you trained them up."

"They haven't seemed interested."

"Well, they are now. Totally on board."

"Then I'd better get to work," Kim said, eyeing her with pain and strength, and headed for Tseng's office.

The security guards helped Doc with lifting Hidalgo and Tseng's bodies onto hover stretchers. Doc covered them in black shrouds and then directed the stretchers out of the room and down the hallway, motioning for the two guards to follow her. Right past Milano. Janey followed quickly, worried for Milano. But he wasn't there. She commed Orlando.

"Are you with Milano?" she asked.

"Yes, we're in my quarters, sharing my special thirty-year-old Glenlivet."

She whistled. "Stay with him."

"It is, and I will," Orlando said.

Janey commed off and headed back to Medical. Soren collected trace and took readings. Kim was at Tseng's computer, gathering the data.

"Need any help?" she asked Soren.

"No, I got it." He didn't look up, instruments in hand.

"Secure the crime scene when you're done."

"Yes, Chief." Soren continued his gathering.

"Can I help you with anything, Investigator McCallister?" Alison asked.

"Yes, anything," John said.

"That's Acting Chief McCallister," Soren said.

Janey shook her head. "Help Soren with whatever he needs." She peered around the room. "I do have some questions."

Alison nodded.

"Why are there medical instruments on the floor?" Janey waved at the mess that had been kicked about by all the traffic.

John bent to pick one up.

"No, stop," Janey said.

He straightened.

"Soren, image all of this." She peered around the room again. "Anything else out of place?"

The medical assistants glanced about and shook their heads, no.

"In answer to your question," Alison said, "I think Tseng knocked a table in her haste to get to Laura."

John nodded. "Yes, it was like this when I rushed over after I heard the explosion."

"Thank you," Janey said. "And where's Kosi?"

Alison and John exchanged glances. Alison spoke first. "Tseng said she was managing Kosi. Had him in isolation."

"Where?" Janey asked.

"He's not in one of the side rooms?" Chivengali said.

"No. We checked." Janey recalled the cot she saw in her sweep. "Soren, check the supply room."

"I'll show you the way," Alison said to Soren and dashed down the side hallway.

TWENTY-EIGHT

FIVE MINUTES LATER, JANEY STRODE DOWN THE corridor to the conference room to wrap up this Venus Hells of a case when her comm beeped. It was Schoeneman.

"Sir?" she answered.

"Where the hell are you?" he spoke harshly. "Time's up, McCallister. I need to get my station ready for the party." Then his tone switched to gentle, and his voice shook with sadness. "I'm sorry. For Laura and Shu-chen."

"Thank you, sir." She opened the conference room door, stepped in, and paused. Schoeneman stared at the murder board, sipping whiskey. "I didn't expect you here."

An image of Shu-chen Tseng had been added to the other four culprits on the board. A near-empty bottle of Aberfeldy Highland Single Malt Scotch Whisky 24-year-Old Exceptional cask sat on the table. Very expensive and rare.

"Do you know why she did it?" Schoeneman brushed an eye. Had he been crying?

Janey shook her head and scanned Tseng's record. "She'd been at the station since its opening."

"I recruited her personally, as I did you. She was my personal physician for years." He gulped down more amber liquid.

"And Laura Hidalgo?"

"A brilliant engineer. Also, a friend from—school." Schoeneman stared at her image.

"She leaked information to the thieves and murderer."

"Why?"

"She was beholden to—" Janey shook her head and stared at the board. "It'll be in the report."

"McCallister, just tell me." He waved his hand in the air and swayed, tipsy. "The report can wait."

Janey eyed him, then took a deep breath. "She was involved in a bombing of the Russian Embassy fifteen years ago that killed four people, as part of the Rhomboid Consortium."

"That can't be true." He narrowed his eyes at her.

Janey held his gaze. "It is, according to the investigative black files of the Sol's Special Investigation Unit. She'd been blackmailed by a man who hates you, and who is the father of her daughter."

"What does this have to do with today's theft and murders?"

"It has everything to do with it. Hidalgo had to have been working with Stephanie and Kocak for a long time to plan this. And with Tseng."

"And Monica." Schoeneman frowned and took another swig. "Damn her." He glared at Janey. "Wait, Laura Hidalgo doesn't have a daughter."

"She does." Janey enlarged the image of Stephanie. "Her."

"She has her mother's eyes," Schoeneman said soberly.

"I'm sorry," Janey said. "For your friends' deaths." Even though they had been involved in theft and murder.

He finished his drink and set it down on the table with a clack. His hand shook as he emptied the rest of the bottle into his glass. "Monica—she—really coordinated the whole thing?"

"I think she took advantage of what Hidalgo and Tseng had been planning."

Kim bustled into the conference room. "And for a long while. Check this out." She opened up a file on the board. Tseng's financials. "Looks like she was siphoning off credits for years."

"Ten years," Janey said. "She had to have been planning this heist with Hidalgo from the start."

"And built the tunnels." Schoeneman shook his head. "Dammit. How could I not see it? How could I not know?" He glared at the board. "Why?"

"Why what, sir?" Janey asked.

"Why did Hidalgo put secret tunnels in my station? Why did she want to steal from me? I gave her everything...introduced her to Daniel..." He glared at Janey. "She got me into the tunnels? I don't believe it. What did she have against me?"

"Maybe she was coerced by Kocak, the father of her daughter. He had a grudge against you," Janey said. "Maybe she believed in what he was doing. Maybe she—"

"That bastard." Schoeneman squeezed the glass in his hands, his knuckles whitening.

"Kocak? You knew him?"

"Are you questioning me, Acting Chief?"

"I am asking you a question."

Schoeneman placed the glass in the sink and spoke, his back to her. "Is my station secure?"

"I'm pretty sure."

"I need you to be one hundred percent sure, Acting Chief McCallister." He spun and glared at her.

"Nothing is one hundred percent, Mr. Schoeneman."

He grunted. "Hire whoever you need. Secure my station. Make sure the guests are not alarmed. As usual. The celebrations go forward as scheduled next week," Schoeneman said. "And get the suspects off my station. Now. Time's up." He strode out of the room.

"He sidestepped the question," Kim said.

"What is he hiding?" Janey asked. "Maybe he owns the Rhomboid Consortium—"

"And was behind the bombing at the Russian Embassy fifteen years ago?"

Janey stared at the door. "I don't know."

After a moment, Kim said, "In Tseng's records, I found out what was going on with Kosi. Thank goodness he's alive. Sending you her private notes. They sum it up nicely." She said that last word with a bite of sarcasm.

"What?"

Janey read the notes and frowned. "Dispassionate. Tseng was intrigued that Kosi survived, wanted to create an antidote, and was also responsible for attempting to kill him. It's all here." She growled, her stomach churning. "She made the poison that killed Ed and Hidalgo."

"Oh, dear lord." Kim sighed. "One more thing."

"Yes?"

Kim fiddled with her necklace. "I sent you the tunnel map."

"Thanks. Will you coordinate the sweep of the

tunnels? We'll probably find the missing cache from the vault," Janey said. "Bring on more staff. Whatever you need. Schoeneman's approved that, so we can secure the station."

"Of course. What will you do?" Kim messed with her hair, re-pinning it up with a stylus.

"Get the suspects on the Special Investigations jet."

"Is Orlando leaving?" Kim eyed the door.

"He doesn't think so."

"But he might."

"Yes."

"Sorry." Kim touched her necklace again.

"Me too." Kim left the conference room.

Janey stared at the murder board live feed of Stephanie, Kocak, and Monica in custody. So many questions still, but at least the culprits were caught. Like where the vault's contents were and how they'd been stolen exactly.

A few minutes later, her comm chimed. "It's Orlando."

Janey asked, "Hey, how's Milano?"

"Passed out in my bed."

"Okay."

"I'm outside the conference room. You locked the door."

"Oh." Janey unlocked the door. "Don't remember doing that."

Orlando entered, clear-eyed, sober. "You okay?"

She shook her head. "No, but I'll be fine."

He strode to her and wrapped her in a fierce hug. He smelled clean, freshly showered, not at all of alcohol. He finally pulled back and eyed her lips, then leaned in to kiss her.

Janey dodged it. "We need to take the three

remaining suspects in interrogation to the space jet. Are you going with them?"

Orlando peered at her and said nothing for a long moment. He finally said, "They haven't asked me to. And I haven't offered."

Janey took his hand and clasped it. "Let's find out, shall we?"

Twenty minutes later, Orlando and another security guard helped her move all three prisoners from the interrogation rooms to Hanger A. Onboard the space jet, Janey and Orlando secured the last prisoner in restraints. The sleek sparse jet could seat fifty, but it only held the three prisoners and a skeleton flight crew.

Doc commed her.

"Yes, Doc."

"I'm here to load the bodies—" Doc cleared her throat. "Laura Hidalgo, Shu-chen Tseng, Larissa Ferreira, and Eduard Kou are secured in the cargo hold of the Sol Security Office jet for my counterpart at headquarters. He'll get his analysis to us by tomorrow."

"Thanks, Doc."

Orlando took her hand.

"I'm heading back to my lab." Doc commed off.

Janey closed her eyes. So much loss.

Orlando let go of her hand and shifted away from her. She opened her eyes.

From the back cabin, an older man strode toward them, filling the aisle with his command air, and nodded to Orlando. "Orlando."

"Captain Kavya, sir." Orlando stood straighter.

"At ease, Investigator."

"I wasn't expecting you," Orlando said.

"Clearly," Captain Kavya said.

Janey held out her hand. "Acting Chief Janey McCallister."

"Captain Sebastian Kavya, Sol Special Investigations Unit, New York, Security Office Precinct." He shook her hand. "Pleased to meet you. Where's Chief Daniel Milano?"

"It will be in my report," Orlando said as Janey said, "The case got personal." She gazed at him.

Kavya looked between them, seeing what was there, maybe knowing already, and then settled his gaze on Orlando. "Maybe you should come with me, Orlando. Don't know if you can complete your case on L'Étoile if you're distracted."

"I can complete it, Captain." Orlando gave his boss a hard look.

"Fine, I'll take your word for it. Now, get off my jet. We're departing as soon as the all-clear is called." He called to the front of the jet, "Captain Jenkins, ready us for takeoff." Kavya said to Janey, "Keep an eye on this troublemaker, Acting Chief."

"Yes, sir."

"When can I expect your report?" he asked her.

"Nine am our local time tomorrow."

"Fair enough." He strode toward the cockpit without a good-bye or backward glance.

Janey clipped down the towable passenger stairway, Orlando right behind her.

The jet taxied into the zero-gravity lock, revved its engines, and took off into a burst of power. Stars shifted. Janey blinked. It was the station that had moved nearly imperceptibly, not the stars.

Orlando grabbed her hand, and together they headed off the hangar toward the service elevator. He eyed the elevator panel. "Can I buy you a drink at SkyBar?"

"I'm exhausted. Rain check?"

"How about"—he pointed up—"our spot?"

She smiled tiredly.

He nodded and pulled her close. "Let's take the night off."

"And not think of anything except—" She leaned into him, eyed his lips, and kissed him. Long and deep.

The elevator door opened. They were still at the hanger level.

It was Doc. "Sorry."

Orlando dropped his arm around Janey's waist.

"Take the next car, Doc," Janey said.

"Of course. I'll update you later."

"I'm taking the night off. Update me now."

Doc shook her head, no. "Good night, you two."

"Thanks, Doc. Good night." Janey bit back a sigh and waved shut the elevator door.

"Alone at last," Orlando said and wrapped his arms around her.

"You're mine for tonight, Orlando Valdez," Janey said.

"And I'm yours for as long as you'll have me, Janey McCallister."

———

AT SOME POINT EARLY THE NEXT MORNING, Janey was awakened by an insistent buzz on her wrist comm, the sound code indicating an urgent recorded message from someone on her team.

Orlando groaned. "Too early."

"I know." She shushed him and spoke to Rhea, her personal AI synched into her room controls. "Rhea, playback message."

"Of course, Janey," Rhea said in her smooth, calm

voice. Then the vid recording played on the ceiling screen. It was from Meilani and Antonia. They were animated, excited, but trying to mask their excitement with professional, serious expressions.

"Boss, Chief," Meilani said. "We figured it out."

"We know where the vault contents are," Antonia jumped in. "Based on Milano's account of what his wife said."

"But we need you to get Hangar Security to cooperate," Meilani interrupted. "We need to search the Estrella Motel, and hangar security on duty says she needs your approval."

"Please and thank you," Antonia added, excitement in her eyes, though her tone was serious. Hurry was implied. The feed ended.

The Estrella Motel was on the hangar level, tucked behind the entry gates, out of view of the hotel casino guests. The small, cheap motel had been part of the first-use waystation for Schoeneman's asteroid business. It was still in operation and only asteroid miners stayed there. The eight-room motel was outside Janey's jurisdiction. Hanger security was in charge of that area.

Time to step up. She needed to be more awake for this. She slipped out of bed and padded to the washroom to splash water on her face.

What did an acting security chief wear in the middle of the night when talking to hangar security? She opted for a short collar blouse, her black formal uniform jacket, and black slacks. She brushed her hair and put it up in its customary ponytail.

It would have to do. She went to a wallscreen in the kitchenette and set up the privacy screen so as not to disturb a sleeping Orlando. She commed the hangar security duty desk. Hannah Chadwick answered, looking alert in her blue uniform.

"Hannah, please let my agents search Estrella. They're pursuing a lead in an open investigation," Janey said without preamble. Hannah had worked with her team before. They all knew each other.

"I need to get approval from my Chief," Hannah said and shrugged, as if to say she was sorry.

"Do it. I'll hold."

Hannah nodded, relaxed a little, perhaps happy that Janey didn't try to jump her chain of command.

The screen blanked, showing the L'Étoile logo—a five-pointed gold star on a blue field.

Hangar Security Chief Scott Edward Ellias shouldn't pose a problem. They cooperated well on their last murder case. He ran a tight ship and was competent at his job, maintaining order at the hangar level for the arriving and departing guests.

A moment later, Hannah was back. "Hangar Chief gives approval but wants one of us to accompany."

"Fine. Tell Scott thanks." Janey commed off. A flash of jealousy zipped through her heart. Normally, she would be the one to run down such an exciting lead. But this was now, a new normal, however awkward. She blew out a breath. She could do this. Had to do this. She spoke to her room AI. "Rhea, take this message for Meilani and Antonia."

"Go ahead, Janey," Rhea's soothing voice intoned.

Janey dictated. "Proceed with caution. Report back as soon as you have something. Hannah will send someone with you."

"Ready to send?" Rhea asked.

"Yes, send."

"Sent, Janey. Shall I start your coffee?"

"No thanks, Rhea. I'm going back to sleep. Sleep mode, resume."

"Yes, Janey. Good night."

Three a.m. was much too early for her after the day they'd just had. She undressed and slipped back into bed.

That hadn't been so hard. Easier than she thought it'd be. Maybe being Acting Chief would be…interesting.

Gentle whooshing waves upon a shore lulled Janey back to sleep.

Some time later, Janey was startled awake by more insistent buzzing on her wrist comm. This time *she* groaned. Felt like she'd hardly fallen back asleep.

Orlando slipped out of bed, stretched, and yawned, looking chipper and well-rested.

"Rhea, play message," Janey commanded.

"Yes, Janey."

It was Meilani whispering. "We found it all, boss. Two dead men dressed in grey sanitation coveralls, mid-twenties. Murdered, looks like, from all the blood. I'm presuming they were the hired help, though their idents aren't in the hotel system. With them was all of the loot and four bots, with retractable arms. Industrial type. Shall we call the Doc? We're collecting evidence right now. What else? Oh yes, taking vids. Shall we call Soren too?"

There was talking in the background, probably Antonia.

"Right, the clue led us to the Estrella Motel, Room Three. Awaiting your orders."

Janey stood too, grabbed her bathrobe, and put it on. May as well start her day, her first official day as Acting Chief. She commed Meilani directly, voice only.

How easily she slipped on her new mantle. A little surprising.

"Chief," Meilani answered.

"Yes, call Doc and Soren," Janey jumped in. "Good job. After everything is documented, get the contents back to the vault—discreetly."

"Yes, Chief."

"We'll debrief at 9 a.m." Janey checked the time. It was only six a.m.

All she had to do now was call Schoeneman. A part of her new job she wasn't looking forward to.

After a quick breakfast, Orlando said he needed to check on his case and left her quarters when she did, disappearing into the staff offices. Janey squared away reports and set up the day's duty assignments in her office. She didn't want to work in Milano's office. Not until... She didn't know when. She called Schoeneman and left a message with his service. He was still asleep and didn't want to be disturbed.

When she got the call from Meilani and Antonia that they were heading back, she met them in the conference room.

"Chief, we found it all," Meilani started.

"Wait," Janey said. "Let's get everyone in here."

"I can call them," Antonia said.

Janey nodded the go-ahead.

A few minutes later, everyone was gathered in the conference room—Antonia, Meilani, Kim, Soren, Natalia, Clark, Anahi, and Orlando, back from doing whatever he'd been doing. Janey took a moment to look at everyone. Then began.

"I know we've had a difficult couple of days, and we've lost people close to us. Tonight we will celebrate their lives." She saw a few tears and nods. Orlando gave

BETH BARANY

her a small smile of encouragement. Kim also. "We're here to wrap up the case, and get ready for the gala."

"Schoeneman is still going ahead with that?" Clark asked.

"As far as I know," Janey said. "Meilani, Antonia, why don't you explain how you figured out where the vault contents were and what you found."

Meilani and Antonia looked at each other soberly, their earlier giddiness under wraps. Meilani started. "Well, Chief Milano said that his wife Laura had confessed something just before Tseng detonated the explosive in Medical." She looked at Janey. "We still don't know why she did that, do we?"

"No, we don't. Not yet," Janey said. She would need to look into that for the report.

Antonia picked up. "I looked into the staffing files for the early days of L'Étoile and saw that Milano came aboard after Laura had been here for some time. Laura stayed in the motel, Room Three. And Milano stayed there with her when he visited before he was hired."

Meilani continued. "So we went to Room Three. Hangar security let us in. And they were as shocked as we were when we saw the two men there." She waved a still image up to a wallscreen. One man lay slumped in a chair, skin pale, face shriveled. The second man was prone on the bed, bruising on his face, as if he'd been in a struggle before he died. "According to Doc's report, the one on the chair died first. Both had been injected by the same poison that killed Ed and Larissa."

"We think Kocak most likely killed them," Antonia said.

Meilani nodded. "Getting rid of the help. We documented the room with Soren and recovered every item that had been taken out of the vault. All the gems, all the contracts, everything. They were packed in suitcases for easy transport."

"Working theory on how they broke into the vault and removed the contents?" Janey asked, pleased that Antonia and Meilani were stepping into a lead investigator role quite naturally and without her prompting.

"Oh, the bots!" Meilani said. "The four bots."

"With retractable arms," Antonia added and waved up to the wallscreen stills of the bots stacked in a corner of the small motel room. "With Soren, we recovered trace on the bots and on the men's hands and feet."

"Same trace that we found in the vault," Soren said.

"These two men with their bots had likely been all over the station using the tunnels," Meilani said.

"I've mapped a good portion of the tunnels with my flyers," Soren said. "They found ones in the lower levels near Aquatics and Hydroponics and one to the back door of the Arboretum."

Janey knew he meant his micro-drones.

"I didn't know the Arboretum had a back door," Natalia said, leaning forward, engaged.

"It's not an official backdoor," Antonia said. "These tunnels were likely construction chutes that Laura didn't have filled in. Could be she'd been planning the heist with Chief Medical Officer Tseng for years."

"Why do you think they wanted to rob the vault?" Clark asked.

"I looked at your interrogation transcripts," Meilani said to Janey. "There was some long-seated resentment between Laura and Schoeneman having to do with Kocak. They practically said as much. I don't know why Tseng was involved."

"She created the poison that Kocak used to kill Ed and Larissa," Janey said. "And the two unidentified helpers. What about the organic compounds? Go back to that."

"Literally what Meilani said," Soren jumped in. "The organic compounds were minute traces from different parts of the station."

"Theories?" Janey asked the group.

"The men were probably stealing food," Antonia said. "The crime scene report of where Larissa died also had these organic traces. From the amount we collected, Kocak and the other two men stayed there too."

Janey nodded.

"If I may," Orlando lifted a finger to indicate he wanted to speak.

"Go ahead," Janey said.

"I took the liberty of searching for the identities of these two men through our system." Orlando flicked his wrist and the profile images, with names, dates of birth, and citizenship appeared on the wallscreen. "They used to work in asteroid mining with Kocak and did some prison time with him."

"That explains the connection between Kocak and these two," Antonia said.

"What about the bots?" Janey asked. "Where did they come from? Where did the algae trace come from?"

"The algae came from walking near the Aquatics," Soren said. "I did look into possible labs where that algae could have been manufactured. The bots could have been packed in containers destined for our Aquatics. Those packing boxes are long gone in the recycler by now."

"Smuggled aboard," Janey muttered. "But how did these two men get the bots to work? The men had to be nearby, right, and the bio-sig was weak inside the vault, as if the men were near but never in the vault."

"Right," Meilani chimed in. "The operator needs to

be within twenty feet of the bot to operate it, sight to sight."

"As for how," Antonia said, her excitement rising. "The bots have retractable arms and are rated to lift one hundred pounds."

"I was studying the schematics of the vault," Meilani said and turned to Soren. "Did you check the air vents at the top of the room?"

Soren's face reddened as if embarrassed. "You know, I scanned them briefly but didn't notice anything odd. Now I see I probably made a mistake. That trace was spread throughout the room. I bet it's on the air vents also. I just assumed I was picking up trace in the air and not from the air vents." He shook his head. "I'll never make that stupid mistake again."

"Good catch Meilani," Janey said. To Soren she said, "Why don't you work with Meilani to check those vents? We'll need to put security on them. I'm not sure why that wasn't done before." As soon as she said that, the answer came to her. She paused, catching each person's eye. "Actually, if Laura was in charge of the original design, construction, and maintenance of the vault, then ..." She let that hang and shook her head. "We will be double checking all systems in the station going forward, starting now."

Her agents sat up taller, more alert. Good. They understood what was at stake. She peered around at everyone again.

"As you go about your daily shift, note any area that does not have active security where you think it should. I will be reviewing everything with a fine-tooth comb." She paused for dramatic effect, though she hardly needed to. Everyone looked thoughtful, serious. Even Orlando.

Now the hard part, making room for grief.

BETH BARANY

"I want to thank everyone for your hard work. Good job," she said soberly.

She didn't know what else to say. It had been the end of a hard case. They were good people. They'd done their best. Now it was time to move forward.

Meilani stood. "I'll see to my shift."

"Me too," Antonia said.

The rest nodded and left the conference room. Except for Soren and Orlando.

"You okay, boss?" Soren asked.

"I will be," Janey said.

———

IN THE COMMISSARY THE NEXT EVENING, THEY played games and sang karaoke late into the night to honor Eduard Kou and Larissa Ferreira. Along with her friends and colleagues, Janey raised her glass and toasted her fallen comrades too many times to count, shedding a few tears too. Informing their families by vid had been hard. The worst.

At least Mom would have Janey's final pre-recorded good-bye video, in the event of...

Orlando glanced at her and squeezed her in a side hug.

She gave him a half-smile, grateful that he didn't make a joke just then.

Mom had looked tired on the vid this morning and brushed it off to the side effects of the new treatment. She'd again tried to dissuade Janey from pursuing a new and improved medicine.

"I feel all right, just a little tired is all. I have a good life, Janey. I have you, a chief now—wow—and my friends. What else could I want?"

"But, Mom…"

Then her mom had made a joke that made her laugh and had deftly changed the subject.

Janey wiped a tear off her cheek. Orlando kissed her cheek and lifted his glass at the nth toast Alison had just given for Ed. Not to be outdone, Antonia topped it with a toast to Larissa.

Late into their cups, Milano arrived and stood at the edge of the festivities that had taken over a corner of the commissary. Leaving the warmth of being surrounded by Kim and Orlando, Janey made her way over to him.

She nodded at him. "Would you like a pint?" She held back from saying sir and chief. Her new role was, well, new, and hopefully temporary.

"No, Janey." He shook his head, weary, but revealed some satisfaction in his tight smile. "Glad to hear your team found the loot. Schoeneman knows, I presume."

"Oh, he knows," Janey said. "None too happy to realize just how long Tseng and Hidalgo…" She didn't finish. If their coded messages were any indication, they'd been planning for years. Janey's team hadn't decoded their messages yet.

Orlando arrived in time to hear that and he shook his head sorrowfully, as if in sympathy. Daniel's shoulders slumped.

"Daniel, would you like a drink?" Orlando asked softly.

"Don't suppose you have another bottle of thirty-year-old Glenlivet lying around?"

"Not on board," Orlando said. "But I can get one…"

Milano frowned. "I'm taking leave."

"When?" Janey asked.

"Tomorrow."

"When will you be back?"

Milano shook his head.

"I'm just Acting Chief," Janey said.

"I know," Milano said. "I'll decide in a month or two. Don't look so worried. I'll be fine. Just need some time away. Keep the chair warm for me."

Janey nodded, not trusting herself to speak past the tears.

"You look out for each other," Daniel said, then he nodded at them, waved at the others, and headed for the commissary as the group burst out in song for Milano, a haunting proud tune Janey could hum but didn't know the words to.

Daniel Milano stopped at the threshold and spun to face the security crew and friends of Larissa and Ed and let himself be serenaded. When the song ended, he touched his heart and surveyed everyone. Then he left. Everyone started singing again, louder than ever.

Janey watched Milano go, and part of her trailed after him like a shadow. The old Janey. The insecure new hire. The not-so-careful investigator. A new dawn was on the horizon. She could feel it coming—warming her and challenging her. New responsibilities. Maybe a new kind of relationship. She slid her hand over Orlando's. He caught her fingers in his, gave her a gentle squeeze, and smiled.

ACKNOWLEDGMENTS

As with the previous books in the Janey McCallister Mystery series, many people helped me create this third book in the series. A huge thank you to all of you! It takes a village to create the world that lives and breathes in this book. Special thanks:

To my Early Reader and Beta Reader teams: Beth Perry, Briana Burgess, Bob Morton, Carol Malone, Catriona Bain, Dodie Coe, Harland Monroe, Jackie Tansky, Kay LaLone, Marilyn Lugner, Mary Van Everbroeck, Sally Stackhouse, and Shelly Small.

To my Patreon supporters: Chloe Adler, Elayne Griffith, Janet Patterson, and Lisa Boragine.

To F.S. for his ongoing support and for his lending of his name for a character in this series.

To Leah Ellias, for asking me to do the honors of naming a recurring character after her husband who passed away in 2019. He would have loved it, she said. Thank you for the permission.

To my students for giving me feedback during our One Hundred-Word Critique classes. You rock!

To my first cover designer, the talented Elayne Griffith, who helped me refine the cover concept and shape the book titles.

To my amazing, diligent, and ever-patient critique partners, Patricia Simpson and Kay Keppler, for their support, encouragement, and critical eye. Bottle of wine coming.

To my mastermind group, Leanne Regalla and Bonnie Johnston, for their moral support and cover feedback.

To my Blurb Babes, Lea Kirk and Tess Rider, for never ever tiring of refining my book blurbs and for the fun brainstorming sessions.

To my proofreader, Paul Martin of Paul Martin Editorial, for his eagle eye.

A massive double thank you to Bonnie Johnston for her friendship, amazing brainstorming sessions, and incredible, tireless support.

To my brother Sam Zoesch for his just-in-time expert input on pharmacology.

And a universe-sized thanks to my husband and fellow creative nebula, Ezra Barany, for all the re-reads, edits, and more edits, geeking out on science right alongside me, and supporting my storytelling instincts every step of the way.

ABOUT THE AUTHOR

Award winning author, Beth Barany writes in several genres including young adult adventure fantasy, paranormal romance, and science fiction mysteries. Inspired by living abroad in France and Quebec, she loves creating magical tales of romance, mystery, and adventure that empower women and girls to be the heroes of their own lives.

For fun, Beth enjoys walking her neighborhood, gardening on her patio, and watching movies and traveling with her husband, author Ezra Barany. They live in Oakland, California with a piano, their cats, and too many books to count.

Sign up here for news on new releases and other goodies: http://bethb.net/gonegreen.